博识英语一百系列

U0132912

总主编 束定芳

博识
初中英语背诵文选 100 篇

初中卷

主　编　王之江　潘春雷

副主编　吴格奇　夏谷鸣　康海凤

本书主编　夏谷鸣　胡跃波

编　　者（按姓氏笔画排列）

王晓琴　方　静　李军宛

郑斐斐　倪骕霜　莫勤勤

韩欣江　鲁蓉蓉　谢慧萍

上海外语教育出版社

外教社 SHANGHAI FOREIGN LANGUAGE EDUCATION PRESS

图书在版编目(CIP)数据

博识初中英语背诵文选 100 篇/夏谷鸣,胡跃波主编.
—上海:上海外语教育出版社,2009
(博识英语一百系列)
ISBN 978 - 7 - 5446 - 0913 - 5

Ⅰ. 博…　Ⅱ. ①夏…②胡…　Ⅲ. 英语课－初中－教学参
考资料　Ⅳ. G634.413

中国版本图书馆 CIP 数据核字(2008)第 105443 号

出版发行：**上海外语教育出版社**
　　　　　　（上海外国语大学内）　邮编：200083
电　　话：021-65425300（总机）
电子邮箱：bookinfo@sflep.com.cn
网　　址：http://www.sflep.com.cn　http://www.sflep.com
责任编辑：陆轶晖

印　　刷：上海外语教育出版社印刷厂
经　　销：新华书店上海发行所
开　　本：787×1092　1/16　印张 19.75　字数 393千字
版　　次：2009 年 4 月第 1 版　2009 年 4 月第 1 次印刷
印　　数：5 000 册

书　　号：ISBN 978-7-5446-0913-5 / G · 0439
定　　价：37.00 元

本版图书如有印装质量问题,可向本社调换

总 序

　　学好外语取决于多方面的因素，一是学习的兴趣，二是学习的资源，三是学习的方法，四是成就感，五是实践的机会。

　　"兴趣是最好的老师"。有兴趣，我们才愿意付出时间、精力和代价，才能"为伊消得人憔悴"但却"无怨无悔"。有学习的资源，就是有各种各样学习外语的材料和机会。大家知道，在中国学习英语，仅靠课堂上的输入，仅靠教材显然是不够的，大量的课外语言实践是必不可少的。这样的课外实践包括听、说、读、写、译等各方面。有些材料学生可以直接通过网络、各类文学作品或媒体获得，还有一些则是经过专家或老师的选择和编排，并附有各种练习的课外阅读或语言训练材料。学习的方法，就是要根据自己的学习的目标，根据自己的现有能力、学习风格和学习条件，选择最适合自己的学习方法，培养自己的自主学习能力，最终成为一个成功的学习者。成就感，就是经常有机会证明自己的学习效果或成就，尤其是通过自己所具备的外语能力获得了其他知识，或者与所学语言国家的人交往，从而改善自己的知识结构，提高了自己的综合素质和能力。实践的机会，就是努力争取和获得外语听、说、读、写、译各方面的实践机会。

　　我们编写这套丛书的理论依据就是以上对成功的外语学习所涉及的重要因素的理解和分析。同时，我们在总体设计中还充分考虑了语言学习的特点，一方面在选材时注意到材料的知识性和趣味性，另一方面在编写各类相关的练习时注意培养学生自主学习的能力，练习的形式充分考虑到各级各类考试的题型和内容。

　　本套丛书的编者由外语教学理论研究者、大学英语教师和中小学教师组成。这样结构的编者队伍有三大好处：一是有一定的理论指导，二是真正了解学生的真实需求，三是可以保证选编的学习材料地道、真实、符合外语学习的规律，所编写的练习能够帮助学生真正提高自己的语言综合能力，达到学习的目标。

　　中小学生学习外语一般有两大目的：一是实用的目的，主要就是应付学校和社会的各类考试，包括升学考试；二是训练自己的思维能力，通过英语扩大自己的知识面，提高自己的综合素质。我们编辑本套丛书，希望兼顾学生这两方面的需求同时把重点放在扩大学生的知识面，提高学生的综合素质方面。并且，通过一定数量的仿真练习，提高学生在各类外语考试中充分发挥自己真实水平，取得好成绩的能力。

　　外语学习没有捷径，只有经过艰苦的实践才能学好外语。更重要的是，贵在坚持。

上海外国语大学教授、博士生导师　束定芳

2008 年 2 月 20 日

《博识英语一百系列》初中卷序言

当前,贯彻实施国家《英语课程标准》(以下简称《课标》)的英语学科教学改革方兴未艾,正在广大基础教育领域里如火如荼地开展着。为了配合进一步深入学习、理解和实践《课标》精神,我们组织编写了《博识英语一百系列》初中卷(以下简称《初中卷》)。我们的宗旨是努力使初中英语教学成为中学素质教育的重要组成部分;我们的终极目的是帮助初中学生逐步提高"综合语言应用能力"(Integrated Language Capability)。我们首先要衷心感谢上海外国语大学束定芳教授和上海外语教育出版社庄智象社长为编写《初中卷》指明了方向,找到了途径并提出了方法。

这套《初中卷》有以下特色:

首先,《初中卷》体现了《课标》的基本理念,即英语教学的人文性目的和工具性目标,也就是:英语教学是为了帮助学生在学会做人的道路上成长,在学会使用英语的过程中成才。重点是帮助学生在学习英语和了解世界的过程中把自己培养成为有知识、有智慧、有志气的学习者。

其次,《初中卷》遵循了"Learn English, learn about English and learn through English"的外语学习准则,就是说,学习英语包括学习英语听、说、读、写的能力,学习英语的语音、词汇、语法等语言知识和通过英语学习丰富的文化内容。

第三,《初中卷》遵照了"听说领先、读写跟上、全面实践、按需提高"的初中英语学习原则。《初中卷》共六册,前四册按《课标》中语言技能的听说读写的顺序排列,后两册则是在全面实践的基础上按照个性化需要为有关测试和初步文学欣赏编写的。

第四,《初中卷》内容的选编坚持"贴近实际、贴近生活、贴近学生"的原则。无论内容或形式都和学生们使用的新《课标》课本相匹配。字里行间渗透着文明、科学等素质教育内容和自主、灵活的解决问题方法。

第五,《初中卷》在小学英语和高中英语之间发挥了过渡阶段的桥梁功能,体现了基础英语教学中承前启后的作用。

最后,《初中卷》的编写既遵循了初中学生的认知规律,又与初中英语学习的实践体系和训练体系要求相配合。《初中卷》中的练习编排和题型设计等充分考虑到初中学生平时作业的规律性和各种测试的规范性。使用《初中卷》能帮助学生在接受作业和测试的挑战时更自信、更熟练、更富有成功感。

《初中卷》由六个分册组成,分别是《博识初中英语听力100课》、《博识初中英语口语 100 句》、《博识初中英语阅读 100 篇》、《博识初中英语仿写 100 篇》、《博识初中英语词语填空 100 篇》和《博识初中英语背诵文选 100 篇》。每本书既各具特点，独立成册，又与其他各册融为一体，形成系列。《初中卷》主要由课堂第一线任教的老师精心编撰，但也不乏基础英语教学专家和高校英语教师的积极指导与参与。《博识初中英语听力 100 课》和《博识初中英语口语 100 句》由浙江省宁波市教育局组织宁波市中学英语教育高级研修班的教师在宁波教育学院康海凤、翁燕文等导师们的指导、帮助和参与下完成；《博识初中英语阅读 100 篇》和《博识初中英语词语填空 100 篇》在杭州师范大学外国语学院几位研究生导师们的指导、帮助和参与下由 2004 级英语教育硕士生（均是英语骨干教师和英语教研员）完成；《博识初中英语仿写 100 篇》和《博识初中英语背诵文选 100 篇》由杭州外国语学校的优秀英语教师们在夏谷鸣、胡跃波等数位浙江省英语特级教师的指导、帮助和参与下完成。全书由杭州师范大学外国语学院王之江教授、潘春雷副教授组织策划、设计、编写、修改和统稿，吴格奇副教授参与了全书的统稿工作。本《初中卷》初稿完成后，由杭州师范大学外国语学院的程亮、吴晓维、沈昌洪三位英语专家进行审阅，并提出了有益的修改意见或建议；外国语学院的青年教师李佳颖、骆玉峰以及英语课程与教学论硕士研究生何立欣、张红玲、张彦芩等积极参与了《初中卷》的编写工作，并在校对、修正和打印过程中做了大量的工作，付出了辛勤的劳动。可以说，《初中卷》是优秀的中学、高校教师和英语教学专家联合打造的专业结晶。因此，也一定会对初中英语师生落实《课标》，提高初中学生的"综合语言应用能力"提供有效的帮助。

我们希望初中学生会喜欢这套《初中卷》，把它当作学好英语的有力帮手，也诚恳希望广大读者对《初中卷》提出批评改进的意见。

王之江
2008 年 5 月 1 日

编者的话

一、编写目标

1. 根据初中学生熟悉和感兴趣的话题,选择英美国家脍炙人口的短诗、儿歌、寓言、电影对白和短文,增强趣味性。

2. 以《英语课程标准》为指导,参照初中英语教学的要求,考虑学生的知识结构和语言能力,力求做到语言实用、内容真实、结构简易,对学生的语言学习起到积极的影响,强化实用性。

3. 选用的文本体裁广泛、不拘一格、形式多样、长短不一,体现多样性,让学生体验各种文体的语言风格。

4.《博识初中英语背诵文选 100 篇》绝大部分都选自英美国家的经典篇目,从语言、文化等方面提升本书的质量。

二、总体设计

1. 全书按照背诵篇目的文体分为五部分,分别为:儿歌、寓言、诗歌、电影对白和短文。

2. 全书内容设计充分体现语言输入与输出的整合、语言体验与文化欣赏的融合、英语原文与汉语译文的结合、语境理解与语篇背诵的组合。

3. 全书结构设计合理,方便阅读、使用。

三、单元结构

1. 篇目呈现:呈现所选经典篇目;

2. 语言注释:解释篇目中的语言难点,包括词义解释、语义说明、结构提炼和语篇分析等;

3. 背景介绍:介绍篇目作者的生平以及创作背景等;

4. 篇目欣赏:分析篇目的深层含义,帮助学生准确理解文字、体验语境并欣赏语篇;

5. 背诵准备:设计各种有针对性的词语或非词语形式的练习,以此帮助学生背诵;

6. 参考译文:本书同时提供参考译文,帮助学生准确理解原文。

编者

2008 年 5 月

目 录

Part 1 儿 歌

Part 2 寓 言

Part 3　诗　歌

Part 4　电影对白

儿 歌

1. The Eensy Weensy Spider

The *eensy weensy spider*

Crawled up the water *spout*，

Down came the rain

And washed the spider out，

Out came the sun and *dried up* all the rain，

And the eensy weensy spider

Crawled up the spout again.

语言注释

1. eensy weensy　很小的

2. spider / ˈspaɪdə / *n*. 蜘蛛

3. crawl / krɔːl / *v*. 爬行

4. spout / spaʊt / *n*. 水管

5. dry up　使……变干

背景介绍

这首儿歌的歌名有多个版本,比如"Itsy Bitsy Spider"和"Incy Wincy Spider"。蜘蛛为什么要爬水管呢? 许多蜘蛛宝宝(spiderlings)会爬上高的物体,比如说水管,用它们的丝乘着风飞离出去,像气球一样,有时会飞好几千英尺。这样能帮助它们飞离兄弟姐妹以避免争夺食物。

篇目欣赏

> 这首儿歌还是一首很好的手指歌谣。儿歌中的动作能帮助小孩子们提高手指的灵敏度。唱的时候拇指,食指交叉摆动模仿蜘蛛上爬,向下甩手表示蜘蛛被雨冲走,以手画圈形容太阳出现,最后又向上移动手指表示蜘蛛往上爬,颇有童趣。可怜的小蜘蛛好不容易爬到高处,谁想被一阵雨冲得稀里哗啦找不着北,还好太阳公公及时赶到,战胜恶势力,晒干了所有的雨水,解救出无辜的小生命。小蜘蛛百折不挠地又爬上老地盘。

背诵准备

这首儿歌里有一些动词词组的用法,有些还是动词副词的倒装结构,试着填填看。

The eensy weensy spider
_____ _____ the water spout,
_____ _____ the rain
And _____ the spider _____,
_____ _____ the sun and _____ _____ all the rain,
And the eensy weensy spider
_____ _____ the spout again.

参考译文

小蜘蛛

小小蜘蛛爬上水管,
大雨来临,把它冲走了。
太阳公公出来了,
晒干了雨水,
小小蜘蛛又爬上水管。

2. The Piper's Son

Tom Tom the *piper*'s son
Stole a pig and away he ran，
The pig was eat
And Tom was beat，
And Tom went *roaring* down the street.

语言注释

1. piper / ˈpaɪpə / *n*. 吹笛手
2. roar / rɔː / *v*. 吼叫,怒吼

背景介绍

这首儿歌的创作要追溯到 18 世纪。歌词里的 "the piper" 指的是当时英国军队里的吹笛手。这首看似胡扯的歌谣其实附带着很深的含义:想想小汤姆挨打之后在街上哭吼着的惨景(went roaring down the street),哪个小孩还敢乱拿人家东西?!

篇目欣赏

这首儿歌有两个韵脚:头两句押 / n / 的韵;第三、四两句从语法上来看,本应使用被动语态"The pig was **eaten** and Tom was **beaten**",可是这里为了保持三句押同一个 / iː / 的韵,便摈弃了语法的规范,而保持了韵律上的优美。

背诵准备

这首儿歌的最后一句有好几个版本。不同之处就在"roar"被替代。那么你能判断一下哪几个词可以替代"roar"吗?

howl, call, shout, cry, bark, whisper

参考译文

吹笛人的娃

汤姆啊汤姆,吹笛人的娃,
偷了一头猪,撒腿赶快跑!
汤姆吃掉猪,他也挨了打,
跑到大街上,放声哇哇哭!

3. I'm a Little Teapot

I'm a little teapot, short and *stout*.
Here is my *handle*, here is my *spout*.
When I get all *steamed up*, hear me shout,
Tip me *over* and *pour* me out!

语言注释

1. stout / staʊt / *adj.* 矮胖的
2. handle / ˈhændl / *n.* 柄
3. spout / spaʊt / *n.* 茶壶嘴
4. steam up   使有蒸汽
5. tip over   使翻倒
6. pour / pɔː / *v.* 倾倒

背景介绍

"I'm a Little Teapot"的歌词用拟人的手法描写了水壶的外形(short and stout)以及水烧开(when I get all steamed up)并从中倒出水(tip me over and pour me out)的情景,风趣可爱,惟妙惟肖,在国外深受小孩子们的喜爱。

篇目欣赏

这首儿歌的背诵和演唱通常都是伴随着肢体动作的。在唱到(here is my handle)的时候,可以将左手放在左臀上模仿茶壶柄;"here is my spout",移动右手模仿壶嘴;最后可以身子向右倾斜模仿"tip me over and pour me out"。

背诵准备

读完这首儿歌,你能发现这首儿歌的韵脚是哪个音吗? 押韵的词又是哪几个呢?

参考译文

我是一把小茶壶

我是一把小茶壶,矮矮又胖胖。
这是我的柄,这是我的嘴。
当我全身都冒蒸汽时,听到我呼喊,
使我倾斜,让我倾吐!

4. A Wise Old Owl

A *wise* old *owl* lived in an *oak*.

The more he saw the less he spoke;

The less he spoke the more he heard.

Why can't we all be like that wise old bird?

语言注释

1. wise / waɪz / *adj*. 聪明的,明智的
2. owl / əʊl / *n*. 猫头鹰
3. oak / əʊk / *n*. 橡树,橡木

背景介绍

动物是大多数儿歌里的主角,特别是小猫、小狗、兔子、鸡、鸭之类外形可爱,小孩子们生活中常见而熟悉的动物更是容易被人们写入儿歌,以激起孩子们的兴趣。可是这首儿歌为什么描写的是一种夜间出没而且外貌稍显吓人的动物呢? 我们来欣赏一下吧。

篇目欣赏

这首儿歌的创作是为了教育小孩子注意保持安静,轻声说话的好习惯。因为猫头鹰通常都是静静地、耐心地守望,等待着猎物。英语中有一条成语就是"a wise old owl",为什么说它聪明呢? 因为在希腊神话中,猫头鹰是智慧的象征,希腊人还选择用猫头鹰来代替他们的智慧女神雅典娜。

背诵准备

　　歌词中有"the + 比较级,the + 比较级"的用法,意为"越……越……"。你能用这种用法完成以下句子吗?

1. _____ carefully she writes, _____ mistakes she'll make.
2. _____ junk food we eat, _____(healthy) we'll be.
3. _____(fast) you drive your car, _____ dangerous it will be.
4. _____ trees we plant, _____(green) our country will be.
5. _____(rich) Bill Gates becomes, _____ money he gives away to the society.

参考译文

一只睿智的老猫头鹰

橡树上住着一只睿智的老猫头鹰。
他看得越多,说得越少;
他说得越少,听得越多。
为什么我们就不能都像睿智的老猫头鹰那样呢?

5. Down by the Station

Down by the station early in the morning,
See the little *Puffer Bellies* all in a row,
See the *engine driver* pull the little handle.
Chug, chug, *toot*, toot,
Off they go.

语言注释

1. puffer / ˈpʌfə / *n.* 吹气的物体(歌中指火车车厢)
2. belly / ˈbelɪ / *v.* 涨满
3. engine driver 火车司机
4. chug / tʃʌg / *v.* 发出轧轧声
5. toot / tuːt / *v.* 发出嘟嘟声

背景介绍

这 是一首曲调轻松,语言活泼的儿歌,描写了火车离站的情景。其中的象声词"chug, chug, toot, toot"的运用,很符合小孩子们的歌唱习惯,使儿歌极富童趣,能激发他们学习的兴趣和表现欲望。

篇目欣赏

在 唱这首儿歌时,一群小孩子可以坐成一排,扮成火车的一节节车厢,最前面的孩子伸出手做往里拉的动作扮演司机拉引擎,然后火车开动,就齐齐向前走并发出"chug, chug, toot, toot"的声音。

背诵准备

这首儿歌中有一些关于火车的语言,你还记得吗?

Down by the station early in the morning,

See the little _____ _____ all in a row,

See the _____ _____ pull the little _____.

_____, _____, _____, _____,

Off they go.

参考译文

去车站

清晨起个早,

来到火车站,

小小车厢站成排,

司机动手把车开。

呜! 呜! 突! 突!

开车!

6. Edelweiss

Edelweiss, Edelweiss,

Every morning you greet me,

Small and white,

Clean and bright.

You look happy to meet me.

Blossoms of snow *may* you *bloom* and grow,

Bloom and grow forever.

Edelweiss, Edelweiss,

Bless my homeland forever.

语言注释

1. edelweiss / ˈeɪdlvaɪs / *n*. 火绒草,雪绒花
2. blossom / ˈblɒsɒm / *n*. 花
3. may / meɪ / *aux*. 祝愿
4. bloom / bluːm / *n*. & *v*. 开花
5. bless / bles / *v*. 保佑

背景介绍

雪绒花就是奥地利的国花火绒草,这种花通常生长在阿尔卑斯山脉海拔1700米以上的地方。在奥地利,雪绒花象征着勇敢,因为野生的雪绒花生长在环境艰苦的高山上,常人难以得见其美丽容颜,所以见过雪绒花的人都是英雄。从前,奥地利许多年轻人冒着生命危险,攀上陡峭的山崖,只为摘下一朵雪绒花献给自己的心上人,因为只有雪绒花才能代表为爱牺牲一切的决心。

篇目欣赏

中国人对雪绒花的了解大都来自美国影片《音乐之声》,片中插曲《雪绒花》已在全世界流行,甚至被称为奥地利的非正式国歌。《雪绒花》的蓝本是一首古老的奥地利民歌,通过对这种美丽国花的歌颂,表达了奥地利人民发自内心的质朴的爱乡之情。在影片中,《雪绒花》的旋律多次响起。第一次是男主人公,冯·特拉普上校借此曲表达对女家庭教师,玛丽亚的接纳,第二次则是全家在家庭沙龙演唱会上,以此曲抒发对祖国的热爱。当拒绝为纳粹服务的上校准备冒险带全家离去时,他为家乡的父老乡亲献上的,还是那首他最喜爱的《雪绒花》。但一曲未了,歌喉已哽咽。玛丽亚默契地接唱下去,并带动全场观众加入大合唱,将影片推向高潮。

背诵准备

这首歌中的形容词用得很美。试着填一填并体会一下。

Edelweiss, Edelweiss,
Every morning you greet me,
_____ and _____,
_____ and _____,
You look _____ to meet me.
Blossoms of snow may you bloom and grow,
Bloom and grow forever.
Edelweiss, Edelweiss,
Bless my homeland forever.

参考译文

雪绒花

雪绒花,雪绒花,每天清晨你问候我。

小而白,洁而亮,见到我你面露喜色。

雪白的花蕾,你快开放,永远鲜艳芬芳。

雪绒花,雪绒花,祝我祖国万年长。

7. Twinkle, Twinkle, Little Star

Twinkle, twinkle, little star,
How I *wonder* what you are.
Up above the world so high,
Like a diamond in the sky.
Twinkle, twinkle, little star,
How I wonder what you are!

When the *blazing* sun is gone,
When he nothing shines *upon*,
Then you show your little light,
Twinkle, twinkle, all the night.
Twinkle, twinkle, little star,
How I wonder what you are!

语言注释

1. twinkle / ˈtwɪŋkl / *v.* 闪烁
2. wonder / ˈwʌndə / *v.* 对……感到惊奇;想知道
3. blaže / bleɪz / *v.* 燃烧,照耀
4. upon / əˈpɒn / *prep.* 在……之上

背景介绍

这 原是一首 18 世纪的法国民歌。法文歌曲并不是关于星星的,而是一个孩子渴望得到糖果的故事。17 岁的莫扎特根据这个旋律,谱写了一首钢琴变奏曲"Ah! Vous Dirai-je, Maman"。这是一首献给孩子们的钢琴变奏曲。而在 1806 年,Jane Taylor 谱写了英文歌词,歌名是"Twinkle, Twinkle, Little Star"。中文歌曲也是根据英文的歌词翻译过来的。大家熟悉的 ABC 字母歌也是同样的旋律呢!

篇目欣赏

歌 词将闪亮的小星星比喻成熠熠的钻石"like a diamond in the sky"，这样可以让小孩子们学会怎样用词语将头脑中的想象生动地描绘出来，也让人体味到英语语言的魅力。歌词将小星星拟人化，对着星星说话并发问，将小星星人性化地展现于眼前，给小星星赋予了很强的生命力。

背诵准备

此歌共有三节，第三节内容如下，只是空出一词，那么你能判断一下这一节描写的是小星星对哪一类人的帮助吗？请填入空格。

Then the _____ in the dark

Thanks you for your tiny spark.

How could he see where to go,

If you did not twinkle so?

Twinkle, twinkle, little star,

How I wonder what you are!

参考译文

一闪一闪亮晶晶

一闪一闪亮晶晶，

神奇可爱的小星星。

高高挂在天空中，

好像宝石放光明。

一闪一闪亮晶晶，

神奇可爱的小星星。

当那太阳落下山，

大地披上黑色夜影。
天上升起小星星,
光辉照耀到天明。
一闪一闪亮晶晶,
神奇可爱的小星星。

8. Oh, Susanna

By Stephen Foster

I came from *Alabama*

With my *banjo* on my knee，

I'm going to *Louisiana*

My true love for to see；

It rained all night the day I left，

The weather it was dry；

The sun so hot I *froze* to death；

Susanna，don't you cry.

Oh，Susanna，

Oh，don't you cry for me，

I've come from Alabama

With my banjo on my knee.

Oh，Susanna，

Oh，don't you cry for me，

'*Cause* I'm goin' to Louisiana，

My true love for to see.

语言注释

1. Alabama /ˌæləˈbæmə / 阿拉巴马州
   (美国州名)

2. banjo / ˈbændʒəʊ / *n*. 班卓琴

3. Louisiana / luˌ(ː)iːzɪˈænə / 路易斯安那
   (美国州名)

4. freeze / friːz / *v*. (froze 为过去式)感觉很冷

5. 'cause / kɔːz / *conj*. 因为(= because)

背景介绍

这首儿歌是美国民谣之父佛斯特（Stephen Foster）的早期作品。佛斯特一生不曾受过正式的音乐教育，其音乐知识，全是自修得来的。因为他的亲人大都居住在美国南方，所以对黑人的生活有深刻的了解。但是佛斯特的歌曲在本质上跟黑人灵歌又是相异的，而更近于英国纯朴的歌谣曲。因此无论是黑人还是白人，身处欧美或远东，各国的人们都非常喜欢他的作品。

篇目欣赏

"哦！苏珊娜（Oh! Susanna）"可能为佛斯特21岁（1847年）时的作品。这是一首二拍子的节奏轻快的歌曲，据说这首用打油诗般的四节歌词写成的曲子（本文节选了两节）是佛斯特为一名黑人卖唱者而写的，那些不合逻辑的句子非常幽默，完全是为了逗引听众哈哈大笑。

背诵准备

你能记得那两个美国的州名以及两句不合乎逻辑的诙谐的句子吗？

I came from ＿＿＿＿＿＿
With my banjo on my knee,
I'm going to ＿＿＿＿＿＿
My true love for to see;
It rained all night the day I left,
＿＿＿＿＿＿ ＿＿＿＿＿＿ ＿＿＿＿＿＿;
＿＿＿＿＿＿ ＿＿＿＿＿＿ ＿＿＿＿＿＿
＿＿＿＿＿＿ ＿＿＿＿＿＿ ＿＿＿＿＿＿;
Susanna, don't you cry.

参考译文

噢！苏珊娜！

我已从阿拉巴马回来，
膝盖上放着我的班卓琴，
我正要到路易斯安那，
去看我的爱人，
我离开的时候整夜下着雨，
天气十分干燥，
太阳如此炎热以至于我差点儿冻死。
苏珊娜，不要哭泣。
噢，苏珊娜，噢，不要为我哭泣。
我已从阿拉巴马回来，
膝盖上放着我的班卓琴。
噢，苏珊娜，噢，不要为我哭泣，
因为我正要到路易斯安那，
去看我的爱人。

9. Do-Re-Mi

Let's start at the very beginning,
A very good place to start.
When you read you begin with A-B-C;
When you sing you begin with Do-Re-Mi
Do-Re-Mi, Do-Re-Mi.
The first three *notes*
Just happen to be
Do-Re-Mi,
Do-Re-Mi,
Do-Re-Mi-Fa-So-La-Ti.

Doe — a deer, a *female* deer;
Ray — a drop of *golden* sun;
Me — a name, I call myself;
Far — a long long way to run;
Sew — a *needle pulling thread*;
La — a note to follow "sew";
Tea — a drink with *jam* and bread.
That will bring us
Back to Do-oh-oh.

语言注释

1. note / nəʊt / *n.* 音符
2. female / ˈfiːmeɪl / *adj.* 女性的, 雌的
3. golden / ˈgəʊldən / *adj.* 金色的
4. needle / ˈniːdl / *n.* 针
5. pull / pʊl / *v.* 拉
6. thread / θred / *n.* 线
7. jam / dʒæm / *n.* 果酱

背景介绍

"Do-Re-Mi"是音乐电影《音乐之声》(1965 年初搬上银幕)里的插曲之一。玛丽亚带着上校的七个孩子出去游玩时教他们唱这首儿歌。有趣的是,玛丽亚让这七个孩子按年龄大小代表"哆来咪发嗦啦梯"这七个音符。

篇目欣赏

这是一首非常欢快的音乐启蒙儿歌,家庭教师玛丽亚采取非常巧妙的方式来启发孩子们对每个音符的记忆。从旋律上讲,这首歌采用了"级进"的方法。老师唱,然后孩子们学唱一遍。接下去,先由孩子们在每个乐曲的第一拍顺序说出七个音符的唱名,老师接唱通俗易懂的词。她找出了与 7 个音符谐音的英文单词,并加以解释,这些词句生动、形象,易学易记。用这种方法教孩子们音乐,真是妙趣横生。

背诵准备

顺序打乱后,你还能准确的记得这些音符吗?

_____ — a long long way to run

_____ — a drink with jam and bread

_____ — a needle pulling thread

_____ — a name, I call myself

_____ — a deer, a female deer

_____ — a note to follow "sew"

_____ — a drop of golden sun

参考译文

哆来咪

让我们从头开始学,有个好开头。读书是从 ABC 开始,

唱歌就从哆,来,咪开始。哆,来,咪。哆,来,咪;哆,来,咪

一开始三个音符。哆,来,咪。哆,来,咪。哆,来,咪,发,嗦,啦,梯。

"哆"是一只小母鹿,"来"是一束金色的阳光,

"咪"是称呼我自己,"发"是道路远又长,

"嗦"是穿针又引线,"啦"是音符跟着"嗦",

"梯"是饮料与茶点,然后我们再唱"哆,噢,噢"。

10. Hush, Little Baby

Hush，little baby，don't say a word，

Mama's going to buy you a *mockingbird*.

And if that mockingbird won't sing，

Mama's going to buy you a *diamond* ring.

And if that diamond ring turns *brass*，

Mama's going to buy you a looking glass.

And if that looking glass gets broke，

Mama's going to buy you a *billy goat*.

And if that billy goat won't pull，

Mama's going to buy you a *cart* and *bull*.

And if that cart and bull turn over，

Mama's going to buy you a dog named Rover.

And if that dog named Rover won't bark，

Mama's going to buy you a horse and cart.

And if that horse and cart fall down，

You'll still be the sweetest little baby in town.

语言注释

1. mockingbird / ˈmɒkɪŋbɜːd / *n*. 嘲鸫
2. diamond / ˈdaɪəmənd / *n*. 钻石
3. brass / brɑːs / *n*. 黄铜
4. billy goat   雄山羊
5. cart / kɑːt / *n*. 大车,兽力车
6. bull / bʊl / *n*. 公牛

背景介绍

这 首儿歌实际是一首摇篮曲。它的节奏模仿摇篮的摆动,曲调舒缓、温馨,让人感到很亲切。

篇目欣赏

在 这首儿歌里母亲对摇篮里的小宝宝许下各种承诺:Momma's going to buy you a mockingbird,可如果出现意外 mockingbird 不唱歌呢? 那就买个 diamond ring 吧。但戒指会失去光泽呀,别急,那么买个 looking glass。虽说小孩子的要求总是千番万番难以满足,但只为能哄小宝宝安静地入睡,又有什么关系呢? 相信这也是天下父母亲都能深切体会到的情感。

背诵准备

妈妈总担心给小宝宝买的东西会出现问题,到底是哪些问题呢?

And if that mockingbird _____ _____,

Mama's going to buy you a diamond ring.

And if that diamond ring _____ _____,

Mama's going to buy you a looking glass.

And if that looking glass _____ _____,

Mama's going to buy you a billy goat.

And if that billy goat _____ _____,

Mama's going to buy you a cart and bull.

And if that cart and bull _____ _____,

Mama's going to buy you a dog named Rover.

And if that dog named Rover _____ _____,

Mama's going to buy you a horse and cart.

And if that horse and cart _____ _____,

You'll still be the sweetest little baby in town.

参考译文

安静，小宝贝

安静，小宝贝，不要说话，妈妈给你买只嘲鸫。

如果鸟儿不唱歌，妈妈给你买钻石戒指；

如果戒指变成黄铜，妈妈给你买镜子；

如果镜子摔碎了，妈妈给你买只雄山羊；

如果山羊拉不动，妈妈给你买牛车；

如果牛车翻了，妈妈给你买只叫流浪者的小狗；

如果小狗不叫唤，妈妈给你买马车；

如果马车倒了，你还是城里最可爱的小宝贝！

11. Mary Had a Little Lamb

Mary had a little *lamb*, its *fleece* was white as snow；

And everywhere that Mary went, the lamb was sure to go.

It *followed* her to school one day, which was *against* the *rule*；

It made the children laugh and play, to see a lamb at school.

And so the teacher *turned* it *out*, but still it *lingered* near,

And waited *patiently* about till Mary did appear.

"Why does the lamb love Mary so?" the *eager* children *cry*；

"Why，Mary loves the lamb, you know," the teacher did *reply*.

语言注释

1. lamb / læm / *n*. 小羊，羔羊
2. fleece / fliːs / *n*. 羊毛
3. follow / ˈfɒləʊ / *v*. 跟随
4. against / əˈgeɪnst / *prep*. 与……相反
5. rule / ruːl / *n*. 规则
6. turn out   驱逐
7. linger / ˈlɪŋgə / *v*. 逗留
8. patient / ˈpeɪʃənt / *adj*. 耐心的
   patiently *adv*. 耐心地
9. eager / ˈiːgə / *adj*. 热切的，渴望的
10. cry / kraɪ / *v*. 叫喊
11. reply / rɪˈplaɪ / *v*. 回答，答复

背景介绍

歌词中描写的故事发生 1815 年 3 月。有一只刚生下来的小羊羔被母亲遗弃,快要死了。当时一个 9 岁的小女孩玛丽向父亲要求将小羊羔带回家。开始她父亲不同意,可后来玛丽终于说服了他。玛丽整晚地照顾小羊,到了第二天早上它能够站起来了,而且很快恢复健康。后来这只羊还生育了三只小羊,其中有一对双胞胎。小羊成了玛丽最好的伙伴,处处跟着她,有一天甚至悄悄跟着她来到学校。幸好老师还没到,她将小羊放在自己座椅下面,并用毯子盖好。小羊趴在下面,一直很安静。过了一会儿玛丽被叫到前面去背诵课文,这时,小羊居然也跟上前去,老师和同学们都哈哈大笑起来。玛丽只好在午饭时将小羊送回了家。那天正好有个叫做约翰·鲁尔斯通的年轻人来学校参观,看到了这一幕。于是第二天他到学校将一张小纸条塞到玛丽手里,纸条上就写着这首歌的大部分内容。关于歌词的创作有两种说法:一是说约翰写了前半部分,另一个叫莎拉·哈尔的波士顿人完成了后半部分;还有种说法是整篇都是莎拉·哈尔创作的。1877 年,爱迪生发明了留声机,他在锡箔圆筒上录下的第一句话就是"玛丽有只小羊羔"。

篇目欣赏

这首儿歌深受小孩子们的喜欢,歌词中有比喻的用法"Its fleece was white as snow"。玛丽像一个母亲一样照顾小羊,小羊也成了玛丽最亲密的小伙伴。当老师将它赶走时它还"lingered near",依依不舍直到玛丽出现。歌词字里行间流露出小羊羔与玛丽的亲密无间。歌词向我们传达了这样一种含义:爱是相互的。

背诵准备

请将歌中描写小羊羔的词语填出来。

Mary had a little lamb its fleece was _____ _____ _____ ;

And everywhere that Mary went, the lamb was _____ ___ __ __ _____ .

It _____ her to school one day, which was against the rule;

It _____ the children laugh and play, to see a lamb at school.

And so the teacher turned it out, but still it _____ _____ ,

And _____ _____ about till Mary did appear.

参考译文

玛丽有只小羊羔

玛丽有只小羊羔,它的毛像雪一样白。

玛丽走到哪里,小羊羔必定跟随。

有一天她跟着玛丽去学校,这可是违背校规的;

伙伴们看到它都笑开了花,还跟它一起玩。

老师要赶它走,可它在一旁逗留不离开,

一直耐心地等到玛丽出现。

"为什么小羊羔这么喜欢玛丽?"小伙伴们急切地问;

"因为玛丽也喜欢小羊羔啊,你们知道的,"老师回答道。

12. London Bridge Is Falling Down

London Bridge is falling down，
Falling down，falling down，
London Bridge is falling down，
My *fair* Lady.
Build it up with wood and *clay*，
Wood and clay will wash away，
My fair Lady.
Build it up with bricks and *mortar*，
Bricks and mortar will not stay，
My fair Lady.
Build it up with iron and *steel*，
Iron and steel will bend and *bow*，
My fair Lady.
Build it up with silver and gold，
Silver and gold will be stolen away，
My fair Lady.
Set a man to *watch* all night，
Suppose the man should fall asleep，
Give him a *pipe* to smoke all night，
My fair Lady.

语言注释

1. fair / feə / *adj*. 美丽的
2. clay / kleɪ / *n*. 黏土
3. mortar / ˈmɔːtə / *n*. 砂浆,灰浆
4. steel / stiːl / *n*. 钢
5. bow / baʊ / *v*. 弯腰
6. watch / wɒtʃ / *v*. 看守,守护
7. suppose / səˈpəʊz / *v*. 假设

8. pipe / paɪp / *n*. 烟斗

背景介绍

就像这首儿歌中唱的那样,历史上的伦敦桥不仅倒塌过,而且倒塌过多次。像伦敦桥这样屡经兴废而依然名声不倒的桥梁实属罕见。

公元 50 年左右,罗马人在泰晤士河上用木头搭建桥梁,这就是最初的伦敦桥。1014 年,英格兰国王埃塞尔雷德二世为了将入侵的丹麦军队一分为二,下令烧毁伦敦桥。这件事据说导致了"*London Bridge Is Falling Down*"这首著名童谣的产生。

自 1176 年开始,人们开始用石头建造伦敦桥。桥面上建起了许多房屋和商店,甚至还建了一座小教堂。这些不仅带来火情隐患,而且增加了桥梁的承重负担。据说 1212 年的大火导致了 3000 人死亡。1633 年的一场大火将一半的桥梁烧毁。

如今的伦敦桥建于 1967 年至 1972 年之间,是座水泥桥。两千年来,伦敦桥不仅见证了人类的历史,其本身就是人类文明的发展史。

篇目欣赏

"*London Bridge Is Falling Down*"这首儿歌就是根据伦敦桥几经磨难的历史而创作的。歌中提到了几次修建伦敦桥的不同材料:一开始因为木头和泥土"will wash away";于是被换用砖头,砖头"will not stay";于是重建时采用了钢铁,钢铁"will bend and bow". 便改用金银,可金银"will be stolen away";人们便安排了人整夜值班来守卫大桥,可又怕他会"fall asleep",于是就给他烟斗抽,这样他就不会打瞌睡误事了。虽然用金银造桥这些情节有些夸张,但却表现出伦敦人对大桥的热爱以及修缮保护它的良好愿望。

背诵准备

记住这首儿歌中不同材质以及它们的特性是背诵的关键。你能填出以下的空格吗？

Build it up with _____ _____ _____,
_____ _____ _____ will wash away;
Build it up with bricks and mortar,
Bricks and mortar _____ _____ _____;
Build it up with _____ _____ _____,
_____ _____ _____ will bend and bow;
Build it up with silver and gold,
Silver and gold _____ _____ _____ _____.

参考译文

伦敦桥要倒了

伦敦桥要倒了,要倒了,要倒了,
伦敦桥要倒了,我的小女孩。
用木头、泥土来造桥,木头、泥土容易被冲走,我的小女孩。
用砖头、砂浆来造桥,砖头、砂浆不牢固,我的小女孩。
用钢和铁来造桥,钢和铁会弯曲,我的小女孩。
用金和银来造桥,金和银会被偷走,我的小女孩。
派一个人整夜守护着桥,可他要打瞌睡呢?
那就给他一支烟斗抽吧,让他整夜抽烟我的小女孩。

13. Hallowe'en Night

When autumn comes,
And the days of *crisp* October,
Then comes a night,
Weird things are seen;
Witches on *broomsticks*,
And *glowing jack-o'-lanterns*,
Peer through the windows —
Hallowe'en!

Then boys and girls
Gather round the fire a-glowing,
Faces are *painted*
Bright blue and green;
Apples are *bobbing*,
And *gypsies telling fortunes*,
Fun and *mystery*,
Hallowe'en!

语言注释

1. crisp / krɪsp / *adj.* 干冷的
2. weird / wɪəd / *adj.* 古怪的
3. witch / wɪtʃ / *n.* 巫婆
4. broomstick / ˈbruːmstɪk / *n.* 扫帚柄
5. glow / ɡləʊ / *v.* 发光
6. jack-o'-lantern / dʒæk əʊ ˈlæntən / *n.* 南瓜灯
7. peer / pɪə / *v.* 凝视,窥视
8. gather / ˈɡæðə / *v.* 聚集
9. paint / peɪnt / *v.* 着色
10. bob / bɒb / *v.* 在水面上下或来回的浮动
11. gypsy / ˈdʒɪpsɪ / *n.* 吉普赛人
12. tell fortune 算命

13. mystery / ˈmɪstərɪ / *adj.* 神秘的

背景介绍

关于万圣节的由来,传说是在基督诞生以前,欧洲的凯尔特人在夏末举行仪式,感激上苍和太阳的恩惠。他们认为 10 月 31 日是秋天正式结束的日子,也就是新年伊始。那时人们相信,故人的亡魂会在这一天回来在活人身上找寻生灵,借此再生。而活着的人则惧怕死魂来夺生,于是人们就在这一天熄掉炉火、烛光,让死魂无法找寻活人,又把自己打扮成妖魔鬼怪把死人之魂灵吓走。当时的占卜者(gypsies)和巫婆(witches)还施巫术以驱赶据说在四周游荡的妖魔鬼怪。时间流逝,万圣节的意义逐渐起了变化,变得积极快乐起来,喜庆的意味成了主流。死魂找替身返世的说法也渐渐被摒弃和忘却。如今,象征万圣节的形象、图画如巫婆、黑猫等,大都有友善、可爱和滑稽的脸。它成了孩子们的节日,年轻人开化装舞会来庆贺。它也是西方人一个很普通的季节性节日。有很多人将此看作秋的结束以及冬的到来。万圣节一过,人们就开始期盼感恩节、圣诞节乃至新年了。

篇目欣赏

万圣节是儿童们纵情玩乐的节目。它在孩子们眼中,是一个充满神秘色彩的节日。夜幕降临,孩子们便迫不及待地穿上五颜六色的化妆服,脸上涂上油彩或是戴上千奇百怪的面具,提上一盏"杰克灯"(jack-o'-lantern)跑出去玩。"杰克灯"的样子十分可爱,它是将南瓜掏空,外面刻上笑眯眯的眼睛和大嘴巴做成的,然后在瓜中插上一支蜡烛,把它点燃,人们在很远的地方便能看到这张憨态可掬的笑脸。万圣节前夜最流行的游戏是"咬苹果"。游戏时,人们让苹果漂浮在装满水的盆里,然后让孩子们在不用手的条件下用嘴去咬苹果,谁先咬到,谁就是优胜者。

背诵准备

请试着填入与万圣节有关的传统事物或习俗。

Weird things are seen;
_____ on _____,
And glowing _____,
Peer through the windows —
Hallowe'en!
Then boys and girls
Gather round the fire a-glowing,
Faces are _____
Bright blue and green;
Apples are _____,
And _____ telling fortunes,
Fun and mystery,
Hallowe'en!

参考译文

万圣节之夜

在秋天来临，
十月干冷的天气里，
有一晚发生着怪异的事情。
乘着扫把的女巫，
闪着荧光的南瓜灯
从窗子里窥视进来——
万圣节！
男孩女孩们
聚集在闪耀的火堆旁，
脸上涂着油彩，

明亮的蓝色和绿色。
苹果在水面上漂动，
吉普赛人在估算着来日，
有趣又神秘，
万圣节！

14. The Twelve Days of Christmas (excerpt)

On the twelfth day of Christmas,

My true love sent to me

Twelve *drummers drumming*,

Eleven *pipers piping*,

Ten *lords* a-*leaping*,

Nine ladies dancing,

Eight *maids* a-*milking*,

Seven *swans* a-swimming,

Six *geese* a-*laying*,

Five *golden* rings,

Four calling birds,

Three French hens,

Two *turtle doves*,

And a *partridge* in a pear tree!

语言注释

1. drummer / ˈdrʌmə / *n*. 鼓手

2. drum / drʌm / *v*. 打鼓, 击鼓

3. piper / ˈpaɪpə / *n*. 吹笛手

4. pipe / paɪp / *v*. 吹笛

5. lord / lɔːd / *n*. 贵族

6. leap / liːp / *v*. 跳, 跳跃

7. maid / meɪd / *n*. 女仆

8. milk / mɪlk / *v*. 挤奶

9. swan / swɒn / *n*. 天鹅

10. geese / giːs / *n*. 鹅 (复数, 单数为 goose)

11. lay / leɪ / *v*. 下蛋

12. golden / ˈɡəʊldən / *adj*. 金色的

13. turtle dove　斑鸠

14. partridge / ˈpɑːtrɪdʒ / *n*. 山鹑

背景介绍

"The Twelve Days of Christmas"是一首旋律轻快、欢乐的圣诞歌曲，在西方国家，小孩子们都耳熟能详。在网上你可以找到许多与圣诞节礼品或游戏有关的网站，可见这12天是多么欢快愉悦的时光！12天指的是从12月25日圣诞节开始到1月5日耶稣显灵日为止的这12天。

这首儿歌起源于16世纪的英国。从1558到1829年间，天主教在英国被禁止，教徒们为了抵抗当权者的压迫并且坚持传颂教义，于是为年轻的教徒们写了这首歌。歌词里的每一天实际上都是有特殊含义的。整首儿歌分12节唱出12天，每一天唱出一样事物，并同时将前面提到的事物依次序累加在里面，这里我们只截取了最后第12天的歌词。

篇目欣赏

现在我们就来破解这12个密码吧！

1. A partridge in a pear tree 即代表耶稣在十字架上

2. turtle doves 指圣经新约和旧约

3. French hens 即 faith, hope and charity, 信仰、希望和慈善这三种美德

4. calling birds 即四位圣经新约福音书的作者 Matthew, Mark, Luke 和 John

5. golden rings 指圣经旧约的开首五卷，又称摩西五书

6. geese a-laying 指创世纪的六天

7. swans a-swimming 指圣灵的七个圣礼

8. maids a-milking 指八个福气(穷人有福了)

9. ladies dancing 指圣灵的九个圣果，即仁爱、喜乐、和平、忍耐、仁慈、善良、忠诚、温柔和自控

10. lords a-leaping 指十诫

11. pipers piping 指十一个忠心门徒

12. drummers drumming 指耶稣十二个使徒信条的十二要点

此外，true love 指上帝，me 指受洗过的人。

背诵准备

这首歌里有很多名词和现在分词的对应，例如：drummers drumming 打鼓的鼓手。先来填写这几组词，有助于我们背诵。

On the twelfth day of Christmas,

My true love sent to me

Twelve drummers _____,

Eleven pipers _____,

Ten _____ a-leaping,

Nine ladies _____,

Eight maids a-_____,

Seven _____ a-swimming,

Six geese a-_____,

Five golden rings,

Four calling birds,

Three French hens,

Two turtle doves,

And a partridge in a pear tree!

参考译文

圣诞假期的十二天(节选)

在圣诞假期的第十二天,

我的真爱送给我,

十二个打着鼓的鼓手,

十一个吹风笛的笛手,

十个在跳跃的贵族,

九个跳舞的淑女,

八个在挤牛奶的少女,

七只在游水的天鹅,

六只在下蛋的鹅,

五只金戒指,

四只啼叫的鸟儿,

三只法国母鸡,

两只斑鸠,

和一只梨树里的山鹑!

寓言

15. The Mosquito and the Bull

By Aesop

A *mosquito settled* on the *horn* of a *bull*，and sat there for a long time. Just as he was about to fly off，he made a *buzzing* noise，and asked the bull if he would like him to go. The bull replied，"I did not know you have come，and I shall not miss you when you go away."

Some men are of more importance in their own eyes than in the eyes of others.

语言注释

1. mosquito / məˈskiːtəʊ / *n*. -toes 蚊子
2. settle / ˈsetl / *v*. 降落，停息
3. horn / hɔːn / *n*. (牛羊等的)角
4. bull / bʊl / *n*. 公牛
5. buzzing / bʌzɪŋ / *n*. 嗡嗡声

背景介绍

《伊索寓言》产生于希腊的古典时期，相传由伊索创作，再由后人收集成书。也有人认为并无伊索其人，只是古人假托其名将一些民间故事集结成书。它通过简短的小寓言故事来体现日常生活中那些不为我们察觉的真理，是人类智慧的结晶。其结构短小精悍，其内容博大丰满，寓永恒真理于短小故事之中，既有深刻丰富的思想性，又有形象生动的艺术性，是一部轻松且充满哲理的永世相传之佳作。

篇目欣赏

"**S**ome men are of more importance in their own eyes than in the eyes of others." 这是说，有些人总以为自己很重要，但别人却不以为然。蚊子无论是在体积还是体重上都无法和公牛相比，它的去留对于公牛来说是不值一提的。对于那些既软弱又无知的人，存在与否，人们都觉得无关紧要。反之如果要引起别人的注意，那就必须先提高自身的水平，不然无论你怎么 buzz 都不能引起他人的关注。

背诵准备

把下面句中直接引语改成间接引语，或把间接引语改成直接引语。

1. Just as he was about to fly off, he made a buzzing noise and asked the bull, "Would you like me to go?"

   _____

   _____

2. The bull replied that he did not know the mosquito had come, and he would not miss him when he went away.

   _____

   _____

参考译文

蚊子和公牛

　　有只蚊子落在牛角上，在那儿呆了很长时间。飞走前，它嗡嗡地问公牛，是否希望它离开。公牛回答道："你来了，我不知道。现在你要走了，我也不会想念你。"

　　有些人总以为自己很重要，但别人却不以为然。

16. The Fox and the Grapes

By Aesop

On one hot summer day，a fox was *strolling* through an *orchard* when he saw *a bunch of ripe* grapes. "It can *quench* my thirst，" thought the fox. Drawing back a few steps，he took a run and a jump，but just missed the bunch. He tried again and again，but still failed to reach the bunch. At last，he had to give up. He walked away with his nose in the air，saying，"I am sure they are *sour*."

语言注释

1. stroll / strəʊl / *v.* 闲逛，溜达
2. orchard / ˈɔːtʃəd / *n.* 果园
3. a bunch of 一串，一束
4. ripe / raɪp / *adj.* (水果或庄稼)成熟的
5. quench / kwentʃ / *v.* 解渴
6. sour / ˈsaʊə / *adj.* 酸的

篇目欣赏

狐狸试了一次又一次，都没有成功。最后，他决定放弃，他昂起头，边走边说："我敢肯定那些葡萄是酸的。"在经历了许多尝试而不能获得成功的时候，有些人往往故意轻视成功，以此来寻求心理安慰。在我们的生活中，常会因为得不到想要的东西而产生这种"酸葡萄"的心里，其实要得到内心真正的快乐，唯有看淡一切的得失，"拿得起、放得下"，那时你会发现其实你拥有的也不少。

背诵准备

请把下面各组中的几个句子合并成一句,写完后对照原文,看看自己写对了吗?

1. A fox was strolling through an orchard.

   The fox saw a bunch of ripe grapes.

   _____

   _____

2. The fox drew back a few steps.

   He took a run and a jump.

   He missed the bunch.

   _____

   _____

3. The fox tried again and again.

   He failed to reach the bunch.

   _____

   _____

4. The fox walked away with his nose in the air.

   He said, "I am sure they are sour."

   _____

   _____

参考译文

狐狸和葡萄

　　一个炎热的夏日,狐狸闲逛到一片果园,看到一串熟透了的葡萄。"正好能让我解渴,"狐狸想。于是他退后几步,助跑,起跳,却没有摘到那串葡萄。他一遍又一遍地尝试,却总摘不到。最后他决定放弃。他高高地昂起头,一边走一边说:"我敢肯定那些葡萄是酸的。"

17. The Prophet

By Aesop

A *prophet*, sitting in the market, was telling the *fortunes* of the *passers-by*. Suddenly a man ran up to him in a hurry, and told him that somebody had *broken into* his house, and was stealing the things inside. He *hastened* home as fast as he could. A neighbor saw him running and said, "Hey, my friend, you say you can *foretell* the fortunes of others, why can't you *foresee* your own?"

语言注释

1. prophet / ˈprɒfɪt / *n*. 预言家
2. fortune / ˈfɔːtʃən / *n*. 运气
3. passer-by / pɑːsəˈbaɪ / *n*. 过路人
4. break into 闯入
5. hasten / ˈheɪsn / *v*. (使)赶紧,(使)急忙
6. foretell / fɔːˈtel / *v*. 预言
7. foresee / fɔːˈsiː / *v*. 预见,预料

篇目欣赏

预言家整天忙着为别人算命,却没有算出自己眼前的灾难,令人不得不怀疑他是否真的能帮别人算出未来。有一点可以肯定每个人的命运都是掌握在自己手中,靠算命是不能给自己带来本质性的变化,何况这世界上也没有谁能真正预知未来。脚踏实地的努力才是避免灾难,获取成功的途径。

背诵准备

请用括号内动词的正确形式填空。

A prophet, _____ (sit) in the market, _____ (tell) the fortunes of the passers-by. Suddenly a man _____ (run) up to him in a hurry, and _____ (tell) him that somebody _____ (break) into his house, and _____ (steal) the things inside. He _____ (hasten) home as fast as he could. A neighbor _____ (see) him _____ (run) and said, "Hey, my friend, you say you can _____ (foretell) the fortunes of others, why can't you _____ (foresee) your own?"

参考译文

预言家

有个预言家在集市给过路人算命,突然有一个人飞奔过来,告诉他他的家被人破门而入,有人正在偷他的东西。预言家一听,就赶紧跑回家,跑得要多快有多快。一位邻居看见他在跑,就说道:"我的朋友,你说能预测他人的祸福,怎么不能预见自己的呢?"

18. The Fox and the Mask

By Aesop

A Fox had *by some means* got into the *storeroom* of a theater. Suddenly he noticed a face *glaring* down on him and began to be very frightened. But looking more *closely* he found it was only a *Mask* like the ones actors use to put over their faces.

"Ah," said the Fox, "you look very *fine*, but it is a pity that you haven't got any *brains*."

语言注释

1. by some means   以某种方法
2. storeroom / stɔːrʊm / *n*. 储藏室、仓库
3. glare / gleə / *v*. 瞪视、怒目注视
4. closely / ˈkləʊzlɪ / *adv*. 近距离地
5. mask / mɑːsk / *n*. 面具
6. fine / faɪn / *adj*. 美丽的
7. brain / breɪn / *n*. 头脑

篇目欣赏

这故事是说那身体魁伟而缺乏思想的人。外表难饰其本质。人是如此,同样在我们周围,许多事情的外表和本质之间存在着差异。有些事情看似很难,其实你真正动手去做了,也能通过自身的努力去实现目标的。相反有些事情看似简单,但当你卷入其中时,却会发现这远远没有你所估计的那样容易。所以我们看人看事不能被其表象所迷惑,要善于发现他们的本质。

背诵准备

请把下面各组中的几个句子合并成一句,写完后对照原文,看看自己写对了吗?

1. Suddenly he noticed a face.

   The face glared down on him.

   _____

   _____

2. He looked more closely.

   He found it was only a Mask.

   The Mask was like the ones actors use to put over their faces.

   _____

   _____

3. You look very fine.

   It is a pity.

   You haven't got any brains.

   _____

   _____

参考译文

狐狸和面具

狐狸用尽方法溜进一家剧院的储藏室。忽然发现一张脸正对自己怒目而视。他大惊失色,凑过去仔细一看,原来是一张演员戴的面具。

狐狸说道:"唉,你看起来挺漂亮,只可惜没长脑子。"

19. The Astronomer

By Aesop

An *astronomer* used to go out at night to *observe* the stars. One evening, while he was *wandering* through the *suburbs* looking up to observe the stars, he fell into a deep *ditch accidentally*. When he got out of the ditch, he found he got *black and blue* all over the body. After his neighbor learned the whole story, he said, "My friend, why do you only keep thinking about the things in the heaven, but not manage to see what is on the earth?"

语言注释

1. astronomer / əˈstrɒnəmə(r) / *n*. 天文学家
2. observe / əbˈzɜːv / *v*. 观察
3. wander / ˈwɒndə / *v*. 游荡，闲逛
4. suburb / ˈsʌbɜːb / *n*. 郊区，郊外
5. ditch / dɪtʃ / *n*. 沟，渠
6. accidentally / ˌæksɪˈdentlɪ / *adv*. 意外地
7. black and blue   青一块，紫一块

篇目欣赏

人 首先要做好最普通的事，才谈得上高深的事。故事里的天文学家能陶醉于上天的美妙，却也因此跌入地上的深沟。人们可能会笑他只顾着探寻遥远的事物，而忽略了眼前最简单，最基本的事情。在生活中许多人都可能急于求成，好高骛远而忽略基础，这真是得不偿失。

背诵准备

请把下面各组中的几个句子合并成一句,写完后对照原文,看看自己写对了吗?

1. He was wandering through the suburbs.

   He looked up to observe the stars.

   He fell into a deep ditch accidentally.

   _____

   _____

2. He got out of the ditch.

   He found he got black and blue all over the body.

   _____

   _____

3. His neighbor learned the whole story.

   After that, he said, "..."

   _____

   _____

参考译文

天文学家

有个天文学家习惯夜观星相。有一天晚上,他来到郊外,全神贯注地望着天空,一不留神跌进了一条深沟。当他从沟里爬出来以后,发现自己浑身上下青一块,紫一块。他的邻居知道了这事后说:"我的朋友,为什么你一心只想着天上的事,不看看地上呢?"

20. The Crow and the Pitcher

By Aesop

A thirsty crow saw a pitcher. He flew to it happily, hoping to find some water in it. But when he reached it, he discovered there was so little water that his beak could not possibly reach it. He tried everything to reach the water, but all his *efforts* were *in vain*. At last, he collected as many *pebbles* as he could carry and dropped them into the pitcher with his beak. The water *rose* and he was able to quench his thirst.

Necessity is the mother of invention.

语言注释

1. effort / ˈefət / *n*. 努力,竭力
2. in vain   徒劳,枉然
3. pebble / ˈpebl / *n*. 细砾,卵石
4. rise / raɪs / *v*. 上升
5. necessity / nɪˈsesɪtɪ / *n*. 需要

篇目欣赏

"Necessity is the mother of invention." 需要是发明之母。因为有了需要,人们会尝试着去实现这个需要。在这个过程中人们也就发现到新生事物。在遇到困难的时候,要动脑筋,想办法。许多人在困难面前放弃了自己的理想,其实这个时候多思考一下,也许会改变自己的命运。

背诵准备

根据文章内容填空,然后对照原文看自己填对了吗?

A thirsty crow saw a _____. He flew to it _____, hoping to find some _____ in it. But when he reached it, he _____ there was so little water that his _____ could not possibly reach it. He tried _____ to reach the water, but all his _____ were in vain. At last, he collected as many _____ as he could carry and _____ them into the pitcher with his beak. The water _____ and he was able to quench his thirst.

Necessity is the mother of invention.

参考译文

乌鸦和水罐

　　一只口渴的乌鸦看到一只水罐,以为找到了水,欢欢喜喜地从天上飞了下来。可到跟前一看,才发现里面只剩下一点点水,他的嘴根本就够不着。乌鸦用尽了一切办法想喝到水,但到头来都是徒劳无功。最后乌鸦找来许多小石头,用嘴衔着一块一块地扔进瓶里。水面上升,他终于喝到了水,解了渴。

　　需要是发明之母。

21. The Boy and the Hazelnuts

By Aesop

A boy put his hands into a pitcher which was full of *hazelnuts*. He *grasped* as many as he could. But when he tried to pull out his hand, he was *prevented from* doing so by the neck of the pitcher. However, he was not *willing* to give up his hazelnuts, and he was not able to pull out his hand either. He *burst into tears* and cried for help. His mother said, "You can take out your hand if you give up half of that."

Do not *attempt* too much at once.

语言注释

1. hazelnut / ˈheɪzlnʌt / *n*. 榛子
2. grasp / ɡrɑːsp / *v*. (用手)抓住,抓紧
3. prevent from　阻止
4. willing / ˈwɪlɪŋ / *adj*. 乐意的
5. burst into tears　突然放声大哭
6. attempt / əˈtempt / *v*. 尝试,企图

篇目欣赏

"Do not attempt too much at once." 切莫急功近利。这个故事告诉我们要学会选择,学会放弃。他放弃半把榛子就能顺利地把手拿出来,可是他并没有这么做,导致整个手被卡在罐子里。有时候也许放弃是最佳的选择。放弃是一种境界,大弃大得,小弃小得,不弃不得。在生活中放弃一些陈旧的观念和习惯,也许你会体会到完全不同的新感觉和成就。

背诵准备

请从故事中找出能够回答下列问题的句子,并在这些句子的帮助下记忆、背诵全文。

1. Where did the boy put his hands?
   _____
   _____

2. Why couldn't he pull his hand out of the pitcher?
   _____
   _____

3. What did he do when he couldn't pull out his hand?
   _____
   _____

4. What did his mother say to him?
   _____
   _____

参考译文

男孩和榛子

有个男孩伸手到装满榛子的罐子里去拿榛子,抓了满满一大把。他想把手从罐子里拿出来的时候,手却被罐口卡住了。他不肯放弃手里的榛子,又无法将手拿出来。他哇哇大哭,请求帮忙。他的妈妈对他说:"只要你丢掉一半的榛子,你的手就能拿出来了。"

切莫急功近利。

22. The Frogs and the Well

By Aesop

Two frogs lived together in a *marsh*. But one hot summer the marsh *dried up*, and they left it to look for another place to live in: frogs like *damp* places. *By and by* they came to a deep well. One of them looked down into it, and said to the other, "This looks a nice cool place. Let us jump in and settle here." But the other, who had a wiser head on his shoulders, replied, "Not so fast, my friend. *Supposing* this well dried up like the marsh, how should we get out again?"

Look before you leap.

语言注释

1. marsh / mɑːʃ / *n*. 沼泽(地带)
2. dry up   干涸
3. damp / dæmp / *adj*. 潮湿
4. by and by   不久后
5. suppose / səˈpəʊz / *v*. 认为可能,猜想
6. Look before you leap.   三思而后行。

篇目欣赏

"Look before you leap."遇事要三思而后行。设想如果这两只青蛙在找到那口井后不假思索地就跳入井内,或许它们能得到暂时的安宁和快乐,但当井再次枯竭的时候他们还能出得来吗? 我们每天都在为做出决定而苦恼,很多时候我们想逃避这个"苦恼"的过程,到时候往往又后悔自己当初的决定。世上没有后悔药,凡事应该首先考虑周到,然后再付诸行动。

背诵准备

请用括号中所给单词的正确形式填空。

Two frogs _____ (live) together in a marsh. But one hot summer the marsh _____ (dry) up, and they _____ (leave) it to _____ (look) for another place to _____ (live) in; frogs _____ (like) damp places. By and by they _____ (come) to a deep well. One of them _____ (look) down into it, and _____ (say) to the other, "This _____ (look) a nice cool place. Let us _____ (jump) in and _____ (settle) here." But the other, who had a wiser head on his shoulders, _____ (reply), "Not so fast, my friend. Supposing this well dried up like the marsh, how should we _____ (get) out again?"

Look before you leap.

参考译文

青蛙和井

沼泽里住着两只青蛙。有一年夏天,天气非常炎热,沼泽干涸了。喜欢潮湿环境的青蛙不得不去寻找一个新家。不久,他们路过一口深井。一只青蛙向下看了看,对另一只说道:"看来井底下又凉爽又舒适,我们不如就跳下去,住在这里吧。"而另一只青蛙则更为明智,答道:"先别急,我的朋友。要是这口井也像沼泽一样干涸了,我们怎么爬出来呢?"

三思而后行。

23. The Hunter and the Woodman

By Aesop

A *hunter*, not very brave, was searching for the *tracks* of a lion. He asked a man *felling oaks* in the forest if he had seen any tracks of the lion or knew where the lion was. "Sure," said the *woodman*, "I will at once show you where the lion is." The hunter, turning very pale and *chattering* with his teeth from fear, replied, "No, thank you. I did not ask that. I'm just in search of the lion's track, not the lion himself."

The hero is brave in *deeds* as well as words.

语言注释

1. hunter / ˈhʌntə / *n*. 猎人
2. track / træk / *n*. 踪迹
3. fell / fel / *v*. 砍,砍伐
4. oak / əʊk / *n*. 橡树
5. woodman / ˈwʊdmæn / *n*. 伐木工
6. chatter / ˈtʃætə / *v*. (因为害怕或寒冷)牙齿打战
7. deed / diːd / *n*. 行为

篇目欣赏

"The hero is brave in deeds as well as words." 语言和行动都勇敢才称得上英雄。有些人总是用豪言壮语来武装自己,使自己在别人眼里显得异常威武,一副英雄气概,但当他付出行动时,他的所作所为却往往是大打折扣,令人倍感失望。故事里的猎人如果能 "Do like a real hunter does."那他一定能得到别人的尊重,反之只能招来别人怀疑的目光。

背诵准备

请把下面各组中的几个句子合并成一句,写完后对照原文,看看自己写对了吗?

1. A hunter was not very brave.

   The hunter was searching for the tracks of a lion.

   _____

   _____

2. He asked a man felling oaks in the forest.

   "Have you seen any tracks of the lion?"

   "Where is the lion? Do you know?"

   _____

   _____

3. The hunter replied.

   He turned very pale and chattered with his teeth from fear.

   _____

   _____

参考译文

猎人和伐木工

　　有个胆小的猎人在森林里寻找狮子的踪迹。他问正在砍橡树的伐木工有没有见过狮子的脚印或者是否知道狮子的巢穴在哪里。"当然知道,"伐木工说,"我这就带你去找狮子。"猎人听了,吓得脸色发白,牙齿打战,哆哆嗦嗦地说:"谢谢,不必了。我要找的只是狮子的踪迹,而不是狮子。"

　　语言和行动都勇敢才称得上英雄。

24. Jupiter and the Monkey

By Aesop

Jupiter issued a *proclamation* to all the *beasts* of the forest, "I will give an *award* to one of you. The one who has the most handsome children will be able to get the award." A monkey came with the other beasts and *presented*, with a mother's *tenderness*, a flat-nose, hairless, ugly, young monkey as a *candidate* for the award. Everyone laughed at her on the *presentation* of her son. She seriously said, "I don't know if Jupiter will give the award to me, but I DO know that in my eyes, my son is the dearest, and the most handsome of all."

语言注释

1. Jupiter /ˈdʒuːpɪtə/ *n*. 朱庇特(希腊神话中的一个神)
2. issue /ˈɪsjuː/ *v*. 发布，公告
3. proclamation /prɒkləˈmeɪʃ(ə)n/ *n*. 公告
4. beast /biːst/ *n*. 兽类
5. award /əˈwɔːd/ *n*. 奖赏
6. present /prɪˈzent/ *v*. 引见
7. tenderness /ˈtendənɪs/ *n*. 温柔
8. candidate /ˈkændɪdɪt/ *n*. 候选人
9. presentation /ˌprezenˈteɪʃən/ *n*. 呈现

篇目欣赏

当 猴妈妈"with a mother's tenderness"(以母亲的万般柔情)推举自己儿子去竞争时，谁都不能否认在妈妈心中，自己的孩子永远是最出色的。母亲对子女的爱是无处不在的，对于这一份沉甸甸的爱，我们准备好给予相应的回报了吗？

背诵准备

请从故事中找出能够回答下列问题的句子，并在这些句子的帮助下记忆、背诵全文。

1. What was Jupiter's proclamation?

_____

_____

2. What did the monkey present? And how did she present it?

_____

_____

3. What did the monkey say when others laughed at her on the presentation of her son?

_____

_____

参考译文

朱庇特和猴子

朱庇特向森林中的百兽发布公告说："百兽中谁的孩子被公认为最英俊，谁就将获得我的奖赏。"猴子与其他野兽一起前来。以母亲的万般柔情，推举她的塌鼻子、无毛、丑陋的儿子为候选人。大家都嘲笑她，可她认真地说道："我不知道朱庇特是否会把这个奖颁给我，可有一点我确实知道，在我的眼里，我的儿子就是最可爱，最英俊的。"

25. The Bat, the Birds and the Beasts

By Aesop

A war was about to *break out* between the Birds and the Beasts. When the two armies were *collected* together, the Bat *hesitated* which to join. Some birds flew over his home, and said, "Come with us!" But he said, "I'm a beast." Later on, some beasts marched below his home, and said, "Come with us!" But he said, "I'm a bird."

Luckily, peace was made at the last moment, and no war *took place*, so the two armies were going to have a party. The bat came to the party too, but both the Bird and the Beast *turned against* him. Therefore the bat hid himself in dark and flew alone at night *ever after*.

语言注释

1. break out   爆发,突然发生
2. collect / kəˈlekt / v. 聚集
3. hesitate / ˈhezɪteɪt / v. 犹豫
4. take place   发生
5. turn against   与……为敌
6. ever after   从此

篇目欣赏

这个故事比喻墙头草两边倒的人下场往往很凄惨。没有自己立场的人也是得不到别人亲近和尊重的。蝙蝠如果能立场坚定帮助其中的一方,那就会避免如今独自夜晚才能出来活动的局面。

背诵准备

请从故事中找出能够回答下列问题的句子,并在这些句子的帮助下记忆、背诵全文。

1. What was about to happen between the Birds and the Beasts?

_____

2. What did the Bat hesitate when the two armies were collected together?

_____

3. What did the Bat say when the Birds and the Beasts invited him to join their armies?

_____

4. What happened at the last moment?

_____

5. Why did the bat hide himself in dark and flew alone at night ever after?

_____

参考译文

蝙蝠、鸟和兽

鸟和兽之间即将爆发一场战争,当双方各自集结自己的队伍的时候,蝙蝠不知道自己应该加入哪一边。鸟们飞过蝙蝠的家,对他说:"加入我们吧。"蝙蝠说:"我是一只兽。"兽们行军经过他家,对他说:"加入我们吧。"蝙蝠说:"我是一只鸟。"

幸好鸟兽双方在最后一刻和解了,避免了战争,双方决定庆祝一下。蝙蝠也来了,可鸟兽双方都与他为敌,从此以后蝙蝠只好躲在暗处,孤单地在夜里飞翔。

26. The Scorpion and the Frog

By Aesop

A *scorpion* and a frog met on the bank of a *stream* and the scorpion asked the frog to carry him across on its back. The frog worried, "How do I know you won't sting me?" The scorpion said, "Because if I do, I will die too."

The frog was *satisfied*, and they set out. But when they were in the middle of the stream, the scorpion stung the frog. The frog felt the *onset* of *paralysis* and started to sink. He knew that both of them would drown, but still he asked at the last minute, "Why?"

The scorpion answered, "It's my *nature* ..."

语言注释

1. scorpion / ˈskɔːpɪən / *n*. 蝎子
2. stream / striːm / *n*. 小河，溪流
3. satisfy / ˈsætɪsfaɪ / *v*. 使某人满意，高兴
4. onset / ˈɒnset / *n*. 攻击，突击
5. paralysis / pəˈrælɪsɪs / *n*. 麻痹，瘫痪
6. nature / ˈneɪtʃə / *n*. 天性

篇目欣赏

蝎子说的"It's my nature"(本性难改)害死了青蛙也害死了自己。但这世界上的确也存在着这种人，多少次他们想改变自己的不良习气，他们努力掩饰着自己的缺点，把幽雅的一面展露出来，可是到了一定时候又会露出狐狸尾巴，害人害己。所以我们一定要看清事物的本质，别被一时的表象所迷惑。

背诵准备

　　这是一则熟悉的寓言故事,故事是怎么发展的呢? 请用文章中的句子回答下面的问题,并在这些句子的帮助下记忆。

1. Where did the scorpion and the frog meet?
_____

2. What did the scorpion ask the frog to do?
_____

3. What did the frog worry about?
_____

4. When did the scorpion sting the frog?
_____

5. How did the frog feel after he was stung by the scorpion?
_____

参考译文

蝎子和青蛙

　　蝎子和青蛙在小河边相遇,蝎子求青蛙背他过河。青蛙很担心,问:"我怎么知道你不会蛰我呢?"蝎子说:"要是我蛰了你,我也活不了。"

　　青蛙放心了,就背着蝎子过河。可当他们到了河中央的时候,蝎子还是蛰了青蛙。青蛙觉得一阵麻木,开始下沉。他知道他们俩都得淹死,在没入水前的最后一刻,他问蝎子:"这是为什么?"

　　蝎子回答说:"本性难改啊……"

27. Hercules and the Wagoner

By Aesop

A *wagoner* was driving a *wagon* along a *country path*, when the wheels sank down deep into a *rut*. The wagoner got frightened. He stood by the wagon and did not know what to do. Suddenly he cried *Hercules* and asked for help. Hercules appeared and *addressed* him, "Put your shoulders to the wheels, my man. *Whip* your horses and never *pray* to me for help."

The wagoner tried hard and finally the wagon got out of the rut, so he thanked Hercules. Hercules said, "It is you who helped yourself."

Self-help is the best help.

语言注释

1. wagoner /ˈwægənə(r)/ *n*. 四轮运货车夫

   wagon /ˈwægən/ *n*. 四轮运货马车(或牛车)

2. country path 乡间小路

3. rut /rʌt/ *n*. 车辙

4. Hercules /ˈhɜːkjuliːz/ 赫丘利斯(罗马神话中的大力神)

5. address /əˈdres/ *v*. 讲话,发表演说

6. whip /(h)wɪp/ *v*. 鞭打

7. pray /preɪ/ *v*. 祈祷

篇目欣赏

"Self-help is the best help." 自助是最好的帮助。很多情况下我们遇到困难时会想起自己的朋友,希望他们能帮助自己,朋友的定义也在于此。不过是不是每件事情都需要别人的帮助才能办到呢? 有时候自己才是真正值得信赖的人,遇到困难首先想想能否通过自己的努力解决问题,或许在每一次的自助中我们会不断地成长。

背诵准备

请用括号中所给单词的正确形式填空。

A wagoner _____ (drive) a wagon along a country path, when the wheels _____ (sink) down deep into a rut. The wagoner got _____ (frighten). He _____ (stand) by the wagon and _____ (not know) what to do. Suddenly he _____ (cry) Hercules and _____ (ask) for help. Hercules _____ (appear) and _____ (address) him, "_____ (put) your shoulders to the wheels, my man. _____ (whip) your horses and never _____ (pray) to me for help."

The wagoner _____ (try) hard and finally the wagon got out of the rut, so he _____ (thank) Hercules. Hercules said, "It is you who _____ (help) yourself."

Self-help is the best help.

参考译文

赫丘利斯和马车夫

赶车人赶着马车走在乡村小路上,车轮忽然陷进了一道深深的车辙印里。车夫被眼前的情况吓呆了,一动不动地站在马车旁,大声地向大力神赫丘利斯求救。赫丘利斯出现在车夫面前,对他说:"伙计,用你的肩膀顶住轮子,拿鞭子赶马,别向我求救。"

车夫用力顶车,终于把车轮推出了车辙。他向赫丘利斯表示感谢,赫丘利斯说:"你该谢的是你自己。"

自助是最好的帮助。

28. The Dog and the Bone

By Aesop

One day, *a dog was out taking a walk*. He was carrying a bone in his mouth. As he was walking across a bridge, he looked down at the river. The dog saw his own *reflection* in the water. But he thought it was another dog. "There's a dog looking up at me." He thought. "And he has a bone, too. That bone looks bigger than my bone. I'll *frighten* that dog and *grab* his bone *away*."

The dog began to *bark*. And, of course, as soon as he opened his mouth, he dropped his bone. It fell into the river and *floated* away. The dog had been very *silly*.

语言注释

1. A dog was out taking a walk. 这个句子中有一个倒装的用法，意思相当于：A dog was taking a walk out.
2. reflection / rɪˈflekʃən / *n*. 反射的影像；倒影
3. frighten / ˈfraɪtn / *v*. 吓走
4. grab away 突然抢走
5. bark / bɑːk / *v*. 吠
6. float / fləʊt / *v*. 漂浮
7. silly / ˈsɪlɪ / *adj*. 傻的

篇目欣赏

很多时候我们会被属于别人的东西而吸引，即便是自己有的，也觉得是对方的好一点。故事里的那条小狗不也就是因为这种心态而做出了一个"愚蠢"的举动吗？当它想通过自己所谓的努力——"bark"来得到别人的东西时，原来属于自己的骨头却从自己口中"溜走"了。这个故事告诉我们：对于你已有的东西要知足。

背诵准备

这个故事也很熟悉，但你是否熟悉故事中介词的用法呢？请用合适的介词填空，并在此基础上背诵。

One day, a dog was _____ taking a walk. He was carrying a bone _____ his mouth. As he was walking _____ a bridge, he looked _____ _____ the river. The dog saw his own reflection _____ the water. But he thought it was another dog. "There's a dog looking _____ _____ me." He thought. "And he has a bone, too. That bone looks bigger than my bone. I'll frighten that dog and grab his bone _____."

The dog began to bark. And, of course, as soon as he opened his mouth, he dropped his bone. It fell _____ the river and floated _____. The dog had been very silly.

参考译文

狗与骨头

有一天，一只狗叼着一根骨头出去散步。走着走着，来到了一座桥上。它站在桥上往下看，看见了自己的倒影。可他以为是另一条狗。它想："有一只狗在看着我，那只狗也有一根骨头。那根骨头好像比我的这一根要大。我得把它吓跑，把它的骨头抢过来。"

于是，它朝那只狗狂吠起来。当然，在它刚张开嘴巴的一刹那，它的骨头就掉到河里，顺水漂走了。这只狗可真傻啊！

29. The Father and His Two Daughters

By Aesop

A man has two daughters, one married to a *gardener*, and the other married to a *tile-maker*. One day he visited the daughter who had married the gardener. He asked, "How are you? How are things with you?" She said, "Everything is fine, but I have only one wish, that there may be a heavy rain, so that the plants may be well watered."

Before long, he went to the daughter who had married the tile-maker. He also asked about her wish. She said, "I want nothing but only one wish. I hope the dry weather may continue, and the sun shines hot and bright, so that the *bricks* might be dried."

The man wondered, "Which *side* shall I *take*?"

语言注释

1. gardener / ɡɑːdnə(r) / *n*. 园丁
2. tile-maker / taɪl ˈmeɪkə / *n*. 瓦匠
3. brick / brɪk / *n*. 砖
4. take side 支持,偏袒

篇目欣赏

我们生活中每个人由于各自的利益而有着不同甚至截然相反的立场。故事中两个女儿一个希望下雨,一个希望干燥的天气,两个人相互矛盾的利益关系使得她们父亲难以做出取舍。其实女儿并没有什么错,谁都会为自己的利益而选择不同的立场,但在这个过程中我们应该尽量避免别人为此而进退两难。

背诵准备

这个父亲真是左右为难,他两个女儿各有什么样的愿望呢?他又该如何做呢?请用文章中的句子填空。

A man has two daughters, one married to a gardener, and the other married to a tile-maker. One day he visited the daughter who had married the gardener. He asked, "_____" She said, "_____
_____"

Before long, he went to the daughter who had married the tile-maker. He also asked about her wish. She said, "_____
_____"

The man wondered, "_____"

参考译文

父亲和两个女儿

有个父亲有两个女儿,其中一个嫁给了园丁,另一个嫁给了瓦匠。有一天,他去看嫁给园丁的那个女儿。他问女儿:"你好吗?一切顺利吗?"女儿说:"我事事顺心,可只有一个愿望,希望老天爷多多下雨,好浇灌那些花花草草。"

不久之后,他又去探望嫁给瓦匠的那个女儿。他也问了那个女儿有什么心愿。她说:"我什么都不缺,只希望干燥的天气能够持续,又热又晒,砖就能快点干了。"

这个父亲很困惑,慨叹到:"我到底该支持谁呢?"

30. The Ant and the Dove

By Aesop

An ant went to the bank of a river to quench its thirst, but was carried away by the water. When he was about to get *drowned*, he was noticed by a dove. The dove was sitting on the tree at that moment. He *plucked* a leaf and let it fall into the water close to the ant. The ant climbed onto the leaf and *floated* safely to the bank.

Before long, a bird catcher came and stood under the tree. He laid his *lime-twigs* for the dove, which was still sitting on the branches. The ant *stung* the bird catcher on the foot. It was so painful that he threw down the twigs. The noise made the dove *aware of* the coming danger.

One good turn deserves another.

语言注释

1. drown / draʊn / v. 溺死
2. pluck / plʌk / v. 摘,采,拔
3. float / fləʊt / v. 漂浮,飘浮
4. lime twig   涂有粘胶的小树枝
5. sting / stɪŋ / v. stung 蛰
6. be aware of   意识到,知道
7. one good turn   一个善举

篇目欣赏

对于蚂蚁,感激的心总会再找机会报恩。对于鸽子,有些朋友也许平时看似微不足道,但却有可能在我们身处困境的时候提供巨大的帮助。平时我们能多向身边的朋友伸出援助之手,等到自己需要的时候,别人就会挺身而出。同样对于那些帮助过自己的人,我们一定不能轻易遗忘,因为 "One good turn deserves another." 好心有好报。

背诵准备

请用括号中所给单词的正确形式填空。

An ant _____ (go) to the bank of a river to quench its thirst, but _____ (carry) away by the water. When he was about to get _____ (drown), he _____ (notice) by a dove. The dove _____ (sit) on the tree at that moment. He _____ (pluck) a leaf and _____ (let) it _____ (fall) into the water close to the ant. The ant _____ (climb) onto the leaf and _____ (float) safely to the bank.

Before long, a bird catcher _____ (come) and _____ (stand) under the tree. He _____ (lay) his lime-twigs for the dove, which _____ still _____ (sit) on the branches. The ant _____ (sting) the bird catcher on the foot. It _____ (be) so painful that he _____ (throw) down the twigs. The noise _____ (make) the dove aware of the _____ (come) danger.

One good turn _____ (deserve) another.

参考译文

蚂蚁和鸽子

蚂蚁口渴了,到河边喝水,不幸被水流卷走,眼看就要淹死了。一只鸽子正巧站在岸边的树上,看到了挣扎着的蚂蚁。他摘下一片树叶,丢在蚂蚁身边的水面上。蚂蚁爬上树叶,安全地漂回了河岸。

没过多久,捕鸟人来到树下,将沾了石灰水的小树枝伸向仍然停在树枝上的鸽子。蚂蚁在捕鸟人的脚上狠狠地蜇了一口。捕鸟人一疼,手里的树枝掉在地上,声音让鸽子意识到即将到来的危险。

好心有好报。

31. The Goose with the Gold Eggs

By Aesop

One day a countryman found a yellow and *glittering* egg in his goose's *nest*. When he took it up, he felt the egg was as heavy as *lead*. He thought it was a *trick* played on him, so he was about to throw the egg away. But he took it home *on a second thought*. He checked the egg again very carefully. To his surprise, he soon found it was an egg of *pure* gold. Every morning, the same thing happened. And he soon became rich by selling these gold eggs. As he grew rich, he grew *greedy*. He wanted to get all the gold eggs at once that the goose could give, so he killed goose and opened it only to find nothing.

Greed often reaches itself.

语言注释

1. glittering / ˈɡlɪtərɪŋ / *adj*. 闪光的
2. nest / nest / *n*. 鸟窝
3. lead / liːd / *n*. 铅
4. trick / trɪk / *n*. 恶作剧
5. on a second thought　转念一想
6. pure / pjʊə / *adj*. 纯的
7. greedy / ˈɡriːdɪ / *adj*. 贪婪的
8. greed / ɡriːd / *n*. 贪婪

篇目欣赏

这个故事告诉我们如果不懂得知足,贪得无厌,我们就会失去已经拥有的东西。贪婪的人往往被贪婪所害。农夫的贪婪导致了他鼠目寸光做出了一个极其荒唐的决定,想想我们日常生活中由于贪婪,是不是也有类似糊涂的事情啊? 如果农夫在做最后一个决定时能再次 second thought, 那么他的幸福生活可能还会继续。

背诵准备

　　这是一则很著名的英语寓言故事,请从故事中找出能够回答下列问题的句子,并在这些句子的帮助下记忆、背诵全文。

1. What did a countryman find in his goose's nest one day?

　　_____

2. What did he think of the egg at first? And what was he about to do?

　　_____

3. What did the countryman soon find?

　　_____

4. How did the countryman become rich?

　　_____

5. Why did the countryman kill the goose with the gold eggs? And what did he find?

　　_____

参考译文

下金蛋的鹅

　　一天,农夫在自家的鹅窝里看到一枚黄澄澄的鹅蛋闪闪发光。他拾起来一掂,那枚鹅蛋竟沉得像铅一样。农夫以为这是有人故意捉弄他,就想把蛋扔了,可转念一想,又把蛋带回了家。他又把这枚鹅蛋仔仔细细地查看了一番,惊喜地发现这居然是一枚纯金的鹅蛋。从此,这只鹅每天早上都产下一枚金蛋。农夫靠卖金蛋很快就发了大财。农夫的钱越多,就变得越贪婪。他想一下子拿到所有的金蛋,于是就把鹅宰了。他剖开鹅的肚子,可里面什么也没有。

　　贪婪的人往往被贪婪所害。

32. The Belly and the Members

By Aesop

The Members of the Body one day suddenly found that they were doing all the work but the *Belly* was having all the food. So they had a meeting, and after a long discussion, they decided to *strike* work till the Belly agreed to work with them. So for a day or two, the Hands refused to take the food, the Mouth refused to receive it, and the Teeth had no work to do. Later on, the Members began to find that they themselves were not in a great *condition*: the Hands could hardly move; the Mouth was dry; and the Legs were unable to *support* the Body. Therefore they learned that the Belly was still doing necessary work for the Body quietly, and all of them must work together or the Body will *go to pieces*.

语言注释

1. belly / ˈbelɪ / *n*. 肚子
2. strike / straɪk / *v*. 罢工
3. condition / kənˈdɪʃən / *n*. 健康状况，适用(适合)状态
4. support / səˈpɔːt / *v*. 支撑，支持
5. go to pieces （由于害怕、悲伤等而)精神崩溃或身体垮下来

篇目欣赏

这则寓言中身体的各个部分都是大写的，这是一种拟人化的方法。我们的身体好比是一个团队。团队里的每一个人都应该有自身的作用。有些人虽然看似无足轻重，其实缺其不可，他们默默地为团队贡献着自己的力量，从来不炫耀自己的能耐。所以我们要善待周围的人，他们都是我们团队中不可缺少的力量。

背诵准备

这是一则很有趣的寓言故事。在开会之前和之后,身体各个部分有什么变化吗?请用文章中的句子填空。

The Members of the Body one day suddenly found that _____
_____.
So they had a meeting, and after a long discussion, they decided to strike work till
the Belly agreed to work with them. So for a day or two, the Hands
_____, the Mouth _____
_____, and the Teeth _____.
Later on, the Members began to find that they themselves were not in a great condition: the Hands _____; the Mouth _____;
and the Legs _____. Therefore they learned that the Belly
_____
_____, and all of them must work together or the
Body _____.

参考译文

肚子和身体器官

身体的各个器官有一天突然发现:所有的工作都是由他们来做,而肚子却独自享用美食。他们召开了一次会议,经过长时间的讨论,大家决定罢工,直到肚子同意分担一部分工作为止。在接下来的一两天里,手拒绝拿食物,嘴也不肯吃东西,就连牙齿也不肯嚼一下。不久后,身体的各个器官都感到有气无力:手酸软无力,嘴又干又渴,腿也快支撑不住身体了。他们这才明白,原来肚子也是在默默地为身体做着必要的工作,大家应该齐心合力,否则,身体就会垮掉。

33. Two Men and the Bear

By Aesop

Two men were traveling together, and they met a bear on their way.

One of them climbed up quickly into a tree and hid himself in the branches. The other found that *he must be attacked*, so he fell flat on the ground. When the bear came up and touched him with his *snout*, and smelt him all over, he held his breath, and *pretended* to be dead.

The Bear soon left him, for it is said he will not touch a dead body. When he was quite gone, the other traveler climbed down from the tree, and joked his friend what the bear had *whispered* in his ear. "He gave me this advice," his *companion* replied. "Never travel with a friend who *deserts* you when the danger comes."

Misfortune tests the sincerity of friends.

语言注释

1. he must be attacked　他一定会遭到袭击,这个句子中的 must 表示一种可能性非常大的猜测。
2. snout / snaʊt / n. (熊等动物的)长鼻子
3. pretend / prɪ'tend / v. (为了骗人而)假装,装作
4. whisper / '(h)wɪspə / v. 低语,耳语,嘀咕
5. companion / kəm'pænjən / n. 同伴,伙伴
6. desert / dɪ'zɜːt / v. 离弃;舍弃
7. Misfortune tests the sincerity of friends. 患难见真情。

篇目欣赏

"Misfortune tests the sincerity of friends." 患难见真情。也可以说 "A friend in need is a friend indeed." 有时候我们会觉得自己有很多朋友,有时候我们又会感到孤单无助。故事里的一个朋友很巧妙地

讽刺了遇难时只顾自己的人。设想如果有一天你需要帮助,你身边的"朋友们"会有多少能挺身而出呢? 同样当你的朋友有难时,你会伸出援助之手吗? 这两者的数量应该是一样的。当我们真心对待朋友时,我们也能从朋友那里得到相同的反馈。

背诵准备

请根据故事内容,用动词的正确形式填空:

Two men _____ (travel) together, and they _____ (meet) a bear on their way.

One of them _____ (climb) up quickly into a tree and _____ (hide) himself in the branches. The other _____ (find) that he must _____ (attack), so he _____ (fall) flat on the ground. When the bear _____ (come) up and _____ (touch) him with his snout, and _____ (smell) him all over, he _____ (hold) his breath, and _____ (prefend) to _____ (be) dead.

The Bear soon _____ (leave) him, for it _____ (say) he not _____ (touch) a dead body. When he _____ quite _____ (go), the other traveler _____ (climb) down from the tree, and _____ (joke) his friend what the bear _____ (whisper) in his ear. "He _____ (give) me this advice," his companion _____ (reply). "Never _____ (travel) with a friend who _____ (desert) you when the danger _____ (come)."

Misfortune _____ (test) the sincerity of friends.

参考译文

两个人和一只熊

两个人一起去旅行,在路上他们遇见了一只熊。

一个人迅速地爬上一棵树,把自己隐藏在树枝里。另一个人发现自己已经来不及躲藏,一定会遭到熊的攻击,就立即平躺在地上。熊走近了,用它的鼻子顶他,把他从头到脚闻了一遍,他始终紧闭呼吸,装成一个死人的样子。

不一会儿,熊就走了。据说,熊是不会吃一个死了的人的。等他走远了,躲在树上的那个旅行者爬了下来,和他的朋友开玩笑。他问:"熊跟你说了什么悄悄话啊?"

他的朋友回答:"熊给了我一个忠告:千万别和在危难时刻舍弃你的朋友一起旅行。"

患难才能见真情。

34. The Milkmaid and Her Pail

By Aesop

Patty the *milkmaid* was going to the market with her milk in a *pail* on her head. As she went along, she began thinking what she would do with the money she would get for the milk. "I'll buy some hens from Farmer Brown," thought she, "and they will lay eggs every morning. And I will sell these eggs to the *priest*'s wife. With the money I'll buy a new dress and a new hat. And I will go to the market. All the young men will come up and speak to me. Polly Shaw will be *jealous*, but I don't care. I will just look at her and *toss* my head like this." As she thought, she tossed her head back, the pail fell off, and the milk was *spilt*. So she had to go home and tell her mother what had happened.

"My girl," said the mother, "Do not count your chickens before they are *hatched*."

语言注释

1. milkmaid / ˈmɪlkmeɪd / *n*. 挤奶女工
2. pail / peɪl / *n*. 桶,提桶
3. priest / priːst / *n*. 神父,牧师
4. jealous / ˈdʒeləs / *adj*. 嫉妒的
5. toss / tɒs / *v*. (使)摇摆
6. spill / spɪl / *v*. (使)溢出;(使)溅出
7. hatch / hætʃ / *v*. (蛋)孵出

篇目欣赏

"Do not count your chickens before they are hatched." 这句话的意思是"小鸡还没有孵出来,先别去数数。"这个故事告诉我们不要过早地打如意算盘。许多事情无法按我们预计的方向发展,别过早地考虑之后会发生的事情,一步一步踏踏实实地走是我们每个人都应该具有的办事风格。

背诵准备

　　帕蒂去市场卖牛奶,那卖牛奶的钱她会派什么用场呢? 在去市场的路上她有很多计划,你还记得吗? 请你用第一人称,按顺序把它们一一写下来,注意使用将来时态。写完之后和原文对照一下,帮助记忆。

1. _____

2. _____

3. _____

4. _____

5. _____

参考译文

挤奶少女和奶桶

　　挤奶少女帕蒂头顶一桶牛奶去赶集。她边走边开始盘算,卖了牛奶得了钱应该干点什么。"我要从农夫布朗手里买几只母鸡。它们每天早上都会下蛋,我把这些鸡蛋卖给牧师的妻子,给自己买一条新连衣裙和一顶新帽子。等我再去集市的时候,所有的小伙子都会凑上来跟我说话。波莉·肖一定会眼红,可我不在乎,我就那么看着波莉,甩一甩头。"她想着,头不由得向后一甩,牛奶桶掉了下来,牛奶洒了个精光,她只好回家把所有发生的事情告诉母亲。

　　"我的孩子,"母亲说,"小鸡还没有孵出来,先别去数数。"

35. The Ants and the Grasshopper

By Aesop

It's summer. The ants are busy collecting grain, while the *grasshopper* is having fun. He *passes* the days in singing. And he laughs at the ants as well, "You silly ants, why not stop for a while and enjoy yourselves?"

Winter has come. The ants have plenty of grain collected in summer. The *starving* grasshopper passes by and *earnestly begs* for a little food. The ants say, "If you were foolish enough to sing all the summer, you must dance *supperless* to bed in summer."

It is thrifty to prepare today for the wants of tomorrow.

语言注释

1. grasshopper / ˈgrɑːshɒpə(r) / *n*. 蚱蜢
2. pass / pɑːs / *v*. 度过(时间),消磨(时间);经过
3. starving / stɑːvɪŋ / *adj*. 饥饿的
4. earnestly / ˈɜːnɪstlɪ / *adv*. 真诚地
5. beg / beg / *v*. 乞求
6. supperless / ˈsʌpələs / *adv*. 没晚饭吃
7. It is thrifty to prepare today for the wants of tomorrow. 未雨绸缪。

篇目欣赏

有储藏才能安然度过寒冬。今天为明天做准备,才能拥有轻松、潇洒的明天。在生活中人们有时沉溺于一时的安逸,以为生活一直是如此美好的。当危险突然降临之时,手足无措,难以应付。"It is thrifty to prepare today for the wants of tomorrow. 未雨绸缪。"我们只有了解自己所处的环境,为今后做好充足的准备,才能从容面对可能遇到的难题。

背诵准备

这是一个脍炙人口的故事。蚂蚁和蚱蜢一劳一逸,给我们警视。冬夏两季他们各自做了什么呢? 请在文章中找出正确的句子填空。

Season	Ants	Grasshopper
Summer		
Winter		

参考译文

蚂蚁和蚱蜢

夏天,蚂蚁们忙着收集粮食,可蚱蜢却游手好闲。他整日唱歌,无所事事,还嘲笑蚂蚁们:"你们这些蠢蚂蚁,干吗不歇一会儿,享受享受?"

冬天来了,蚂蚁们因为夏天辛勤劳作,有足够的粮食。饥肠辘辘的蚱蜢正好经过蚂蚁的家,只好向蚂蚁乞讨。蚂蚁说:"你真蠢,整个夏天都被你唱过去,那么到了冬天,你就该从早到晚饿着肚子跳舞了吧。"

未雨绸缪。

36. The Sick Lion

By Aesop

A lion had grown old and weak. He *pretended* to be sick，but in fact it was just a *ruse* to make the other animals come *pay their respects*. As soon as they entered his cave，he jumped at them and *ate* them *up*，one by one. The fox also came to see the lion，but she *greeted* him from outside the cave. The lion asked the fox why she didn't come in. The fox replied，"*Because I see the tracks of those going in，but none coming out*."

He is *wise* who is warned by the *misfortunes* of others.

语言注释

1. pretend / prɪˈtend / *v*. 假装
2. ruse / ˈruːseɪ / *n*. 诡计；诈术
3. pay one's respect 致敬；此处有"探视，探望"的意思
4. eat up 吃光
5. greet / griːt / *v*. 问候，致意
6. Because I see the tracks of those going in, but none coming out. 因为我只看到动物们进去的足印，却看不到出来的足印。句子中的 those 指代那些去探望狮子的动物们。
7. wise / waɪz / *adj*. 明智的
8. misfortune / mɪsˈfɔːtʃən / *n*. 不幸

篇目欣赏

"He is wise who is warned by the misfortunes of others."聪明人懂得以他人的不幸为鉴。狐狸显然是非常聪明的，没有盲目地跟风。在生活中我们会因为看到许多人都在做某件事情而动心，有的甚至在没有仔细思考前就全身心地投入其中，结果发现是个大骗局，如果能像狐狸一样多观察，多思考，那么就能避免不少损失。

背诵准备

请从故事中找出能够回答下列问题的句子，并在这些句子的帮助下记忆、背诵全文。

1. Why did the lion pretend to be sick?

_____

2. What happened to the animals as soon as they entered the lion's cave?

_____

3. Where did the fox greet the lion?

_____

4. Why didn't the fox enter the lion's cave?

_____

5. What do you learn from this story?

_____

参考译文

生病的狮子

狮子年老体弱。他假装生病了，然而，这只是狮子的诡计，他想骗百兽来探望他。一旦动物进入他的洞穴，他就扑上去，把他们一个个吃掉。狐狸也来探望狮子，可她只在洞口问候狮子。狮子问她怎么不进来，她说："因为我只看到动物们进去的足印，却看不到出来的足印。"

聪明人懂得以他人的不幸为鉴。

37. The Farmer and the Snake

By Aesop

One winter day, a farmer found a snake *stiff* and frozen with cold. The farmer thought the snake was so poor that he put it under his clothes just near his *chest*. Before long, the snake *came to life gradually*.

The warmth of the farmer had not changed its *cruel* nature. It opened its mouth and bit at the farmer right at the chest.

"My god! How cruel you are! I saved you, but you bit me. Why?" As he was saying, he took out the snake and threw it on the ground. But the farmer was already *poisoned* and was dying.

The greatest kindness will not bind the *ungrateful*.

语言注释

1. stiff / stɪf / *adj*. 僵硬的
2. chest / tʃest / *n*. 胸口
3. come to life 复苏,苏醒
4. gradually / ˈgrædjʊəlɪ / *adv*. 逐渐地
5. cruel / ˈkrʊəl / *adj*. 残酷的,残忍的
6. poison / ˈpɔɪzn / *v*. 毒杀,使中毒
7. ungrateful / ʌnˈgreɪtfʊl / *adj*.忘恩负义的

篇目欣赏

每次看完农夫和蛇的故事,都要为农夫而惋惜,同时痛恨蛇的冷酷无情。蛇的忘恩负义让帮助它的农夫丢了性命,那么离开了农夫的蛇又能走多远呢? 还会有第二个农夫去救它吗? 虽说心地再善良也感动不了忘恩负义的人,但那些人也不可能走得太远。

背诵准备

根据文章内容给下列句子排序。

_____ The farmer put it under his clothes just near his chest.

_____ A farmer found a snake stiff and frozen with cold.

_____ The snake opened its mouth and bit at the farmer right at the chest.

_____ The farmer was already poisoned and was dying.

_____ The snake came to life gradually.

_____ The farmer took out the snake and threw it on the ground.

根据上面提示,请简单地复述这个故事,尽量用文章中的原句。

_____

_____

_____

_____

_____

参考译文

农夫和蛇

一个冬日,农夫发现了一条被冻僵了的蛇。他觉得蛇很可怜,于是就把蛇放在自己怀里。不久,蛇就慢慢苏醒了。

农夫的温暖并没有改变蛇残酷的本性。它张开嘴,狠狠地在农夫胸口咬了一口。

"天哪! 你真是太没良心了。我救了你,你却咬我,这是为什么呀!"他边说边掏出蛇,把它重重地扔在地上。可农夫中了蛇毒,奄奄一息。

心地再善良也感动不了忘恩负义的人。

38. The Wolf and the Stork

By Aesop

A long, long time ago, the wolf and the *stork* were friends. One day, the wolf asked the stork to come to his house to eat.

When the stork arrived at the wolf's house, the wolf put two bowls of soup on the table. The wolf ate his bowl of soup quickly. When he finished, he asked the stork, "Did you like my soup?"

But the stork was angry because he couldn't eat the soup. His *beak* was too long! When the stork went home, he was still hungry. The wolf laughed and laughed.

Then the stork had an idea. He asked the wolf to come to dinner. He filled two tall pitchers with good soup. They began to eat. When the stork finished eating, he asked the wolf if he wanted more to eat.

But the wolf was angry. His mouth was so big that he couldn't get it into the *pitcher*. The wolf went home hungry, and the stork laughed and laughed.

语言注释

1. stork / stɔːk / *n*. 鹳
2. beak / biːk / *n*. 喙
3. pitcher / ˈpɪtʃə / *n*. 陶制大水罐

篇目欣赏

狼和鹳是朋友,狼邀请鹳来做客,它准备了美味佳肴,并把它们放入了一个鹳无法吃到的器具里,令鹳非常难堪。它没有想到鹳也会用同样的计策来对付自己。事实上,在对待朋友时会有"山谷回音现象"。你朝着山谷放声歌唱,听到的也同样是亲切的歌声,如果你冲着大山怒吼一声,听到的同样也是愤怒的。对待朋友同样如此,虚情假意换回不了真心真意。

背诵准备

根据故事内容用合适的词语填空。

A long, long time ago, the wolf and the _____ were friends. One day, the _____ asked the stork to come to his house to eat.

When the stork _____ at the wolf's _____, the wolf put two _____ of soup on the table. The wolf ate his bowl of soup _____. When he finished, he _____ the stork, "Did you like my _____?"

But the stork was _____ because he couldn't eat the soup. His _____ was too long! When the stork went home, he was still _____. The wolf laughed and _____.

Then the stork had an _____. He asked the _____ to come to dinner. He filled two tall _____ with good soup. They began to eat. When the stork finished _____, he asked the wolf _____ he wanted more to eat.

But the wolf was angry. His _____ was _____ big _____ he couldn't get it into the pitcher. The wolf went home _____, and the _____ laughed and laughed.

参考译文

<h3 style="text-align:center">狼和鹳</h3>

从前,狼和鹳是朋友。有一天,狼请鹳到家里吃饭。

鹳到了狼家里,狼端出两碗汤。狼很快就喝完了汤,喝完之后他问鹳:"你喜不喜欢我的汤?"

可是鹳很生气,因为他的嘴太长了,根本不能从碗里喝到汤。鹳饿着肚子回到家里,可是狼却哈哈大笑。

鹳心生一计,也请狼来吃饭。他把汤装在两个大陶罐里。这一次,鹳很快就吃完了,他问狼要不要再来一罐。

可这一回轮到狼生气了,他的嘴太大了,根本没有办法喝到罐里的汤。狼饿着肚子回家了,鹳哈哈大笑。

39. Belling the Cat

By Aesop

Once，some mice *were frightened of* a cat that lived in their house. The mice decided to hold a meeting and talk over the problem.

"That cat is always *sneaking up* and surprising me，" said the first mouse，"Right！" said the second mouse. "We have to run for our lives every day." "I have an idea，"said the third mouse. "Let's tie a bell around the cat's neck. Then we can hear him coming，and have plenty of time to run and hide."

The mice agreed it was a great idea. They got a bell and a piece of *ribbon*. "Now，" said the first mouse. "Who is going to tie the bell on the cat?"

"Not I！" said the second mouse.

"Not I！" said the third mouse.

None of them was brave enough to *bell* the cat.

语言注释

1. be frightened of　害怕
2. sneak up　偷偷地接近；蹑手蹑脚地靠近
3. ribbon / ˈrɪbən / n. 丝带，缎带
4. bell / bel / v. 系铃于

篇目欣赏

这是一则经典的伊索寓言。猫总是蹑手蹑脚地走到老鼠后面,给老鼠一个致命的打击。为此老鼠非常头痛。几只老鼠商量怎么能使自己摆脱这样的窘境,最后他们决定给猫系上一个铃铛,这样大老远就能听到猫走近的声音了,但就是这个听上去很简单的方法却难倒了他们。因为有哪只老鼠能有那样的胆量去做这件事情呢? It is easy to suggest impossible solutions. (不切实际的办法是最容易想到的。)有些事情说起来容易,做起来却很难。你说是吗?

背诵准备

这是一则很著名的伊索寓言,请从故事中找出能够回答下列问题的句子,并在这些句子的帮助下记忆、背诵全文。

1. How did the mice feel about the cat that lived in their house?
_____

2. What did the mice decide to do then?
_____

3. Why did the first mouse hate the cat?
_____

4. How about the second mouse?
_____

5. What was the third mouse's idea?
_____

6. What did the mice get since they agreed it was a great idea?
_____

7. Why none of the mice was going to bell the cat?
_____

参考译文

谁去给猫系铃铛?

从前一群老鼠很害怕同住一屋檐下的猫。老鼠们决定开会讨论这个问题。

"那只猫总是蹑手蹑脚地靠近我,害我吓一跳。"第一只老鼠说。

"就是啊! 我们每天都四处逃命。"第二只老鼠说。

"我有个主意!"第三只老鼠说,"我们在猫的脖子上挂一个铃铛吧,这样他一来,我们就能听到,并有足够的时间藏起来。"

老鼠们都觉得这个主意不错。他们找来了一个铃铛和一条带子。

第一只老鼠说:"那么,谁去给猫系铃铛呢?"

"我不去！"第二只老鼠说。

"我也不去！"第三只老鼠说。

没有一只老鼠有勇气去给猫系铃铛。

40. The Crow and the Partridge

By Aesop

One day, a *crow* was flying across a road. She looked down and saw a *partridge*. The partridge was *strutting* along, looking very beautiful.

"Oh," thought the crow. "*I wish I could walk as beautifully as the partridge.*" The crow flew down to the road and started walking behind the partridge. The crow tried to copy the partridge's wonderful strut.

The partridge turned around. "What do you think you're doing?" the partridge *demanded*.

"Don't be angry," replied the crow. "I'm just trying to learn to walk like you."

"Foolish bird!" answered the partridge. "You're a crow. Walk like a crow!"

But the crow didn't listen to the good advice. She kept trying to strut like a partridge. She never did learn how to strut. And she forgot how to walk like a crow!

语言注释

1. crow / krəʊ / n. 乌鸦
2. partridge / ˈpɑːtrɪdʒ / n. 山鹑
3. strut / strʌt / v. 趾高气扬地走；n. 高视阔步
4. I wish I could walk as beautifully as the partridge.
   我希望我走路的姿态能够像山鹑那么优雅。
5. demand / dɪˈmɑːnd / v. 要求；询问

篇目欣赏

"I wish I could walk as beautifully as the partridge."乌鸦的愿望是非常美好的，美丽的事物人人都向往。但是山鹑的忠告"You're a crow. Walk like a crow!"也是言之有理。那么问题究竟在哪里呢？"copy"

一词道出了其中的缘由。其实每个人都有自己的可取之处,一味地"copy"别人的东西只能让别人鄙视自己,而且还掩盖了自己本身的优点。事实上并非所有看似优美的东西都适合自己。在坚持自我的同时,不断吸收适合自身特点的事物才是我们应该选择的。少一点单纯的"copy",也许你的生活将更加有特色。

背诵准备

你一定从这则寓言中得到了不少启示吧?请从故事中找出能够回答下列问题的句子,并在这些句子的帮助下记忆、背诵全文。

1. What was the partridge doing when the crow was flying across a road?

_____

2. What was the crow's wish?

_____

3. What did the crow try to do then?

_____

4. What did the partridge demand?

_____

5. What was the partridge's good advice?

_____

6. Did the crow learn how to walk like a partridge? What was the result?

_____

参考译文

乌鸦与山鹑

有一天,乌鸦飞过一条大路,低头看到了一只山鹑。山鹑正昂首阔步,走路的姿态十分优雅。

乌鸦心想:"要是我走路的姿态能够像山鹑那么优雅就好了。"于是乌鸦飞落到大路上,走在山鹑的身后。乌鸦努力模仿山鹑优雅的姿态。

山鹬回过头来，质问乌鸦："你究竟在干什么呀？"

"别生气，"乌鸦回答，"我正试着学你走路呢！"

"你真傻！"山鹬说，"你是一只乌鸦，应该走得像只乌鸦！"

可是乌鸦并没有接受山鹬的忠告。它继续挺着胸，学山鹬走路的样子。可是它始终没有学会山鹬那种昂首阔步的样子，也忘了应该怎样走得像只乌鸦。

41. The Lion and the Mouse

By Aesop

One day, the Lion was sleeping. The Mouse ran across the Lion's *paws*. The Lion woke up, and was angry. He *grabbed* the Mouse and opened his huge *jaws*.

"Don't eat me!" the Mouse begged. "Please! I'm sorry. Let me go, and maybe someday, I can help you in some way." The Lion laughed. "How could you help me?" But he let the Mouse go.

Some time later, the Mouse heard the Lion *roaring* angrily. The Mouse ran to see what was wrong. The Lion was caught in a hunter's net.

The Mouse said, "Don't worry. I'll get you out of there." He began to *nibble* on the net. He nibbled and nibbled, and finally, there was a hole in the net. The Lion *squeezed* through the hole. He was free again. "Thank you, Mouse." "You are welcome, Lion. And let this be a lesson to you."

语言注释

1. paw / pɔː / *n*. (动物之)脚爪
2. grab / græb / *v*. 抓住,攫取
3. jaw / dʒɔː / *n*. 上/下颚
4. roar / rɔː / *v*. 怒吼,咆哮
5. nibble / ˈnɪbl / *v*. 小口小口地吃;一点一点地咬
6. squeeze / skwiːz / *v*. 挤出

篇目欣赏

当第一次狮子放了老鼠的时候他怎么都不会相信有那么一天小小的老鼠能帮助他。在他的眼里老鼠始终是一只只会 nibble things 的小动物,成不了什么气候。可是就是这只渺小的老鼠却救了自己的性命。最后老鼠对狮子说的那句"Let this be a lesson to you."中的 lesson,是何意? 大家都会有自己的判断。"毋以善小而不为"的道理也在于此。

背诵准备

这是一则非常能发人深省的寓言故事。由于使用了不同的动词,使得故事的情节发展也更为跌宕起伏,请用文章中的动词的正确形式填空,并在此基础上背诵这则寓言故事。

One day, the Lion _____ (sleep). The Mouse _____ (run) across the Lion's paws. The Lion _____ (wake) up, and was angry. He _____ (grab) the Mouse and _____ (open) his huge jaws.

"Don't eat me!" the Mouse _____ (beg). "Please! I'm sorry. Let me go, and maybe someday, I can help you in some way." The Lion _____ (laugh). "How could you help me?" But he _____ (let) the Mouse _____ (go).

Some time later, the Mouse _____ (hear) the Lion _____ (roar) angrily. The Mouse _____ (run) to _____ (see) what was wrong. The Lion _____ (catch) in a hunter's net.

The Mouse _____ (say), "Don't _____ (worry). I'll _____ (get) you out of there." He _____ (begin) to nibble on the net. He _____ (nibble) and _____ (nibble), and finally, there was a hole in the net. The Lion _____ (squeeze) through the hole. He was free again. "Thank you, Mouse." "You are welcome, Lion. And let this be a lesson to you."

参考译文

狮子和老鼠

有一天,狮子正在睡觉,老鼠正好碰到狮子的爪子。狮子被惊醒,生气地一把抓住老鼠就张大嘴巴。

"求求你,千万别把我吃掉。"老鼠向狮子恳求,"真是抱歉。可是求你放了我吧,也许有一天,我还能帮助你呢!"狮子大笑起来,"你怎么帮得了我?"不过他还是放了老鼠。

又有一天,老鼠听到狮子愤怒的咆哮声,他跑去看究竟发生了什么事,原来狮子被困在猎人的捕兽网里。

老鼠说:"别着急,我能把你救出来。"他开始一点一点地咬网上的绳子。他咬啊,咬啊,终于在捕兽网上咬出了一个洞。狮子从这个洞里挤了出来,他又自由了。"谢谢你,老鼠。""不用谢,狮子。就让这件事成为你的一个教训吧!"

42. The Boy Who Cried Wolf

By Aesop

Once, a shepherd boy was watching his *flock* of sheep. He got *bored*, and decided to *have some fun*.

"Help, help!" he cried. "Wolf! Wolf! The wolves are *attacking* my sheep."

The people in the village came running to help. The shepherd boy laughed and said, "There are no wolves. I was just *fooling*." The villagers were back to their work.

But the shepherd boy cried "Wolf! Wolf!" *three more times*. Three more times, the villagers came running. And three more times the boy laughed. He thought it was a great joke. The villagers did not.

Soon after, *some wolves really did come*. The shepherd boy cried "Wolf! Wolf!" But the villagers didn't come. The boy ran to the village.

"Help! The wolves are attacking my sheep!" he cried. "You won't fool us again." said the villagers. And so the boy lost all of his sheep.

语言注释

1. flock / flɒk / *n*. 群

2. bored / bɔːd / *adj*. (觉得)无聊

3. have some fun 找点乐子

4. attack / əˈtæk / *v*. 袭击

5. The people in the village came running to help. 村里的人都跑来帮忙。句子中其实有两个动作，一是 come，一是 run。由于这两个动作是同时发生，所以其中一个用现在分词的形式，表示伴随。

6. fool / fʊl / *v*. 欺骗

7. three more times 又三次。在这一段中，出现了三次 three more times，避免了重复叙述之前发生过的事情。

8. soon after 不久以后

9. Some wolves really did come. 确实来了许多狼。这是一个强
调句。Really 和 do 同时出现,加重语气。

篇目欣赏

在这则寓言故事中,孩子说了谎,一而再,再而三,结果导致他的羊群真的被狼吃掉了。显然这孩子是因为无聊才开了这么一个"愚蠢的玩笑",多次撒谎的结果给自己带来巨大的损失。在生活中我们类似的"愚蠢玩笑"还有很多很多,有些甚至连自己都难以意识到,不过我们可以牢记一点:我们要对自己所做过的一切事情负责,做一个有责任心的人。

背诵准备

这是一个耳熟能详的寓言故事,请重点记忆文章中放羊娃和村民说的话,通过对话记忆背诵全文。

Once, a shepherd boy was watching his flock of sheep. He got bored, and decided to have some fun.

"_____" he cried. "_____"

The people in the village came running to help. The shepherd boy laughed and said, "_____" The villagers were back to their work.

But the shepherd boy cried "_____" three more times. Three more times, the villagers came running. And three more times the boy laughed. He thought it was a great joke. The villagers did not.

Soon after, some wolves really did come. The shepherd boy cried "_____" But the villagers didn't come. The boy ran to the village.

"_____" he cried. "_____" said the villagers. And so the boy lost all of his sheep.

参考译文

狼来啦

从前有个放羊娃正在放羊,他觉得无聊,就想找点乐子。

"救命啊!救命啊!"他喊道,"狼来啦!狼来啦!狼来抢我的羊啦!"

村里的人听到放羊娃的呼救就跑来帮忙。可是,放羊娃却笑着对他们说,"哪里有狼啊,我跟你们闹着玩呢。"村民们又回去干活了。

可是放羊娃又连喊了三次"狼来啦",村民们跑来了三次,可每次放羊娃都笑着告诉他们这是个玩笑,但村民们一点也不觉得这个玩笑好玩。

又过了不久,狼真的来了。放羊娃又大声地呼救:"狼来啦!狼来啦"可是村民们再也不上当了,放羊娃只好逃回了村子。

"救命啊!狼来抢我的羊啦!"他喊道。"你别再骗我们了。"村民们回答。放羊娃所有的羊都被狼吃掉了。

43. The Tortoise and the Hare

By Aesop

A long, long time ago, a *hare* and a *tortoise* wanted to have a race. The hare was very fast. The tortoise, of course, was very slow.

The hare laughed at the tortoise, and was far ahead at the beginning, so he stopped to talk with some friends. He was so busy talking that he didn't see the tortoise run past him.

The tortoise ran and ran. But the hare ran faster. Soon the hare *caught up with* the tortoise. He thought that he had a lot of time, so he stopped to eat a big lunch. He was too full to run fast after the lunch, so he stopped to rest. Soon he fell asleep. While he was sleeping, the tortoise passed him again.

When the hare woke up, he ran very fast. But it was too late. The tortoise had won the race.

Slow but *steady* wins the race.

语言注释

1. hare / heə / *n*. 兔子
2. tortoise / ˈtɔːtəs / *n*. 乌龟
3. catch up with 赶上
4. steady / ˈstedɪ / *adj*. 稳健的

篇目欣赏

虽然乌龟和兔子的速度是无法比较的,但是乌龟通过自己锲而不舍的努力最终获得了比赛的胜利。这是一则我们耳熟能详的寓言故事。故事中最后一句"Slow but steady wins the race." Steady 是稳健的意思。

如果在生活中我们能稳健地对待任何事情,那么胜利就不会和我们擦肩而过。兔子虽然跑得快但它却嘲笑自己的对手,放松警惕,从而把胜利拱手相让。

背诵准备

把下面每组句子合成一句,写完后对照原文,看看自己写对了吗?

1. The hare laughed at the tortoise.

   The hare was far ahead at the beginning.

   The hare stopped to talk with some friends.

   _____

2. He was so busy talking.

   He didn't see the tortoise run past him.

   _____

3. He thought.

   He had a lot of time.

   He stopped to eat a big lunch.

   _____

4. He was too full.

   He couldn't run fast after the lunch.

   He stopped to rest.

   _____

5. He was sleeping.

   At that time, the tortoise passed him again.

   _____

参考译文

龟兔赛跑

很久以前,兔子和乌龟决定要举行一次赛跑。大家都知道,兔子跑得很快,乌龟却跑得很慢。

兔子嘲笑乌龟跑得慢,并且在比赛一开始就遥遥领先,因此他停下来和朋友们聊天。他聊得兴起,没有看到乌龟已经超过了他。

乌龟跑啊跑,可兔子轻而易举地又超过了他。兔子心想自己有的是时间,于是就停下来饱餐一顿。可是他吃得太多了,跑不快,于是停下来休息,不一会儿,他就睡着了。在他熟睡的时候,乌龟再一次超过了他。

等兔子醒来的时候,他跑得飞快,可是无济于事,乌龟已经赢得了比赛。

锲而不舍才能取得胜利。

44. The Little Sheep and the Wolf

By Aesop

A little sheep was returning home alone, and she was followed by a wolf. *Seeing she could not escape, she turned around*, and said, "Well, Mr. Wolf, I know that I shall be your *prey*, but before I die, could you just *do me a favor*?" "What do you want?" said the wolf. "I really like dancing. Could you play me a piece of music, so I can dance with the music?" asked the little sheep. The wolf agreed, and while he was *piping* and the little sheep was dancing, some *hounds* heard the music. They ran up and began *chasing* the wolf. The wolf *sighed*, "I am a *butcher*, but not a *piper*. I *deserve* it."

In case of emergency, clever thinking is the key.

语言注释

1. Seeing she could not escape, she turned around and said, "...": She found that she could not escape, so she turned around to the wolf and said, "..." 她发现自己跑不了了,就回过头对狼说:"……"
2. prey / preɪ / *n*. 被捕食的动物,猎物
3. do sb. a favor 帮某人一个忙
4. pipe / paɪp / *v*. 吹笛子
   piper / ˈpaɪpə / *n*. 吹笛子的人
5. hound / haʊnd / *n*. 猎狗
6. chase / tʃeɪs / *v*. 追赶,追捕
7. sigh / saɪ / *v*. 叹息
8. butcher / ˈbʊtʃə / *n*. 屠夫
9. deserve / dɪˈzɜːv / *v*. 应得
10. in case of 万一发生……
11. emergency / ɪˈmɜːdʒnsi / *n*. 紧急情况,突发事件

篇目欣赏

很多人在遇到紧急事情的时候都缺少像故事里小羊那样的 clever thinking。小羊之所以能保命就是在于在危急时刻还能保持清醒的头脑和敌人周旋。身陷险境的时候,关键是要有智谋。生活中其实很多情况下要有一种智慧和谋略。平时需要,遇到危机的时候更需要,这样我们往往会取得主动。

背诵准备

这是一个很有趣的故事,小羊的机智给我们留下了十分深刻的印象。请重点记忆文章中小羊和狼的对话,通过对话记忆背诵全文。

A little sheep was returning home alone, and she was followed by a wolf. Seeing she could not escape, she turned around, and said, "_____ _____" "_____" said the wolf. "_____" asked the little sheep. The wolf agreed, and while he was piping and the little sheep was dancing, some hounds heard the music. They ran up and began chasing the wolf. The wolf sighed, "_____ _____"

In case of emergency, clever thinking is the key.

参考译文

小羊和狼

小羊独自回家,路上被狼跟踪。眼看着无法脱身,她转过身来对狼说:"狼先生,我知道我今天注定要成为你的猎物。临死前,我想请您帮我一个忙,可以吗?""你想要什么?"狼问道。"我非常喜欢跳舞。您能为我吹奏一曲,让我再跳个舞吗?"小羊问道。狼同意了,就吹起笛子来。

小羊翩翩起舞。几只猎狗听到音乐,跑来追赶狼。狼叹息道:"我本来就是个屠夫,又不是吹笛子的。我真是自作自受啊。"

身陷险境的时候,关键是要有智谋。

45. Dreams

By Langston Hughes

Hold fast to dreams
For if dreams die
Life is a *broken-winged* bird
That cannot fly.

Hold fast to dreams
For when dreams go
Life is a *barren* field
Frozen with snow.

语言注释

1. hold fast   紧紧地抓住
2. broken-winged / ˈbrəʊkənwɪŋd / *adj*. 折断翅膀的
3. barren / ˈbærən / *adj*. 荒芜的
4. frozen / ˈfrəʊzn / *adj*. 结冰的；冻结的

背景介绍

生于密苏里州乔普林的兰斯顿·休斯（Langston Hughes，1902－1967）从读高中时就开始写诗。1921 年他曾就读于哥伦比亚大学，但一年后便辍学。由于渴望周游世界，他便在一艘远洋货轮上当水手，并借此机会游历非洲和欧洲，曾在巴黎当过饭馆厨师和夜总会看门人。1925 年，他回美国后在华盛顿市一家旅馆当侍者期间，正在那儿举行巡回朗诵会的诗人维切尔林赛发现了他的诗歌才能。此后他便开始在文坛上崭露头角，并最终成为哈莱姆文艺复兴运动的领袖人物和最著名的美国诗人之一。他的主要诗歌作品还有《抵押给犹太人的好衣服》（*Fine Clothes to the Jew*，1927）、《梦乡人》（*The Dream Keeper and Other Poems*，1932）和《哈莱姆的莎士比亚》（*Shakespeare in Harlem*，1942）。

篇目欣赏

人们常常以"梦想"这个词来代表美好的理想和希望,并且强调假如没有梦想,人生就会失去目标和方向。休斯这首短诗正是描写了这样一个主题。当然,这儿的梦想还有特殊的含义,它们是饱受种族歧视之苦的美国黑人对自由、平等和民权的向往,它们也是黑人们忍受压迫、剥削和社会不公正待遇所不可缺少的精神支柱。诗人写这首诗的本意正是为了鼓励美国黑人憧憬未来,增添生活的勇气。

诗中的语言非常精练,诗人为了说明梦想的重要性而特地运用了两个生动的比喻。失去梦想,人生就像是断了翅膀的鸟儿,永远不能再飞翔;失去梦想,人生就像冰雪封冻的荒野,充满悲哀和凄凉。言简意赅,回味无穷。

背诵准备

人生需要梦想。如果没有梦想,我们的生活将会怎样呢?

Dreams

_____ _____ to dreams

For if dreams _____

Life is a _____ bird

That cannot fly.

_____ _____ to dreams

For when dreams _____

Life is a _____ field

_____ with snow.

参考译文

梦想

兰斯顿·休斯

要坚信你的梦想
因为如果梦想死亡
人生就像一只断翅的鸟儿
无法飞翔。

要坚信你的梦想
因为当梦想逝去
人生就像一片荒野
遍布冰雪。

46. Border Line

By Langston Hughes

I used to *wonder*
About living and dying —
I think the difference *lies*
Between tears and crying.

I used to wonder
About *here and there* —
I think the *distance*
Is nowhere.

语言注释

1. border / ˈbɔːdə / *n*. 边界
2. wonder / ˈwʌndə / *v*. 思考
3. lie / laɪ / *v*. 在于
4. here and there   人间与地狱
5. distance / ˈdɪstəns / *n*. 距离

篇目欣赏

休斯通常被认为是一个温和派诗人,从不用狂暴的呐喊和激愤的言词来表达他对美国社会含蓄的抗议和诅咒。但在这首微型短诗中,他对于美国黑人生活在水深火热之中这一现状的激愤之情却已溢于言表。诗中叙述者告诉读者,他过去常常思考生与死的差别,可是他最终却发现,对于美国黑人来说,这种差别只是程度上的差异而已,就像抽泣和号啕大哭。他过去也常冥思人间与地狱的距离,但他现在认为这种差距几乎已经不复存在,因为黑人的悲惨生活状况与人间地狱无异。

背诵准备

休斯在诗中表达了对生与死的差别、人间与地狱的距离的思考。请在诗中找出有关内容。

1. _____

   _____

2. _____

   _____

参考译文

分界线

兰斯顿·休斯

我过去常思考
生与死
如同
抽泣与号啕大哭。

我过去也常冥思
人间与地狱
几乎
没有距离。

47. The Red Wheelbarrow

By William Carlos Williams

So much *depends*
upon

a red wheel
barrow

glazed with rain
water

beside the white
chickens.

语言注释

1. wheelbarrow / ˈwiːlbærəʊ / *n*. 手推车
2. depend upon 依靠；依赖
3. glazed / gleɪzd / *adj*. 表面光滑的，具光泽的

背景介绍

生于新泽西州鲁瑟福德的威廉·卡洛斯·威廉斯(William Carlos Williams, 1883－1963)是 20 世纪最著名的美国诗人之一。他的诗歌常常描写日常生活中人们不大注意的东西。由于他所从事的医生职业，使他有机会看到在各种条件下生活的人们，从他们的出生一直到死亡的那一刻。这样细致入微的观察使他的诗歌具有深刻的洞察力和丰富的内容。埃兹拉·庞德以及其他意象派诗人对于他的诗歌创作有很大的影响。同时他还步惠特曼的后尘，积极发展了自由诗的形式。由于坚持用美国本土的语言写作，他的诗歌具有浓郁的乡土气息。他的抒情诗主要收集在《近期诗集》(*Collected Latter Poems*, 1950)和《早期诗集》(*Collected Early Poems*, 1951)这两部书中。

篇目欣赏

威 廉斯的这首短诗也经常被推崇为意象派诗歌的名篇。它从儿童的视角出发来观察一个极其普通的农家院落一角,用写意的笔触描绘出一幅色彩清新的图画。画面的中心是一辆独轮手推车,它是农民日常的劳动工具,因日晒雨淋和主人每天的使用,手推车的木头已经磨得很光滑,并呈现出红色。车身上罩着一层闪光的雨点,更加突出了颜色的鲜亮。与手推车形成对比的是周围一群嬉戏觅食的雪白雏鸡。两者一静一动,一红一白,构图生动,情趣隽永。

背诵准备

整首诗只有一个标点符号,实际上就是一个句子。你能在脑海里想象诗中的画面吗?

The Red Wheelbarrow

So much _____

_____

a _____ wheel

barrow

_____ with rain

water

beside the _____

chickens.

参考译文

红色手推车

威廉·卡洛斯·威廉斯

这么多的事

全靠
一辆红色的手推车

给雨水擦得
晶亮

旁边有些
白色鸡雏。

48. I'm Nobody!

By Emily Dickinson

I'm nobody! Who are you?
Are you nobody, too?
Then there's a pair of us — don't tell!
They'd *banish* us, you know!

How *dreary* to be somebody!
How public, like a frog
To tell your name the livelong day
To an *admiring bog*!

语言注释

1. banish / ˈbænɪʃ / v. 放逐,驱逐
2. dreary /ˈdrɪərɪ / adj. 沉闷的
3. admiring / ədˈmaɪərɪŋ / adj. 赞赏的;钦佩的
4. bog / bɒg / n. 泥塘,沼泽

背景介绍

跟 惠特曼一样,埃米莉·狄金森(Emily Dickinson,1830–1886)及其诗歌远远超出了她所在时代的局限。虽然她给后人留下了1775首诗歌,但其中只有很少一部分是在她生前发表的。狄金森一生都没有离开过自己的家乡,马萨诸塞州的阿默斯特。从1861年秋天起,她开始大量写诗。对她的诗歌风格产生直接影响的是爱默生的诗歌。狄金森虽然生前几乎足不出户,但其诗歌表明她有着丰富的精神生活。很多评论家认为,她的诗歌预示了20世纪诗歌的诞生。

篇目欣赏

这首诗采用了戏剧性独白的形式,诗中叙述者以第一人称出现,与同是无名之辈的读者说悄悄话。谈话的主题是名声所带来的累赘。一旦声名鹊起,成为明星,你就会变成一个公众人物,那时就再也无个人隐私可言。而且为了取悦于那些盲目崇拜明星的乌合之众,你就得整天在外抛头露面,喋喋不休地吹嘘自己。叙述者庆幸自己仍然默默无闻,并要求读者不要暴露她身份,否则她俩就会遭到社会的唾弃。

贯穿于整首诗的是一种自嘲和讥讽的语调。令人感兴趣的是诗人究竟是否真正看破了红尘,安心于自己默默无闻的隐居生活;或只是借题发挥,表达了对一种可望而不可即的社会生活的向往。

背诵准备

在埃米莉·狄金森的眼里,那些大人物是个什么形象呢? 从这首诗里可见一斑。

I'm Nobody!

I'm _____! Who are you?
Are you _____, too?
Then there's a pair of us — don't tell!
They'd _____ us, you know!

How dreary to be _____ !
How public, like a _____
To tell your name the livelong day
To an admiring _____!

参考译文

我是无名之辈!

埃米莉·狄金森

我是无名之辈,你是谁?
你也是无名之辈吗?
那么,咱俩是一对——且莫声张!
你懂嘛,他们容不得咱俩!

做个名人多无聊!
像只青蛙到处招摇
向一洼仰慕的泥塘
把自己的大名整天宣扬!

49. To Make a Prairie ...

By Emily Dickinson

To make a prairie it takes a *clover* and one bee,

One clover and a bee,

And *revery*.

Revery alone will do,

If bees are few.

语言注释

1. prairie / ˈpreərɪ / *n*. 草原
2. clover / ˈkləʊvə / *n*. 红花草,草原上很常见的苜蓿属植物
3. revery / ˈrevərɪ / *n*. 幻想,遐想

篇目欣赏

狄　金森的诗歌特点是短小精悍,言简意赅。这首诗歌就是一个典型的例子。诗的大意是强调想象力在诗歌创作中的重要性。这是一个很大的题目,但诗人并没有落入俗套,去咬文嚼字地搬弄术语,或是连篇累牍地论证文学创作的全过程。相反,她只是打了一个简单的比方:要描绘一片草原,你只需要一株草原上常见的红花草和一只蜜蜂,再加上一点遐想。但假如情况不允许,连红花草和蜜蜂都找不到的话,那也没有关系。只要你闭上眼睛,想象一下,那片草原马上就会浮现在你的眼前。诗歌虽然很简单,但却很有说服力。

诗歌的形式不拘一格,不押韵,诗行也长短不一。第二行是第一行后半部分的重复,但是重复中也有变化,把“one”和“a”的位置颠倒了一下,显得语气灵活,自然洒脱。第三行末尾和第四行开始的“revery”一词的重复,突出地表现了“遐想”这个诗歌主题的重要性。

背诵准备

闭上眼睛,狄金森诗中的草原能浮现在你的脑海里吗?

To Make a Prairie ...

To make a _____ it takes a _____ and one _____,

One clover and a bee,

And _____.

_____ alone will do,

If _____ are few.

参考译文

要描绘一片草原……

埃米莉·狄金森

要描绘一片草原,只需要一朵红花和一只蜜蜂,

红花一朵,蜜蜂一只,

还有遐想。

光遐想也行,

假如蜜蜂找不到。

50. In a Station of the Metro

By Ezra Pound

The *apparition* of these faces in the crowd;
Petals on a wet, black bough.

语言注释

1. metro / ˈmetrəʊ / *n.* 地铁
2. apparition / ˌæpəˈrɪʃən / *n.* 幽灵，幻象
3. petals on a wet, black bough　湿漉漉黑色枝条上的众多花瓣

背景介绍

生于爱达荷州、长在宾夕法尼亚州的埃兹拉·庞德(Ezra Pound, 1885 –1972)是 20 世纪美国文坛上一位极有争议的人物。这主要是由于在第二次世界大战期间，庞德曾经在意大利的电台上为墨索里尼作过亲法西斯的宣传，战后受到了美国政府的审判，但被判定患有精神病，在精神病院里度过了后半生的大部分时光。然而他同时也是一位英美现代诗歌的先驱和领路人，曾孜孜不倦地提携了一批新人，其中包括后来在英美诗坛崭露头角的罗伯特弗罗·斯特和托马斯·斯特恩斯·艾略特。1908 年，为了逃避在他看来是褊狭和令人窒息的美国社会和文化，庞德来到了欧洲大陆，并投身于意象主义等先锋派的运动。作为芝加哥《诗歌》(*Poetry*)杂志的驻外记者，他积极推动了美国诗歌的振兴。他自己的诗歌作品包括 1909 年在伦敦出版的《狂喜》(*Exultations*)和《人物》(*Personae*)这两部诗集，1915 年问世的中国古诗英译本《中国》(*Cathay*)，以及被他称作"现代史诗"的一部鸿著《诗章》(*Cantos*)。后者包括了 109 首诗歌和 8 首未完成的草稿，内容涉及世界文学与历史的方方面面。庞德的诗学为现代英美诗歌的发展奠定了基础，他还编辑了《意象派诗选》(*Des Imagistes*, 1914)，为现代诗的崛起作出了很大的贡献。

篇目欣赏

庞德曾经说过:"意象主义的要旨,在于不把意象当作装饰品,意象本身就是语言。"这首小诗就是一个以意象作为叙述语言的典型范例。全诗只有短短的两行,甚至还不能构成一个完整的句子,但它却展示了一幅色彩丰富、构图生动的画面:雨过天晴,地铁车站前涌动着熙熙攘攘的人群;在湿漉漉的黑色沥青地面的映衬下,无数行人的脸庞与色彩绚丽的雨伞和雨衣交相辉映,宛如一个姹紫嫣红、花团锦簇的花园。诗人在创作这首作品时,明显受到了俳句这种短小日本诗歌形式的影响。据庞德本人回忆,诗的灵感来自巴黎地铁车站,当时他写下了一首31行的诗,但觉得很不满意。半年后,他将这瞬间的印象压缩到了15行,可是仍觉得表现力欠佳。直到再过了一年,他在俳句的启发下,将该诗浓缩成两行,才感觉差强人意。这首意象派诗歌名篇堪称是东西方文化交融的典范。

背诵准备

英文原诗只有短短的两句,你能试着翻译这首诗吗?

参考译文

地铁车站

埃兹拉·庞德

人群中这些面孔幻景般闪现;
湿漉漉的黑枝条上朵朵花瓣。

51. A House of My Own

By Sandra Cisneros

Not a flat. Not an apartment in back. Not a man's house. Not a daddy's. A house all my own. With my *porch* and my pillow, my pretty purple *petunias*. My books and my stories. My two shoes waiting beside the bed. Nobody to shake a stick at. Nobody's garbage to pick up after.

Only a house quiet as snow, a space for myself to go, clean as paper before the poem.

语言注释

1. porch / pɔːtʃ / *n*. 门廊, 走廊
2. petunia / pɪ'tjuːnjə, -nɪə / *n*. 矮牵牛花

背景介绍

桑 德拉·希斯内罗丝(Sandra Cisneros, 1954 —   ), 美国当代女诗人。本文选自她的成名作《芒果街上的小屋》*(The House on Mango Street, 1984)*

希斯内罗丝是墨西哥移民的女儿。她成长于六十年代的芝加哥移民社区, 受政府资助上了大学。因为出众的写作天赋, 她被推荐进了国际知名的爱荷华大学研究生写作班。毕业后, 她当过中学教师和大学辅导员, 与少数族裔的贫困学生有许多接触。面对他们经历着的相似的困境和迷惘, 她联想到自己的成长历程, 酝酿五年, 在三十岁时, 采用一种诗歌与小说的混合文体完成了《芒果街上的小屋》。

《芒果街上的小屋》讲述一个少女的成长经历, 描绘移民群落的生存状况。在 20 世纪后期美国知识界高度重视族裔问题的文化氛围里, 这本书引起了相当大的反响和争论。1984 年出版, 次年便获得了"前哥伦布基金会"颁发的美国图书奖, 又陆续进入大中小学课堂, 后来兰登书屋取得了版权并推出其平装本。

篇目欣赏

进入芒果街,房子是主人公小埃斯佩朗莎的梦想,也是全书的核心象征。随着小埃斯佩朗莎渐渐长大,她的梦中房子不断有所变化。她羡慕"住在山上、睡得靠星星如此近的人",但是也明确意识到,那些高高在上的人"忘记了我们这些住在地面上的人"。于是,她想:有一天她自己在山上有了房子,要在阁楼里收留无家可归的流浪者。接近收尾之处,在"*A House of My Own*(自己的一栋房)"中,她再一次描述了心目中的房子:

不是小公寓。也不是背阴的大公寓。也不是哪一个男人的房子。也不是爸爸的。是完完全全我自己的……

只是一所寂静如雪的房子,一个自己归去的空间,洁净如同诗笔未落的纸。

如诗的语言构筑起的房子承载的是更加成熟的埃斯佩朗莎的精神追求。不过,它们传达的,很可能仍只是某一特定时段的感受,而非最终的结论。

背诵准备

在希斯内罗丝诗歌与小说混合的文体中,我们很好地体会了语言的音韵与意象的美。你能根据她的描绘,用纸笔画出她的小屋吗?

文章以两个比喻句结尾:

Only a house quiet as snow, a space for myself to go, clean as paper before the poem.

你能试着用这样的句式描述一下你的小屋吗?

Only a house _____ as _____ , a space for myself to _____ , _____ as _____ .

参考译文

一所我自己的房子

桑德拉·希斯内罗丝

不是小公寓。也不是背阴的大公寓。也不是哪一个男人的房子。也不是爸爸的。是完完全全我自己的。那里有我的门廊我的枕头,我漂亮的紫色矮牵牛花儿。我的书和我的故事。我的两只等在床边的鞋。不用和谁去作对。没有别人扔下的垃圾要拾起。

只是一所寂静如雪的房子,一个自己归去的空间,洁净如同诗笔未落的纸。

52. Auld Lang Syne

By Robert Burns

Should auld *acquaintance* be forgot,

And never brought to mind?

Should auld acquaintance be forgot,

And days of auld long syne?

And here's a hand, my *trusty* friend,

And gie's a hand o' thine;

We'll take a cup o' *kindness* yet,

For auld lang syne.

语言注释

1. acquaintance / ə'kweɪntəns / *n*. 相识,熟人
2. trusty /'trʌstɪ / *adj*. 可信赖的
3. kindness / 'kaɪndnɪs / *n*. 亲切,善意

背景介绍

苏格兰诗人罗伯特·彭斯(Robert Burns,1759－1796)在英国文学史上占有很重要的地位,他复活并丰富了苏格兰民歌;他的诗歌富有音乐性,可以歌唱。彭斯生于苏格兰民族面临被异族征服的时代,因此,他的诗歌充满了激进的民主、自由的思想。诗人生活在破落的农村,和贫苦的农民血肉相连。他的诗歌歌颂了故国家乡的秀美,抒写了劳动者纯朴的友谊和爱情。著名的抒情诗有《一朵红红的玫瑰》(*A Red Red Rose*),《高原玛丽》(*Highland Mary*)等。

篇目欣赏

A uld Lang Syne 原本是罗伯特·彭斯的一首诗,歌唱真挚的友谊,后被人谱以曲调。1940 年美国电影《魂断蓝桥》(*Waterloo Bridge*)用这首歌作主题曲。然后,这首歌传遍世界各地。在每年新年零点到来之时,全欧美都会齐唱这首不朽之作。歌词中有许多是古苏格兰语,分别对应英语中的

Auld Lang Syne = Old Long Since, times gone by

gie's = give us

o'thine = of yours

tak' = take

o' = of

背诵准备

以下是此歌的其中一段,你能根据中文判断出斜体字苏格兰古语对应的英文吗?

We *twa hae* run about the braes,(我们俩曾游遍山冈,)

And *pou'd* the gowans fine;(并把野菊来采摘;)

But we've wander'd *monie* a weary *fit*,(我们已历尽艰辛,)

Sin auld lang syne.(远离过去的好时光。)

twa :_____ *hae* :_____

pou'd :_____ *monie* :_____ *fit* :_____

参考译文

友谊地久天长

罗伯特·彭斯

老朋友怎能被遗忘,

永不再放心上?

老朋友怎能被遗忘，
还有过去美好时光？
老朋友，我已伸出手，
请你也伸手相握；
让我们干一杯友谊之酒，
为了过去美好时光。

53. Stopping by Woods on a Snowy Evening

By Robert Frost

Whose woods these are I think I know.

His house is in the village，though；

He will not see me stopping here

To watch his woods fill up with snow.

My little horse must think it *queer*

To stop without a farmhouse near

Between the woods and frozen lake

The darkest evening of the year.

He gave *the harness bells* a shake

To ask if there is some mistake.

The only other sound's the sweep

Of *easy wind* and *downy flake*.

The woods are lovely，dark，and deep，

But I have promises to keep，

And miles to go before I sleep，

And miles to go before I sleep.

语言注释

1. queer / kwɪə / *adj*. 奇怪的
2. the harness bells   马挽具上的铃铛
3. easy wind   微风
4. downy flake   绒羽般的雪花

背景介绍

罗伯特·弗罗斯特(Robert Frost,1874－1963)，美国二十世纪最重要的诗人之一，是最具美国风格的美国诗人。他的诗可分为抒情诗和叙事诗两大类，前者隽永绝妙，深沉感人，以《雪夜林边小驻》为代表。弗罗斯特敏于观察自然，深谙田园生活，他的诗往往以此为题材，但在朴实、平凡中，别有哲理寓意。诗人根植于传统，但不泥古；不附庸时尚，却能把握方向。1914年在庞德的帮助下，出版《波士顿以北》(*North of Boston*)。此诗集不但迅速走红大西洋两岸，并且成为弗罗斯特无韵诗(blank verse)诗艺的代表作。成名后，弗罗斯特将自己塑造成质朴、温柔的新英格兰庄园诗人，并以此形象稳固了他在美国文学史上独特的地位。

篇目欣赏

新英格兰乡间的雪夜具有一种震撼人心的自然美。鹅毛大雪给大地披上了厚厚的一层银装，在寂静无声的原野里，人们仿佛置身于另一个神奇的世界，忘却烦恼。弗罗斯特在这首诗里描写的正是这样一种超然脱俗的境界。诗人在一个雪夜驾着马车赶路，路经一个树林时，为林间的幽深和黑暗所吸引，一瞬间竟忘却了时间，停下来出神地凝望着雪夜的美景。马脖上的铃铛声把它的思绪重新带回到了现实之中。诗人恋恋不舍地告别树林，因为长夜漫漫，他还得抓紧时间赶路，以便早点回家休息。

正如评论家们所指出的那样，诗中所描写的雪夜赶路蕴含着浓郁的象征意义。旅行向来是人生的一种比喻，而披星戴月的长途跋涉也是对现实生活艰辛的真实写照。在另一方面，树林深处的黑暗可以被解释成死亡或彼岸世界的象征。诗人被这种黑暗所吸引，似乎是潜意识中一种对脱离污浊尘世牵挂的向往。而他及时被马儿的铃声惊醒，重新上路，更显示出他对人生的执著和责任感。

背诵准备

这首小诗是弗罗斯特最负盛名的代表作。诗歌为四步抑扬格，韵脚异常严密又特别自然，前三节一二四行同韵，第三行和下一节的一二四行同韵，最后一节四行同韵。最后一节语音上还有独到之处，多处出现的长元音与双元音，从声响方面传达了旅途的单调和沉闷。全诗用语极为简单朴素，绝大多数是单音节单词。你能找出这些韵脚吗？

参考译文

雪夜林边小驻

罗伯特·弗罗斯特

这是谁家的林子，我想我知道 。
虽说他的农舍在村子另一头；
他不会看到我停留在这儿，
望着他的林子积雪有多厚。

我那小马一定会感到奇怪：
停留在附近没有村舍的地方
在森林和冰湖之间，
在这一年最昏暗的黄昏。

他摇了摇马具上的挂铃，
想问问到底有没有弄错。
此外只听得一阵微风吹过，
和一阵鹅毛似的雪片卷过。

树林真可爱，幽暗而深远。
可是我还得赶赴一个约会，
还得赶好多里路才能安睡，
还得赶好多里路才能安睡。

54. The Road Not Taken

By Robert Frost

Two roads *diverged* in a yellow wood,
And sorry I could not travel both
And be one traveler, long I stood
And looked down one as far as I could
To where it *bent* in the *undergrowth*;

Then took the other, as just as *fair*,
And having perhaps the better *claim*,
Because it was grassy and wanted wear;
Though as for that the passing there
Had worn them really about the same,

And both that morning equally lay
In leaves no step had *trodden* black.
Oh, I kept the first for another day!
Yet knowing how way leads on to way,
I *doubted* if I should ever come back.

I shall be telling this with a *sigh*
Somewhere ages and ages hence:
Two roads diverged in a wood, and I —
I took the one less traveled by,
And that has made all the difference.

语言注释

1. diverge / daɪˈvɜːdʒ / *v.*(道路等)分岔
2. bend / bend / *v.* 使转弯,转向
3. undergrowth / ˈʌndəɡrəʊθ / *n.*
   矮树丛树林中长在树下的矮小植物,幼苗和灌木

4. fair / feə / *adj*. 干净的,纯洁的

5. claim / kleɪm / *n*. 要求权

6. tread / tred / *v*. 在……上走,走过……,沿……走

7. doubt / daʊt / *v*. 对……怀疑

8. sigh / saɪ / *n*. 叹息声

篇目欣赏

写 诗对于弗罗斯特来说,是一种"暂时阻挡混乱"的艺术,并且可将其失序的现实生活,重新纳入正规。因此弗罗斯特不仅带给世人诗的全新风貌,并且借着写诗排解他的不安、焦虑从而重整生命中的秩序,达到一种和谐的境地。弗罗斯特的诗歌最常描述新英格兰。他的诗结合诗人、农夫与哲学家的特色:既清晰、简单、自然、富哲理,又根植于新英格兰的土壤,描绘自然与人的存在。*The Road not Taken* 是描述清晨站在树林岔路上所做的选择。在作者描述熟悉的景物的背后,寓含更深的思想,不断启迪着人们对于人生的深层次的思考。

背诵准备

这是一首很美的描写乡间风景的小诗。诗中语言简单而淡雅地展现着恬静的自然风情。大家在背诵时,可以在脑中勾画出一副同样优美的画面,那么背诵这首诗也就不是一件很困难的事情了,下面我们根据图片,来试着填写诗中的词语吧。

Two roads __A__ in a yellow wood,

And sorry I could not travel both

And be one __B__ , long I stood

And looked down one as far as I could

To where it bent in the __C__ ;

A

B

C

参考译文

未选之路

罗伯特·弗罗斯特

黄树林里岔开两条路，
很遗憾我不能都涉足，
我孤单地站立良久，
向其中一条极目望去，
看它弯没在林荫深处。

然后走另一条路，同样清幽，
也许还多些魅力：
那绿草茵茵似乎更盼望人迹，
虽然这两条小路上，
都很少留下旅人的足迹。

那个早晨落叶满地，
两条路都未经脚印踏践，
啊！第一条改天再走吧！
只是来路延绵无尽头，

我恐怕无法再回到原点。

多年后的某时某地，
我回忆此刻将轻轻叹息：
树林里岔开两条路 而我——
我走了人迹较少的那一条，
因此有了完全不同的人生。

55. I Wandered Lonely as a Cloud (excerpt)

By William Wordsworth

I *wandered* lonely as a cloud

That *floats* on high o'er *vales* and hills,

When all at once I saw a crowd,

A host, of golden *daffodils*;

Beside the lake, *beneath* the trees,

Fluttering and dancing in the *breeze*.

Continuous as the stars that shine

And twinkle on the milky way,

They stretched in never-ending line

Along the *margin* of a bay:

Ten thousand saw I at a glance,

Tossing their heads in sprightly dance.

语言注释

1. wander / ˈwɒndə / *v*. 徘徊,游荡

2. float / fləʊt / *v*. 漂浮

3. vale / ˈveɪliː / *n*. 谷;通常指由溪流冲积而成的山谷

4. daffodil / ˈdæfədɪl / *n*. 水仙花

5. beneath / bɪˈniːθ / *prep*. 低于;在……下方

6. flutter / ˈflʌtə / *v*. 飘动,晃动

7. breeze / briːz / *n*. 微风,轻风

8. margin / ˈmɑːdʒɪn / *n*. 边缘,边界

9. toss / tɒs / *v*. 使颠簸,来回振动

背景介绍

威廉·华兹华斯(William Wordsworth,1770-1850)生于英格兰西北部的湖区,童年时,他在湖光山色、草坡积雪之间不但沐浴着自然的美景,同时也领略了神秘的崇拜,体会了与大自然合一的境界。但随着时光的逝去,他觉得童年时见到的大自然的神秘光彩也随之渐去渐远了,于是他归纳出这样一条道理:婴儿刚刚来自天堂,与自然是合一的;童年离天堂不远,能在自然中望见天堂的荣光;到成人后却再也望不见了。所以华兹华斯的自然主题,并不仅仅是对自然的欣赏,而是在自然中寻找失去的时光,寻找失去的天堂。尽管人与自然完全契合的境界已不可追回,但诗人还能从反思中悟到永生的信息,用心灵的眼睛(inward eye)看到那不可见的世界。

篇目欣赏

《我好似一朵云独自漫游》是华兹华斯抒情诗的代表作,也是华兹华斯描写自然的诗中最美的一首了。1902年4月15日,华兹华斯等数人沿湖散步,这天风比较大,湖水漾起层层波纹。他们在林间发现几株水仙,再往前走水仙越来越多,后来走到湖湾边,突然见到一条狭长的湖湾地带开满了水仙,摇曳生姿,迎风舞蹈,这一从未见过的美景使诗人惊呆了。后来经过追忆,华兹华斯写成此诗,表现了自我与自然的交流,诗人从中找到了一点未泯的童心,窥见了一种永恒的契机,并把这种极乐与读者共享;不但要享受一时,还要把这一境界贮存起来,作为永久的食粮。各种物象都在翩翩起舞——花朵、波浪、直到诗人的心情,都仿佛统一在舞蹈(dancing)的意象中了。

尽管华兹华斯是如此推崇情感与想象,他的诗中还是保持着"情"与"理"间的平衡,保持着"诗教"的因素。在此诗中,他就似乎是在以泛神论的祭司的身份向读者进行诗教,以抵制人对自然的异化,使心灵从自然中获取安慰和治疗。理性的演绎,仍是华兹华斯诗中的重要成分。

背诵准备

这首优美的诗中有很多景色的描写,将自然景观和诗人的感觉融为一体,自然景物的描述栩栩如生,请将下面这些名词放入到诗中合适的位置,这样可以帮助你记忆全文哦!

breeze	hills	trees	vales	daffodils	lake

I wandered lonely as a cloud

That floats on high o'er _____ and _____,

When all at once I saw a crowd,

A host, of golden _____;

Beside the _____, beneath the _____,

Fluttering and dancing in the _____.

参考译文

我好似一朵云独自漫游(节选)

威廉·华兹华斯

我孤独地漫游,像一朵云

在山丘和谷地上飘荡,

忽然间我看见一群

金色的水仙花迎春开放,

在树荫下,在湖水边,

迎着微风起舞翩翩。

连绵不绝,如繁星灿烂,

在银河里闪闪发光,

它们沿着湖湾的边缘

延伸成无穷无尽的一行:

我一眼看见了一万朵,

在欢舞之中起伏颠簸。

56. The Tyger (excerpt)

By William Blake

Tyger! Tyger! burning bright
In the forests of the night,
What *immortal* hand or eye
Could *frame* thy fearful *symmetry*?

In what distant deeps or skies
Burnt the fire of *thine* eyes?
On what wings dare he *aspire*?
What the hand dare *seize* the fire?

And what shoulder, and what art,
Could twist the sinews of thy heart?
And when thy heart began to beat,
What dread hand? and what dread feet?

What the hammer? What the chain?
In what furnace was thy brain?
What the anvil? What dread grasp
Dare its deadly terrors clasp?

语言注释

1. immortal / ɪˈmɔːtl / *adj.* 永恒的,不朽的, 不会被遗忘的
2. frame / freɪm / *v.* 构造,构筑
3. symmetry / ˈsɪmɪtrɪ / *n.* 对称,相称
4. thine / ðaɪn / *pron.* (古)你的东西,你的
5. aspire / əsˈpaɪə / *v.* 渴望,追求
6. seize / siːz / *v.* 抓住,捉住

背景介绍

威廉·布莱克(William Blake,1757-1827)是位英国诗人。布莱克与农民诗人彭斯同时出现在英国诗坛,曾是一名印刷刻版匠。他生活贫困,以刻版为生,却非常富于创造性,后来成为一流的诗人兼画家,他的诗集全是自己刻版的,配以精美的插图,如《天真之歌》、《经验之歌》、散文诗集《天堂与地狱的婚姻》和规模宏大的一系列《先知书》。

布莱克和彭斯一样,也有鲜明的启蒙主义思想。他的许多抒情诗都带有政治倾向性,还专门写了《法国革命》和《亚美利加》等诗,歌颂革命潮流和自由、平等、博爱的理想,批判封建和殖民主义。

篇目欣赏

《老虎》选自《经验之歌》,是布莱克的代表作,诗中含有神秘而辉煌的力和美。诗中语句描写坚挺有力,节奏明快清晰,凸现出兽中之王老虎的高贵威猛及其常人对于它的敬畏。其格律是扬抑格四步,和我国的七言诗节奏相近,这种格律与其内在节奏配合起来,表现了铁匠捶打铁砧般的铿锵有力。将铁匠与老虎进行类比,更体现出作者对于底层劳动人民的歌颂和崇敬。

背诵准备

诗中作者形象地描述了老虎的威猛,对于它的身体各个部位都加以生动而夸张的描述,请找出诗中的形容词,并填到下面适当的空格处,使诗句完整。

Tyger! Tyger! burning bright
In the forests of the night,
What _____ hand or eye
Could frame thy _____ symmetry?

And what shoulder, and what art,

Could twist the sinews of thy heart?

And when thy heart began to beat,

What _____ hand? and what _____ feet?

参考译文

老虎(节选)

威廉·布莱克

老虎! 老虎! 光焰闪耀,

在那深夜的丛莽中燃烧。

是什么超凡的手或眼睛

塑造出你这惊人的匀称?

你眼中的火焰

取自深海,还是高天?

凭什么翅膀有此胆量?

凭什么手掌敢攫取这火光?

什么样的臂力,什么样的技艺

才能拧成你那心脏的腱肌?

什么样的手,什么样的脚,

才使得你的心脏开始搏跳?

什么样的铁锤,什么样的铁链?

什么熔炉把你的脑子烧炼?

什么样的握力? 什么样的铁砧?

敢把这无人敢碰的材料握紧?

57. So, We'll Go No More A-Roving

By George Gordon Byron

So，we'll go no more a-*roving*

So late into the night，

Though the heart be still as loving，

And the moon be still as bright.

For the *sword outwears* its *sheath*，

And the *soul* wears out the *breast*，

And the heart must pause to *breathe*，

And love itself have rest.

Though the night was made for loving，

And the day returns too soon，

Yet we'll go no more a-roving

By the light of the moon.

语言注释

1. roving / ˈrəʊvɪŋ / *n*. 流浪, 漫游
2. sword / sɔːd / *n*. 剑
3. outwear / aʊtˈwɛə / *v*. 穿旧, 穿破；用旧；用完
4. sheath / ʃiːθ / *n*. (刀、剑等的)鞘
5. soul / səʊl / *n*. 灵魂
6. breast / brest / *n*. 胸部
7. breathe / briːð / *v*. 呼吸

背景介绍

乔治·戈登·拜伦(George Gordon Byron,1788 - 1824),英国诗人。出生于伦敦破落的贵族家庭,10 岁继承男爵爵位。他曾在哈罗中学和剑桥大学读书,深受启蒙主义的熏陶。成年以后,正逢欧洲各国民主、民族革命运动蓬勃兴起。反对专制压迫、支持人民革命的进步思想,使他加入英国的工人运动,并成为 19 世纪初欧洲革命运动中争取民主自由和民族解放的一名战士。

篇目欣赏

拜伦个性极强,是浪漫主义第二浪潮的核心人物。在第二浪潮中,他以追求自由的磅礴激情,孤独忧郁的悲剧气质,愤世嫉俗的冷嘲热讽这三大特点风靡了整个欧洲,形成了"拜伦主义"的旋风。拜伦主义,一方面是民族解放的风暴,一方面又是个人主义的颂歌。拜伦是以叛逆者的姿态登上诗坛的,一开始就向英国的现实进行无情的抨击,但因他同时又蔑视群众,所以笔下塑造出的又是一些孤傲而厌世的个人反抗者——拜伦式的英雄。拜伦著名作品大都是长诗,包括《恰尔德·哈罗德游记》、《唐璜》和许多描写拜伦式英雄的叙事诗。

1816 年,拜伦因私生活受到上流社会的排斥,愤而移居意大利。在意大利,他写了《恰尔德·哈罗尔德游记》的第 3、4 两章(1816、1818 年)。这部抒情叙事长诗和未完成的巨著《唐璜》是他最著名的代表作。《我们将不再携手漫游》作于意大利,是拜伦创作的一首爱情诗。与一般爱情诗不同的是,诗中表现的不是对幸福的追求和贪恋,而是"不可贪恋"和不可名状的惆怅。这种留待读者猜测体味的"悖理",赋予诗歌以独特的魅力。

背诵准备

这首诗中有多句都是以-ing 作为韵脚。这是动词的-ing 形式,由动词转化而来。下面已经把动词的原形给你了,试着对照原文先把它变成-ing 的形式,然后再填入合适的位置。

rove   love

So，we'll go no more a-_____

Though the heart be still as _____

Though the night was made for _____

Yet we'll go no more a-_____

参考译文

我们将不再携手漫游

乔治·戈登·拜伦

我们将不再携手漫游,

从黄昏直到夜阑人静,

尽管爱情依旧涌上心头,

而月色也依旧那么明净。

因为利刃会把剑鞘磨破,

灵魂也会把胸腔磨损,

心房需要喘息一刻,

爱情也需要休息的时辰。

尽管良宵专为爱情而设,

而白昼又来得太早,太快,

但我们将不再依依难舍

在明媚的月色里徘徊……

58. The Song of the Shirt (excerpt)

By Thomas Hood

With fingers *weary* and worn,
With eyelids heavy and red,
A woman sat, in unwomanly rags,
Plying her needle and thread —
Stitch! stitch! *stitch*!
In *poverty*, hunger, and dirt,
And still with a voice of *dolorous* pitch
She sang the "Song of the Shirt."

"Work! work! work!
While the cock is crowing aloof!
And work — work — work,
Till the stars shine through the roof!
It's Oh! to be a slave
Along with the *barbarous* Turk,
Where woman has never a soul to save,
If this is Christian work!

"Work — work — work
Till the brain begins to swim;
Work — work — work
Till the eyes are heavy and dim!
Seam, and gusset, and band,
Band, and gusset, and *seam*,
Till over the buttons I fall asleep,
And sew them on in a dream!

语言注释

1. weary / ˈwɪərɪ / *adj.* 疲倦的,体力或智力上疲倦的
2. ply / plaɪ / *v.* 使用;操作
3. stitch / stɪtʃ / *v.* 缝,用针线来固定或连接
4. poverty / ˈpɒvətɪ / *n.* 贫穷,贫困
5. dolorous / ˈdɒlərəs / *adj.* 忧伤的,悲痛的
6. barbarous / ˈbɑːbərəs / *adj.* 野蛮的
7. seam / siːm / *v.* 缝合

背景介绍

托 马斯·胡德(Thomas Hood, 1799 – 1845)是 19 世纪英国著名诗人。他1799 年生于伦敦,父亲是书商,由于经营失利,家庭陷入困境。胡德只读了 9 年书,便向报刊(特别是幽默杂志)投稿谋生。他不仅写诗,也写杂文,作漫画,并从事雕刻,在当时颇有名。

在胡德生命的最后一年多时间内,他在病重情况下写了《衬衫之歌》、《劳工之声》和写被凌辱的卖笑少女投泰晤士河自尽的《叹息桥》等诗,这些作品都是他的代表作。胡德去世后第七年,英国缝衣女工、其他一些工人和人民群众捐款为他立墓碑,上面刻着胡德遗嘱指定的碑文:"他唱了《衬衫之歌》。"

篇目欣赏

《衬 衫之歌》全长近百行,它以现实主义的笔法,真实地描绘了一个缝衣女工悲惨辛酸的生活。在 19 世纪的英国,这首诗首先直截了当地喊出了被剥削的劳工的呼声,在当时影响极大,被喻为"社会抗议文学"。

胡德的诗揭示了劳动者的苦难,批判了社会的不平,为被剥削压迫的

人们大声疾呼,然而他在诗末呼吁的却仅仅是:"但愿这调子传进富人耳朵",显得软弱无力,这就显露了人道主义的弱点。因此恩格斯在肯定《衬衫之歌》是一首优秀的诗的同时,也指出"这首诗使资产阶级女郎们流了不少怜悯的但毫无用处的眼泪。"

背诵准备

在节选诗中的最后一节,诗人为了突出工人工作的艰苦和机械,频繁使用"work"这个词来加强语气,同时为了表现工人工作的单调和枯燥,诗人又使用了一个回环,将三个表示工作的动词反复使用。请对照原诗,将下面空缺的动词填入,并体味诗人这样写的深刻用意。

_____ — _____ — _____
Till the brain begins to swim;
Work — work — work
Till the eyes are heavy and dim!
_____, and _____, and _____,
_____, and _____, and _____,
Till over the buttons I fall asleep,
And sew them on in a dream!

参考译文

衬衫之歌(节选)

托马斯·胡德

手指磨破了,又痛又酸,
眼皮沉重,睁不开眼,
穿着不像女人穿的褴褛衣衫,
一个女人在飞针走线。

——缝啊！缝啊！缝啊！
穷困污浊，忍饥受饿，
但她仍在用悲凉的调子
吟唱着这支《衬衫之歌》！

"劳动！劳动！劳动！
当远处的公鸡刚刚报晓！
劳动！劳动！劳动！
直到星光在漏屋上闪耀！
啊！这简直是当奴隶，
在野蛮的异教国家做工，
那儿女人没有灵魂可超升；
难道这是基督徒的劳动？

劳动——劳动——劳动
直到头脑眩晕；
劳动——劳动——劳动
直到眼睛昏沉。
接缝，角料，带子，
带子，角料，接缝，
直到我钉扣子时睡着了，
一面做梦一面还在缝！

59. Under the Harvest Moon

By Carl Sandburg

Under the harvest moon,
When the soft silver
Drips *shimmering*
Over the garden nights,
Death, the gray *mocker*,
Comes and whispers to you
As a beautiful friend
Who remembers.

Under the summer roses
When the *flagrant crimson*
Lurks in the *dusk*
Of the wild red leaves,
Love, with little hands,
Comes and touches you
With a thousand memories,
And asks you
Beautiful, unanswerable questions.

语言注释

1. shimmer / ʃɪmə / *v.* 闪闪发光
2. mocker / ˈmɔkə / *n.* 嘲弄者
3. flagrant / ˈfleɪɡrənt / *adj.* 燃烧着的,燃烧正旺的
4. crimson / ˈkrɪmzn / *n.* 深红色
5. lurk / ləːk / *v.* 潜藏
6. dusk / dʌsk / *n.* 黄昏

背景介绍

卡尔·桑德堡(Carl Sandburg,1878－1967),1878年1月6日出生在美国伊利诺斯州盖尔斯堡一个瑞典裔贫苦劳动者家庭。从13岁起,就不得不中断学业,开始从事各种各样的体力劳动:赶车送牛奶、擦皮鞋、洗碗碟、在理发店打杂、为戏院装换布景、给砖厂运送砖块、进陶瓷厂当徒工、还在麦收季节到农田里去卖苦力。1904年卡尔·桑德堡出版了一本薄薄的诗集《轻率的狂喜》,但是,直到1914年哈蕾特·芒罗主编的《诗刊》发表他的一组诗,他才开始引起诗坛的注意。1916年,他的《芝加哥诗集》出版,引起一片争议,也使他名声大振,并奠定了他作为具有独创精神和独特风格的诗人的地位。

篇目欣赏

桑德堡生前素有"工业美国桂冠诗人"之称。他广泛取材于现实生活的作品,为我们展示出一幅视野广阔的美国工业社会的生动画卷。在形式上桑德堡继承了惠特曼所开创的那种粗犷、豪放,不拘音节、不用脚韵而有自然节奏的自由诗传统,而且在增强其音乐性方面作出了自己的贡献,给予自由诗运动以新的推动;在精神上,也继承了惠特曼对于普通人民的爱和对于他们有能力应付一切的信赖,因而,桑德堡又被公认为"普通人民的诗人"。他是人民的歌手,也是人民的辩护师、代言人和教育者,在人们抨击和揭露芝加哥的丑恶和黑暗的同时,他满怀自豪、理直气壮地为之歌唱,因为他还看到了芝加哥的劳动人民及其力量和乐观的未来。他的语言直接来源于口语、方言、民歌,简朴、有力、感情真挚而强烈,和广大劳苦人民有着一致的爱憎。他的诗歌题材,直接取之于他们的生活,像惠特曼一样,他善于使用重复和累积来形成诗篇的内在韵律,取得增强诗篇气势和感染力的效果。《中秋月下》这首诗,作者将中秋满月的夜景描写得安静、美妙、祥和,在夜景的衬托中引出人生的死与爱,看似两个及其矛盾的对象,在诗中却是那样的和谐,死这样一个沉重的话题被放到这样的环境当中也不免让读者对于人生的内涵有了一个别样的认识和思考。

背诵准备

　　作者美丽的语言将自然的柔美景色描绘到了字里行间,用语言将他们描绘得栩栩如生。读诗的同时仿佛就是在欣赏一副美丽的夜景图,请将下列图片和诗中的单词对应起来。这些图片能够帮助你更好地体会诗中的内涵。

A
_____

B
_____

C
_____

参考译文

中秋月下

长尔·桑德堡

中秋月下,
当柔柔银辉
滴滴闪光
笼罩着花园的夜色时,
死神,这灰色的嘲弄者,
像个长得英俊
爱怀旧的朋友
前来与你窃窃低语。

夏日玫瑰下,
当芬芳绯红
隐隐约约
藏匿在红叶丛丛的暗影里,

爱神,伸出纤纤小手,
来撩动你,
激起你千种思绪,
并向你提出
妙不可答的问题。

60. Between the Sunset and the Sea

By Algernon Charles Swinburne

Between the sunset and the sea

My love laid hands and lips on me;

Of sweet came *sour*, of day came night,

Of long *desire* came brief delight:

Ah love, and what thing came of thee

Between the sea-downs and the sea?

Between the sea-mark and the sea

Joy grew to grief, *grief* grew to me;

Love turned to tears, and tears to fire,

And dead delight to new desire;

Love's talk, love's touch there seemed to be

Between the sea-sand and the sea.

Between the sundown and the sea

Love watched one hour of love with me;

Then down the all-golden water-ways

His feet flew after yesterday's;

I saw them come and saw them flee

Between the sea-*foam* and the sea.

Between the sea-strand and the sea

Love fell on sleep, sleep fell on me;

The first star saw *twain* turn to one

Between the moonrise and the sun;

The next, that saw not love, saw me

Between the sea-banks and the sea.

语言注释

1. sour / ˈsaʊə / *n*. 酸味
2. desire /dɪˈzaɪə / *n*. 希望,渴望
3. grief / griːf / *n*. 悲伤,悲痛
4. foam / fəʊm / *n*. 泡沫
5. twain / tweɪn / *pron*. 二

背景介绍

阿尔杰农·查尔斯·斯温本(Algernon Charles Swinburne,1837－1909)生于伦敦。他对当时艺术萎靡板滞和充满道德说教的状况深感不满,而表现出对中古艺术的向往和追求感官美的倾向。但斯温本又是一个革命民主主义者,这使得他脱离"为艺术而艺术"的"象牙之塔"而为民主和自由高唱赞歌。同时,斯温本的激烈的无神论世界观也使他的诗洋溢着异教精神。正因为斯温本的诗既带有感官美的性质和蔑视传统道德的颓废色彩,同时又洋溢着激进的革命民主主义激情,所以引来批评界保守势力的群起围攻。

在诗艺上,斯温本以重感性而著称。他注重于用细腻柔和的文笔描绘客观事物的形状与色彩,给读者以视觉方面的刺激。但他更重视诗的音乐之美,刻意追求词本身的声音以及词的组合所产生的节奏。他试用过各种诗歌节奏,如大规模地运用"抑抑扬"等英语诗中少见的三拍子音步,并用它恰到好处地显示大海动荡起伏变化万千的韵律。他还喜欢采用回旋曲、幻想曲等源的音乐盖过了诗的内容的倾向。但他在诗歌音乐性方面的开拓和追求,毕竟极大地丰富了英语诗的音律,为英语诗歌形式的发展作出了贡献。

篇目欣赏

《在夕阳和大海之间》选自诗剧《夏斯特拉》，这是斯温本早期作的诗歌之一，是写苏格兰玛丽女王的故事的；这首抒情诗插曲则是剧中人玛丽·彼顿唱的歌，颇有先拉斐尔派特色。斯温本从小爱海，在他的诗里，我们经常可以听到大海动荡起伏、变化万千的音韵，这也是他被骂作"八爪海怪"的由来。他是个重感性的诗人，他丰富的英国抒情诗及其音律固然也有让过多音乐盖过诗的内容的倾向。

背诵准备

作者在描述夕阳和大海之间的美妙风景和情感之时使用了很多类似于 sunset 这样的复合名词。在每节诗的第一句和最后一句都有这样的词语出现，试试看，能把这些词语从诗中找出来吗？

Between the _____ and the sea

Between the _____ and the sea

Between the _____ and the sea

Between the _____ and the sea

Between the _____ and the sea

Between the _____ and the sea

Between the _____ and the sea

Between the _____ and the sea

参考译文

在夕阳和大海之间

阿尔杰农·查尔斯·斯温本

在夕阳和大海之间，

爱人的手和唇抚爱了我。
昼带来夜,甜带来酸,
长久的愿望带来短暂的欢乐,
爱情啊,你带来的是什么,
在沙丘和大海之间?

在潮线和大海之间,
喜化为悲,悲化为我,
爱变为泪,泪变为火,
逝去的欢乐变为新的心愿,
恍惚听得情话,感到抚摸,
在沙滩和大海之间。

在日没和大海之间
爱守着我度过爱的一刻,
然后踏着那金灿灿的水道
他飞步而去,追随着日没。
我看到他的脚步来了又去
在海沫和大海之间。

在海滨和大海之间,
爱笼罩梦,梦笼罩我。
第一颗星看见二变为一
在月升和日落之间;
第二颗星不见爱,只见我,
在海岸和大海之间。

61. Sudden Light

By Dante Gabriel Rossetti

I have been here before,

But when or how I cannot tell:

I know the grass beyond the door,

The sweet *keen* smell,

The sighing sound, the lights around the shore.

You have been mine before, —

How long ago I may not know:

But just when at that *swallow*'s *soar*

Your neck turned so,

Some *veil* did fall, — I knew it all of *yore*.

Has this been thus before?

And shall not thus time's *eddying* flight

Still with our lives our love *restore*

In death's *despite*,

And day and night *yield* one delight once more?

语言注释

1. keen / ki:n / *adj.* 好的

2. swallow / ˈswɔləʊ / *n.* 燕子

3. soar / sɔ: / *n.* 高飞,翱翔

4. veil / veɪl / *n.* 面纱

5. yore / jɔ: / *n.* (书)很久以前

6. eddy / ˈedɪ / *v.* 起漩涡

7. restore / rɪsˈtɔ: / *v.* 恢复

8. despite / dɪsˈpaɪt / *prep.* 不管,不顾

9. yield / ji:ld / *v.* 产生,获得

背景介绍

但 丁·迦百列·罗塞蒂（Dante Gabriel Rossetti, 1828 – 1882）享有"美的崇拜者"之称。他在美术史和诗歌史上占有同等重要的地位。他的诗如其画，画如其诗，都表现出南方人的热情、真挚和艺术性的个性，而且特别强调声、色、光、影的神秘朦胧的官能美，富于象征意味。

篇目欣赏

这 篇《顿悟》是一首神秘诗，讲的是通过直觉突然进入悟境，这与禅宗颇有点相像。罗塞蒂依据的是这样一种心理体验：忽然间觉得这个地方我似乎来过，这个场景我恍惚经历过，但其实却并无其事。在几乎人人体验过的这种心理现象基础上，罗塞蒂作出了时间轮回的神秘主义推测。但与佛教关于轮回和解脱的观念不同，罗塞蒂的"时间飞旋"只不过是一种美好的诗的幻想。诗人不想从轮回中解脱，而只是在诗中祈求这明知不可能的轮回出现。

背诵准备

作者在整首诗中讲述自己的心灵体验，有些是他自己知道的，而有些又是他不知道的，以下这些诗句都谈到了知与不知。请认真阅读原诗，找出这些诗句并将下面空格补充完整。

Know

1. I know ＿＿＿＿＿＿＿＿＿＿＿＿＿＿＿＿，

　　＿＿＿＿＿＿＿＿＿＿＿＿＿＿＿＿＿，

2. ＿＿＿＿＿＿＿＿＿＿＿＿＿＿＿＿＿，

　　＿＿＿＿＿＿＿＿＿， — I knew it all of yore.

Not know

3. _____ I cannot tell：

I know _____,

4. _____, —

_____ I may not know：

参考译文

顿　悟

但丁·迦百列·罗塞蒂

我一定到过此地，

何时，何因，却不知祥。

只记得门外芳草依依，

阵阵甜香，

围绕岸边的闪光，海的叹息。

你曾属于我——

只不知距今已有多久，

但刚才你看飞燕穿梭，

蓦然回首，

纱幕落了！——这一切我早就见过。

莫非真有过此情此景？

时间的回旋会不会再来一次

恢复我们的生活与爱情，

超越了死，

日日夜夜再给我们一次欢欣？

62. A Girl

By Ezra Pound

The tree has entered my hands，

The *sap* has *ascended* my arms，

The tree has grown in my breast —

Downward，

The branches grow out of me，like arms.

Tree you are，

Moss you are，

You are *violets* with wind above them.

A child — so high — you are，

And all this is *folly* to the world.

语言注释

1. sap / sæp / *n*. 树液

2. ascend / əˈsend / *v*. 上升;向上走或移动

3. moss / mɔs / *n*. 苔藓

4. violet / ˈvaɪələt / *n*. 紫罗兰

5. folly / ˈfɔlɪ / *n*. 愚行,荒唐事

背景介绍

艾兹拉·庞德(Ezra Pound),1885 年出生于美国爱达荷州海莱市。21 岁时获宾夕法尼亚大学文学硕士学位,早期从事意象派的写作。在《意象派诗选》的序言中,庞德提出诗歌创作的三条新原则:提倡用准确的日常语言,创造新的韵律以及自由选材。这些主张对现代自由体诗的发展起了重大的作用,也为庞德之后改写现代派诗作了准备。1917 年之后他开始了现代派诗歌的写作。除此之外,庞德还是一个热衷于介绍中国古典诗歌和哲学的翻译家。他迷恋中国的诗歌及文字,并提倡用意象来表达诗人情感。

篇目欣赏

庞德这首诗通过对一名年轻女性的描写,抒发了庞德对于历史和文化的看法:干涩垂死毫无生气的文明与自然异教世界的反差巨大。古罗马的作品中(如奥维德的 *Metamorphoses*)有许多妇女化身植物或动物的例子。这首诗中被追求的女孩为了躲避她的追求者变成了一棵树。第一节是女孩在变化过程中的言语;第二节是爱她却无法得到她的男子(或者是神)的话语。

背诵准备

短短十句诗分成两节。前一节中有形象的动作描写,后一节中有恰当的比喻。你能找出相应的动作和比喻完成以下的填空吗?

A Girl

The tree has _____ my hands,

The sap has _____ my arms,

The tree has _____ in my breast —

Downward,
The branches _____ out of me, like arms.

_____ you are,
_____ you are,
You are _____ with wind above them.
A _____ — so high — you are,
And all this is folly to the world.

参考译文

女　孩

艾兹拉·庞德

这树透入我的手掌，
顺着血液蔓延，
扎根在我的胸腔——
扩散，
穿透肉体，又将我缠绕——手臂一样。

你是树，
又是苔藓，
你是柔风中的紫罗兰。
你只是个孩子啊，却让我仰视，
这一切，
在这个世界里显得如此荒诞。

63. Auguries of Innocence (excerpt)

By William Blake

To see a world in a *grain* of sand
And a heaven in a wild flower,
Hold *infinity* in the *palm* of your hand
And *eternity* in an hour.

语言注释

1. augury / ˈɔːgjʊrɪ / *n.* 预兆
2. innocence / ˈɪnəsəns / *n.* 单纯，天真无邪
3. grain / greɪn / *n.* 颗粒，细粒
4. infinity / ɪnˈfɪnɪtɪ / *n.* 无限远
5. palm / pɑːm / *n.* 手掌
6. eternity / ɪˈtɜːnɪtɪ / *n.* 永恒；无限的时间

背景介绍

威廉·布莱克(William Blake，1757－1827)，英国浪漫主义诗人、画家和雕刻家。他的很多书都是自画插图，自行出版。布莱克出生于伦敦，他在那度过了他生命的大部分时间。他的父亲，是当时伦敦成功的针织品商人。他鼓励布莱克发展艺术潜能。1767 年，他被送去亨利·帕斯美术学校。他记录到，从孩提时代起，他就看到了天使和魔鬼的修道士的幻象。他看到天使加百利，圣母玛丽亚和各种历史人物，并且和他们交谈。1783 年，布莱克的第一本诗集《诗的素描》(*Poetical Sketches*)问世，1789 年，他出版《天真之歌》(*Songs of Innocence*)，1794 年出版了《经验之歌》(*Songs of Experience*)。这些作品都是通过孩子的眼睛看世界，但是同样也代表了成年人的体验。

篇目欣赏

诗选自《天真之歌》。布莱克意图在《天真之歌》中用"土气的笔",饱蘸清清的溪水,为天真无邪的孩子们写下优美动听的歌曲,以表现未被"经验"玷污以前的天真世界里的自由、仁爱、欢乐和幸福。诗歌简洁明快,自然流畅,但在箴言式的诗句中,蕴涵对于人生和宇宙的深刻思考。布莱克认为极微小的东西如一粒细沙,都含有神秘的意味。如果一个人能够真正懂得一件极细微的东西,他也就领悟了宇宙的真谛。因而,从一粒细沙里可以看穿宇宙,从一朵野花里可看到天堂;瞬间和无限也是相通的;你可以把无限掌握在你的掌心里,把永恒存在一个瞬间。

佛教中也有与之心意相通的禅偈——《心是莲花开》。

一花一天堂　一草一世界

一树一菩提　一土一如来

一方一净土　一笑一尘缘

一念一清净　心是莲花开

背诵准备

弘一法师(李叔同)曾经翻译过这首诗。译文如下:

一花一世界,

一沙一天国;

君掌盛无边,

刹那含永劫。

译文将哲学与文学结合,清澈隽永。不过,这里有一处和原诗有出入的翻译。你能对照诗歌找出来吗?

参考译文

纯真预言（节选）

威廉·布莱克

从一粒细沙中窥探世界，
在一朵野花里寻觅天堂，
掌中握无限，
刹那成永恒。

64. Crossing the Bar

By Alfred Tennyson

Sunset and evening star，
And one clear call for me!
And may there be no *moaning* of the bar，
When I put out to sea，

But such a tide as moving seems asleep，
Too full for sound and *foam*，
When that which drew from out the *boundless* deep
Turns again home.

Twilight and evening bell，
and after that the dark!
And may there be no sadness of farewell，
When I *embark*；

For though from out our bourne of Time and Place，
The flood may *bear* me far，
I hope to see my *Pilot* face to face，
When I have crossed the bar.

语言注释

1. bar / bɑː(r) / *n*. 沙洲，沙滩
   crossing the bar 渡过沙洲，诗中用作
   比喻，指走向死亡
2. moan / məʊn / *v*. 呻吟
3. foam / fəʊm / *n*. 泡沫
4. boundless / ˈbaʊndlɪs / *adj*. 无限制的
5. twilight / ˈtwaɪlaɪt / *n*. 黄昏
6. embark / ɪmˈbɑːk / *v*. 登机，上船
7. bear / beə(r) / *v*. 推挤
8. pilot / ˈpaɪlət / *n*. 导航员

背景介绍

丁尼生(Alfred Tennyson, 1809 - 1892)是维多利亚时期最受欢迎的诗人。惠特曼称他为"人民的诗人"。在丁尼生去剑桥读书前,他在写诗方面就已经初露锋芒,与他的兄弟合作出版了一本诗集 *Poems by Two Brothers*。在剑桥,他对政治和学术问题的参与,使他开阔了视野,增长了知识。1850 年,他发表了《悼念》,获得巨大成功,成为继华兹华斯之后的又一位桂冠诗人。他的主要作品有长诗 *In Memoriam*《悼念》,独幕剧 *Maud*,长诗 *Idylls of the King*,以及短抒情诗 *Break*,*Break*,*Break* 等。

篇目欣赏

写这首诗时作者已 80 岁高龄。令人惊叹的是,此时的桂冠诗人仍能灵感勃发。据说诗人完成这首诗只用了不到 10 分钟。诗人在暮霭中想象自己渡过沙洲的情景。"渡过沙洲"是比喻,指诗人在经历了人生的风霜后,平静地迎接死亡的来临,毫无恐惧和哀伤。这首诗表现了作者关于死亡的传统的基督教思想,强调了他自己坚定的宗教信仰。正如娴熟的领航会引导船安然渡过沙洲一样,上帝也会引导我们平安地渡过险恶的浅滩。诗的前两行以视觉景色和声音开关,以鲜明的感观形象吸引读者注意力。同作者的其他诗一样,在这首诗中,诗人也成功地把身外的自然景色与诗人的心态融合在一起,用景物衬托心情。落日的余晖,寥寥闪烁的星辰,好似沉睡的退潮,悄然涌动的浪花,以及暮霭钟鸣,使全诗笼罩着一种沉静、凝重、肃穆的气氛,这正与诗人的心态相吻合。在诗的押韵上,长元音 /ɑ:/ /i:/以及辅音 /m/ /n/ /s/ /l/ /w/ 都制造出一种宁静柔和的音乐效果。

背诵准备

有批评家说丁尼生对诗歌音乐感的把握是继弥尔顿之后最好的。请放上一曲班德瑞的《月光水岸》,反复吟读这首诗,体会其中的音律美。特别注意长元音的发音。

参考译文

越过沙洲

阿尔费雷德·丁尼生

太阳沉没,晚星闪烁,
一个清晰的呼声在召唤我!
愿海滩不要哀泣呜咽,
当我出海的时刻。

浑然流动的潮水似已睡去,
潮太满了,反而无声无息,
从无边的海洋里汲取的,
如今又复归去。

暮色茫茫,晚钟轻轻.
接着是黑暗降临!
但愿不要有诀别的悲痛
当我起航的时辰;

虽然潮水会把我带到无限遥远,
越出我们的时间、空间,
我希望见到领航人,面对着面,
当我越过了海滩。

65. Days

By Philip Larkin

What are days for?
Days are where we live.
They come，they wake us
Time and time over.
They are to be happy in：
Where can we live but days?

Ah，solving that question
Brings the *priest* and the doctor
In their long coats
Running over the fields.

语言注释

1. time and time over   反复地,不断地
2. They are to be happy in.   日子应该快活地过。
3. priest / priːst / *n*. 神父,牧师

背景介绍

菲 利浦·拉金(Philip Larkin, 1922 – 1985)是第二次世界大战以后涌现出来的优秀诗人。许多评论者认为,五十年代以来英国出了两位大诗人,一位是塔特休斯,一位是拉金。

拉金成名于"福利国家"时期,他的同伴是一些对政治有幻灭感的"愤怒的年轻人"。他自己也无特别的热情,但关心社会生活的格调,喜欢冷眼观察世态。在技巧上他则一反流行于五十年代之初的狄兰·托马斯等人的浪漫化倾向,深受哈代的影响,务求写得具体、准确。这两点使他成为一个很好的世态记录者。

篇目欣赏

这首发人深省的诗以简单直白的语言谈论时间和死亡,暗示着视野之外具有前瞻的某种关系。其中一个细节,牧师与医生的长袍给整首诗带来了灰黑色的色调。这和拉金一贯以来具体写实风格有所差异,但是,他忧郁却不沉沦,嘲讽,感性,低调,坚执,浸入骨髓的悲观,在这一切之下,仍是对人生、对生命严肃的沉思:"日子本该快乐入住:除了日子,我们还有何处安身?"拉金的诗十分讲究技巧,即使后期诗歌中引入了粗鄙的俚语和口语,他的诗仍遵循传统的英诗格律,在二十世纪英语诗越来越漠视用韵的大时代里,这一点尤其难能可贵。他的诗歌结构与韵律都极为讲究,字里行间充满了和谐的节奏美。他善用双关词,押头韵,尾韵等诗歌技巧。本诗中他却一反常态,用平易亲切的语调,随意却自有一种拉金式的独特的感性与隽永。

背诵准备

这首诗意象简单而又深远。诗中有两句重要的问句。你能把它们找出来并仔细体会它们的意义吗?

参考译文

日 子

菲利浦·拉金

日子有什么用?
日子是我们的栖身之所。
它们来了,唤醒我们
一次又一次。
日子本该快乐入住:

除了日子,我们还有何处安身?

啊,解答这个问题
得有劳神父和医生
身着长袍
在野地里飞奔。

66. Pippa Passes

By Robert Browning

The year's at the spring,
And day's at the morn;
Morning's at seven;
The hillside's *dew-pearled*;
The *lark's on the wing*;
The *snail's* on the *thorn*;
God's in His heaven —
All's right with the world!

语言注释

1. dew-pearled / djuːpəld / *adj*. 露珠像珍珠般的
2. lark / lɑːk / *n*. 云雀
3. on the wing 展翅飞翔
4. snail / sneɪl / *n*. 蜗牛
5. thorn / θɔːn / *n*. 刺;皮刺,这里是指蜗牛的壳针

背景介绍

罗伯特·布朗宁(Robert Browning,1812–1889)出生于伦敦郊区,19世纪60年代以后,他被公认为与丁尼生并驾齐驱的最重要的维多利亚诗人之一。他的早期作品,自我表白性太强,太主观性和个人化。他从失败中总结教训,首创了"戏剧独白"这一诗歌体裁。布朗宁的诗歌洋溢着一种乐观自信的精神。实际上,他的乐观并不盲目。他也探讨信仰与怀疑,善与恶等复杂的人性问题。他的很多作品体现了他对人物心理活动的敏锐的洞察力。总的来说,生机和活力是布朗宁作品的根本特征。

篇目欣赏

> **P**ippa Passes 是布朗宁的一部诗集。Pippa 在一个压榨工人血汗的工厂做工。一天放假时,她在大街上唱起了这首歌。这首诗的语言极其简单,朗朗上口。诗人运用了排比结构,使整首诗视觉上整齐、简单,这正与儿童的语言趋势一致。从逻辑上看,这首诗开头三行,在时间上从大到小有规律地排列,紧接下来的三行主要从地点上从高到低有序地排列。Pippa 眼前的景物井然有序,呈现出一片生机和活力,同时,万物和谐,各得其所。最后两行是诗的升华。Pippa 的视线从具体的景物转移到上帝,并且进而归结出"世界万物均无恙"。但这只是 Pippa 自己天真的幻想,并不是诗人自己的真实态度。诗人用 Pippa 的单纯与现实世界的邪恶和不和谐相对照,目的还是要暴露和鞭挞丑恶的世界。

背诵准备

在赏析中我们已经分析了这首小诗的逻辑顺序。你能根据这些来填空吗?

Pippa Passes

The _____ 's at the spring,

And _____ 's at the morn;

_____ 's at seven;

The _____ 's dew-pearled;

The _____ 's on the wing;

The _____ 's on the thorn：

_____ 's in His heaven —

All's right with the _____!

参考译文

皮巴走过

罗伯特·布朗宁

一年之计在于春
一日之计在于晨
晨曦之计在七时
山坡之上露珍珠
云雀展翅空中飞
小小蜗牛正在爬
上帝在他的天堂
世界万物均无恙

67. She Dwelt Among the Untrodden Ways

By William Wordsworth

She *dwelt* among the *untrodden* ways
Beside the springs of Dove，
A maid there were none to praise
And very few to love；

A violet by a *mossy* stone
Half hidden from the eye！
Fair as a star，when only one
Is shining in the sky.

She lived unknown，and few could know?
When Lucy *ceased* to be；
But she is in her grave now；and oh，
The difference to me！

语言注释

1. dwell / dwel / *v*. 居住
2. untrodden / ˌʌnˈtrɒdən / *a*. 人迹罕至的
3. mossy / ˈmɒsɪ / *v*. 生满苔藓的
4. fair / feə (r) / *adj*. 美丽的
5. cease / siːs / *v*. 终止；停止：

背景介绍

威廉·华兹华斯(William Wordsworth, 1770 - 1850)是"湖畔诗人"(Lake Poets)的领袖,在思想上有过大起大落——初期对法国大革命的热烈向往变成了后来遁迹于山水的自然崇拜,在诗艺上则实现了划时代的革新,以至有人称他为第一个现代诗人。

华兹华斯的小诗清新,长诗清新而又深刻,一反新古典主义平板、典雅的风格,开创了新鲜活泼的浪漫主义诗风。他的十四行诗雄奇,他的《序曲》(1805)首创用韵文来写自传式的"一个诗人的心灵的成长",无论在内容和艺术上都开了一代新风。华兹华斯关于自然的诗歌优美动人,他的这类诗歌的一个突出特点就是——寓情于境,情景交融。这种风格的体现是作者通过对诗歌的题材、诗歌所用的语言以及对诗歌所用的格律、诗体和作者对诗歌词汇的选择体现出来的。

篇目欣赏

在这首诗中,诗人向我们展现了一位住在人迹罕至的荒野的姑娘。第一节说明露茜住在白鸽泉边,是一位无人称颂,少人怜爱的姑娘。第二节,诗人用两个比喻来形容露茜的非同一般:苔藓石旁的一株紫罗兰,半藏着没有被人看见!美丽得如同天上的星点,一颗唯一的星,清辉闪闪。第三节表明了露茜生时不为人所知,死亦不为人所晓。最后一句只有寥寥四字,却包含强烈深沉的感情。

背诵准备

本诗采用了传统的 **ABAB** 的韵脚,读来含蓄隽永。请找出诗中出现的韵脚,并给出符合诗歌意象的其他韵脚。

参考译文

悼露茜

威廉·华兹华斯

她居住在白鸽泉水的旁边，
无人来往的路径通往四面；
一位姑娘不曾受人称赞，
也不曾受过别人的爱怜。

她是苔藓石旁的一株紫罗兰，
半藏着没有被人看见！
美丽得如同天上的星点，
一颗唯一的星清辉闪闪。

她生无人知，死也无人唁，
不知何时去了人间；
但她安睡在墓中，哦可怜，
对于我可是个地异天变！

68. Song

By Christina Rossetti

When I am dead, my dearest,
Sing no sad songs for me;
Plant thou no roses at my head,
Nor *shady cypress* tree:
Be the green grass above me
With showers and *dewdrops* wet;
And if thou *wilt*, remember,
And if thou wilt, forget.

I shall not see the shadow,
I shall not feel the rain;
I shall not hear the *nightingale*
Sing on, as if in pain;
And dreaming through the *twilight*
That doth not rise not set,
Haply I may remember,
And haply may forget.

语言注释

1. shady / ˈʃeɪdɪ / *adj*. 遮阴的
2. cypress / ˈsaɪprəs / *n*. 柏树
3. dewdrop / ˈdjuːdrɒp / *n*. 露水
4. wilt / wɪlt / *vt*. 使枯萎
5. nightingale / ˈnaɪtɪŋgeɪl / *n*. 夜莺
6. twilight / ˈtwaɪlaɪt / *n*. 黄昏
7. haply / ˈhæplɪ / *adv*. 偶然地

背景介绍

克 里斯蒂纳·罗塞蒂(Christina Rossetti, 1830 – 1894)的父亲是一位从意大利流亡英国的爱国者,会做诗。他们的家庭是当时流亡英国的意大利人聚会的场所,那里经常举行的政治和文化讨论,活跃的家庭气氛,使她耳濡目染,从小就显示出对艺术和文学的热爱,并且学着作诗。罗塞蒂终生都用严格的宗教原则约束自己的生活,极少参加娱乐活动。由于宗教原因,她还主动取消了两次婚约。她一生过着严正克己、虔诚朴实的平静生活,喜欢参加慈善活动。诗集 *Goblin Market and Other Poems*(1862)包括了各种诗歌体裁:纯粹的抒情诗、叙事体寓言、民谣以及宗教诗。她的诗歌表现出一种自我克制的精神。现代派作家沃尔夫对她的诗歌评价甚高。

篇目欣赏

诗 的上半部分,是死者对自己的所爱交代后事。她不要哀歌与玫瑰松柏,只要自己的头上有那沾满雨露的芳草。这和中国的古诗"死后何所惧,托体同山阿"有异曲同工之处。然而,她的心境,其实很矛盾。心灵的深处,她仍希望,自己能够永远活在他的心中。所以,终于,她还是不自觉地说了出来:唉,随你吧。愿意,就想起我;不愿意,就忘却。她把自己无法解决的矛盾,就这样转移给了自己的爱人,同样的万般无奈。

　　诗的下半部分,死者设想自己从此是要进入一个万古如长夜的梦里。既然自己不会看得到婆娑的树影,所以你也不必在我的坟头种植松柏和玫瑰;既然我不会听到杜鹃啼血,所以嘱咐你也不必在我坟前悲哀;既然我不会感觉到风雨的凄凉,那么,就让雨露尽情地沾染我坟头的青草。这些,原来竟是和上半部分都是一一有呼应的!诗人自吟自唱,意图悄无声息地遁入另外一个世界,没有丝毫的勉强。

　　另外,诗人还运用了押头韵,如 "sing no sad song"和"green grass",给人一种绵延不断的感染力。

背诵准备

罗赛蒂"*Song*"最后两句,徐志摩曾作过改写,音步与诗意一并搬过来略作编译,即成名诗《偶然》一首。请看下面这两句,

> 您记得也好
>
> 最好您忘掉
>
> Haply I may remember,
>
> And haply may forget.

徐志摩还作过一首《歌》,由罗大佑作曲演唱,韵味却是和原诗不同,不妨找来听听。

参考译文

临去嘱所爱

克里斯蒂纳·罗塞蒂

> 临去嘱所爱, 勿为歌哭哀!
>
> 玫瑰与松柏, 慎勿庐前栽。
>
> 绿草覆玉骨, 白露湿冢台。
>
> 劝君且随意, 忆念或释怀。
>
> 夕岚不可见, 惆怅雨云来;
>
> 夜莺不复闻, 凄凄声悲徊。
>
> 朦朦华胥境, 魂梦优游哉。
>
> 身后孰可知? 忆念或释怀。

69. The Waste Land (excerpt)

By T. S. Eliot

April is the cruelest month, *breeding*
Lilacs out of the dead land, mixing
Memory and *desire*, stirring
Dull roots with spring rain.
Winter kept us warm, covering
Earth in forgetful snow, feeding
A little life with dried *tubers*.

语言注释

1. breed / briːd / *v.* 繁殖,旺盛生长
2. lilac / ˈlaɪlək / *n.* 丁香花
3. desire / dɪˈzaɪə (r) / *n.* 希望,渴望
4. dull / dʌl / *adj.* 迟钝的,反应不迅速的
5. tuber / ˈtjuːbə (r) / *n.* 块茎

背景介绍

艾略特(T. S. Eliot,1888－1965)出生于美国的密苏里州。1906 年进入哈佛大学,期间受到的文学影响是多方面的。他尤其对英国唯心主义哲学兴趣浓厚,强调个体经验的私人性。1922 年他发表了《荒原》(*The Waste Land*)。除诗歌外,艾略特还发表了重要的文学评论。他终生所追求的诗歌目标是使诗歌更微妙,更具有暗示性,同时又更精确。他从意象派那里汲取营养,学来了清晰精确、令人震惊的意象;从庞德那里领悟到诗歌的媒介而不是诗人的个人性情是至关重要的因素。他在诗中成功地把机智(wit)和情感(passion)糅合到一起,使二者浑然一体。他憎恶华丽的辞藻,偏爱把正式的词语与口语结合使用。他的诗歌主题主要是现代西方文化的衰败以及欧洲文明的危机。

篇目欣赏

《荒原》被誉为现代诗的里程碑。意象是该诗的主要艺术手法之一。它们种类繁多,来源广泛,看似彼此无涉,实际上都有着或隐或显的内在关联,构成了围绕和深化主题的意象链,体现了诗人的创作理念,艺术地反映出"一战"后欧洲衰微破败的客观现实和混乱无着的精神状态。节选的部分来自第一节"死者葬礼"。诗中出现了"荒地,丁香,春雨,根芽"等客观现实的意象,以生命的蠢动来昭示残忍。其中"四月是最残忍的一个月"成为名句传颂。

同样的丁香与春雨出现在诗人戴望舒的《雨巷》中,是否也一样带着残忍的意味呢?

背诵准备

本首诗几乎每一行都以动词的进行式结尾,在音律和格式上做到了工整上口。你能大声朗诵以后来完成下面的填空吗?

The Waste Land (excerpt)

April is the cruelest month, _____

Lilacs out of the dead land, _____

Memory and desire, _____

Dull roots with spring rain.

Winter kept us warm, _____

Earth in forgetful snow, _____

A little life with dried tubers.

参考译文

荒原（节选）

艾略特

四月是最残忍的一个月，荒地上
长着丁香，把回忆和欲望
掺和在一起，又让春雨
催促那些迟钝的根芽。
冬天使我们温暖，大地
给助人遗忘的雪覆盖着，又叫
枯干的球根提供少许生命。

70. When You Are Old

By William Butler Yeats

When you are old and gray and full of sleep，

And nodding by the fire，take down this book，

And slowly read，and dream of the soft look

Your eyes had once，and of their shadows deep；

How many loved your moments of glad grace，

And loved your beauty with love false or true，

But one man loved the *pilgrim* soul in you，

And loved the sorrows of your changing face；

And *bending* down beside the *glowing* bars，

Murmur，a little sadly，how love *fled*

And *paced* upon the mountains overhead

And hide his face *amid* a crowd of stars.

语言注释

1. pilgrim / 'pɪlgrɪm / *n*.朝圣者
2. bend / bend / *v*. 使弯曲
3. glow / gləʊ / *v*. 发热,发光
4. murmur / 'mɜːmə (r) / *v*. 发出很小的声音
5. flee / fliː / *v*.消失；消亡
6. pace / peɪs / *n*. 行走时跨出的一步
7. amid / ə'mɪd / *prep*. 被……包围；在……中间

背景介绍

威廉·勃特勒·叶芝(William Butler Yeats,1865－1939)是爱尔兰著名诗人和剧作家,生于都柏林一个画师家庭,自小喜爱诗画艺术,并对乡间的秘教法术颇感兴趣。1884年就读于都柏林艺术学校,不久违背父愿,抛弃画布和油彩,专意于诗歌创作。1888年在伦敦结识了萧伯纳、王尔德等人。1896年,叶芝又结识了贵族出身的剧作家格雷戈里夫人,叶芝一生的创作都得力于她的支持。他这一时期的创作虽未摆脱19世纪后期的浪漫主义和唯美主义的影响,但质朴而富于生气,著名诗作有《茵斯弗利岛》(1892)、《当你老了》(1896)等。1899年,叶芝与格雷戈里夫人、约翰·辛格等开始创办爱尔兰国家剧场活动,并于1904年正式成立阿贝影院。这期间,他创作了一些反映爱尔兰历史和农民生活的戏剧,主要诗剧有《胡里痕的凯瑟琳》(1902)、《黛尔丽德》(1907)等,另有诗集《芦苇中的风》(1899)、《在七座森林中》(1903)、《绿盔》(1910)、《责任》(1914)等,并陆续出版了多卷本的诗文全集。叶芝及其友人的创作活动,史称"爱尔兰文艺复兴运动"。1923年,"由于他那些始终充满灵感的诗,它们通过高度的艺术形成了整个民族的精神",叶芝荣获诺贝尔文学奖。

篇目欣赏

1889年1月30日,23岁的叶芝遇见了美丽的女演员茅德·冈,诗人对她一见钟情。这种强烈爱慕之情给诗人带来了真切无穷的灵感,《当你老了》就是那些著名诗歌中的一首。

在诗的开头,诗人设想了一个情景:在阴暗的壁炉边,炉火映着已经衰老的情人的苍白的脸,头发花白的情人度着剩余的人生。在那样的时刻,诗人让她取下自己的诗,在那样的时刻也许情人就会明白:诗人的爱是怎样的真诚、深切。那些庸俗的人们同样爱慕着她,为她的外表,为她的年轻美丽——他们怀着假意或者怀着真心去爱。但是,诗人的爱不是这样。

诗人爱着情人的灵魂——那是朝圣者的灵魂；诗人的爱也因此有着朝圣者的忠诚和圣洁；诗人的爱不会因为情人的衰老而有任何的褪色，反而历久弥新，磨难越多爱得越坚笃。

诗人的爱已经升华。在密集的群星中间，诗人透过重重的帷幕，深情地关注着情人，愿情人在尘世获得永恒的幸福。

背诵准备

音乐和诗歌是奥林匹斯山上美丽而智慧的缪斯女神钟爱的艺术。水木年华组合有一首歌，歌名叫做"一生有你"。歌词是这样的：

以为梦见你离开

我从哭泣中醒来

看夜风吹过窗台

你能否感受我的爱

等到老去的一天

你是否还在我身边

看那些誓言谎言

随往事慢慢飘散

多少人曾爱慕你年轻时的容颜

可是谁能承受岁月无情的变迁

多少人曾在你生命中来了又还

可知一生有你我都陪在你身边

当所有一切都已看平淡

是否有一种精致还留在心田

喔哦～～～～～～

对照 *When You Are Old* ，你能找出哪些词句是化身而来的吗？

参考译文

当你老了

威廉·勃特勒·叶芝

当你老了，白发苍苍，睡意蒙眬，
在炉前打盹，请取下这本诗篇，
慢慢吟诵，梦见你当年的双眼
那柔美的光芒与青幽的晕影；

多少人真情假意，爱过你的美丽，
爱过你欢乐而迷人的青春，
唯独一人爱你朝圣者的心，
爱你日益凋谢的脸上的哀戚；

当你佝偻着，在灼热的炉栅边，
你将轻轻诉说，带着一丝伤感：
逝去的爱，如今已步上高山，
在密密星群里埋藏它的赧颜。

71. My Favorite Things

from *the Sound of Music*

Raindrops on roses and *whiskers* on *kittens*,

Bright *copper kettles* and warm woolen *mittens*,

Brown paper package tied up with strings,

These are a few of my favorite things.

Cream colored *ponies* and *crisp* apples *strudel*,

Door bells and sleigh bells and *schnitzel* with noodles,

Wild geese that fly with the moon on their wings,

These are a few of my favorite things.

Girls in white dresses with blue *satin sashes*,

Snowflakes that stay on my nose and *eyelashes*,

Silver white winters that melt into springs,

These are a few of my favorite things.

When dogs bites,

When the bee *stings*,

When I am feeling sad,

I simply remember my favorite things,

And then I don't feel so sad.

语言注释

1. whisker / ˈhwɪskə / *n*. 胡须
2. kitten / ˈkɪtn / *n*. 小猫
3. copper kettle 铜壶
4. mitten / ˈmɪtn / *n*. 手套

5. pony / ˈpəʊnɪ / *n*. 小马

6. crisp / krɪsp / *adj*. 脆的

7. strudel / ˈstruːdl / *n*. 果馅卷

8. schnitzel / ˈʃnɪtsəl / *n*. 炸肉排

9. satin sash 绸带

10. eyelash / ˈaɪˌlæʃ / *n*. 睫毛

11. sting / stɪŋ / *v*. (蜜蜂等昆虫)蛰

背景介绍

来到萨尔茨堡,玛丽亚发现孩子们活泼可爱,各有各的性格、爱好和理想。他们不愿意过这种严加管束的生活,总设法捉弄历届的家庭教师,不让她们待下去。对玛丽亚自然也不例外:一会儿出其不意地把蛤蟆放在她的口袋里;一会儿趁她不备将松球放在她的座位上。但玛丽亚自己就具有孩子般的性格,她能理解孩子们在成长过程中的所作所为。她引导他们,关心他们,帮助他们,赢得了他们的信任,很快就成了他们的知心朋友,建立了深厚的感情。这首歌曲是玛丽亚为了安慰因为雷雨而受到惊吓的孩子们并教他们唱出自己喜爱的事物。

篇目欣赏

在身处困境的情况下回忆一下自己最喜欢的事物是一种很好的解除焦虑的方法。歌词简洁优美,犹如一首诗歌,同学们可以背诵,特别是文中最后几句"When I am feeling sad, I simply remember my favorite things. And then I don't feel so sad."更是一种行之有效的缓解紧张的方法。

背诵准备

玛丽亚为了安慰因为雷雨而受到惊吓的孩子们并教他们唱出自己喜爱的事物,那么他们究竟喜欢什么东西呢? 请用正确词语填空:

_____ _____ _____ and whiskers on kittens,
Bright copper kettles and _____ _____ _____,
_____ _____ _____ _____ _____ _____ _____,
These are a few of my favorite things.

_____ _____ _____ and crisp apples strudel,
_____ _____ _____ _____ and schnitzel with noodles,
_____ _____ _____ _____ _____ _____ _____ _____,
These are a few of my favorite things.

Girls _____ _____ _____ _____ _____ _____ _____,
Snowflakes that _____ _____ _____ _____ _____ _____,
_____ _____ _____ that melt into springs,
These are a few of my favorite things.

When dogs _____,
When the bee _____,
When I _____ _____ _____,
I simply remember my favorite things,
And then I don't feel so _____.

参考译文

我最喜欢的东西

玫瑰花上的雨珠,小猫咪的胡须;
亮闪闪的铜壶,毛茸茸的手套;
细绳系着的棕色纸盒多玲珑;
我最喜爱的东西远不止这些。

乳白色的小马驹,清脆的苹果馅卷饼;

门铃、雪橇铃、面条里的炸肉片;

大雁高飞,翅膀托着月亮;

我最喜爱的东西远不止这些。

白衣少女,腰系蓝绸带;

片片雪花,落在鼻尖,落在睫毛;

冰雪融化,春天来临;

我最喜爱的东西远不止这些。

当小狗咬,蜜蜂蜇,

当我不快乐的时候,

只要我想起我喜爱的东西,

我就不再难受。

72. Garfield

Luca:	You're on the wrong side of the street, fat cat. *Beat it*!
Garfield:	And you, Luca, the wrong side of the *evolutionary curve*.
Luca:	Okay, that's it. You're gonna *get it good* today.
Garfield:	I *make a point to* get it good every day. The real question, Luca, is how shall I *outwit* you this time?
Luca:	What?
Garfield:	Shall I *baffle* you *with* simple math?
Luca:	I know how to spell.
Garfield:	Or should I *distract* you *with* something shiny?
Luca:	Now you're making fun of me.
Garfield:	I hope so. You're no fun to look at.
Luca:	You'll never *get the best of* me!
Garfield:	I think I just did.
Luca:	Not the *duck*s again!
Garfield:	Jump back! And kiss myself.
Luca:	If l ever get off this chain, you're going down. Everybody back up! I don't know how wild this thing is gonna get.
Garfield:	I love the smell of *cinnamon*-apple in the morning. (Sniffs) It smells like ... victory.
Luca:	OOOh! I hate this fat cat.

语言注释

1. Beat it!　走开, 滚蛋!
2. evolutionary / ˌiːvəˈluːʃənərɪ / *adj*. 进化的
3. curve / kɜːv / *n*. 曲线
4. get it good　得到教训
5. make a point to do sth. = make a point of doing sth.　坚持做某事

6. outwit / aut'wɪt / v. 以机智获胜,以诡
   计击败

7. baffle ... with ...　(以)难倒,难住

8. distract with ...　转移注意力,使分心

9. get the best of　战胜,胜过(某人)

10. duck / dʌk / n. 头部或身体迅速俯下
    或侧闪的动作

11. cinnamon / ˈsɪnəmən / n. 肉桂

背景介绍

《加菲猫》(Garfield)是 2004 福克斯公司根据同名畅销漫画改编的电影。加菲猫自从 1978 年 6 月 19 日问世以来,它就以四格漫画的形式登上了全世界各种报纸,关于它的漫画销售一路攀升,在全世界拥有上亿肥猫迷。大概是因为它看破红尘,语出惊人的独特魅力和人性化的享乐主义,这只一脸傲气表情的猫,这只完全自由的猫,这只爱说风凉话、贪睡午觉、牛饮咖啡、大嚼千层面、见蜘蛛就扁、见邮差就穷追的猫,这只世界上最懒惰的猫成了全世界最受欢迎的猫。

就像漫画家吉姆·戴维斯(Jim Davis)所评价的那样:"大家爱加菲猫是因为它说出来的话与做出来的事,人们也想说,也想做,却因为环境所限不能完成。"我们从加菲猫身上看到很多平凡人身上的品质,同时又能够在它身上实现我们无法达到的随心所欲。

篇目欣赏

《加菲猫》中,动物间的对话妙趣横生,教会我们很多用英语"拌嘴"的诀窍。本片段就是 Garfield 与对门邻居家养的大狗 Luca 间的吵架实录,当时,馋嘴的 Garfieild 正看上 Luca 家窗台上那香喷喷刚出炉的

诱人蛋糕,打算偷来一饱口福。Luca 对 Garfield 说:You're gonna get it good today.(要让他吃不了兜着走,小心点。)而 Garfield 故意将其话曲解说道:I make a point to get it good every day.(我每天都是吃不了兜着走的。)Luca 感到被 Garfield 耍了之后说道:Now you're making fun of me.却不料,又一次被耍,Garfield 立刻回道:I hope so. You're no fun to look at. Garfield 真是脑快嘴也快,句句不饶人。

背诵准备

加菲猫能言善辩,嘴下从不留情。他还有许多经典语录,你来猜猜他会如何说,看看你与加菲猫有几分相似。请选择框内的词填入下列句子中,并将句子翻译成中文。

hard work	hate	waking up	money	tasty
work	go to sleep	put off	forget	relatives

1. I _____ Mondays.

2. _____ is not everything. There's Mastercard & Visa.

3. Never _____ the work till tomorrow what you can _____ today.

4. "Your future depends on your dreams." So _____.

5. There should be a better way to start a day than _____ every morning.

6. Success is a relative term. It brings so many _____.

7. "_____ never killed anybody." But why take the risk?

8. "_____ fascinates me." I can look at it for hours!

9. The more you learn, the more you know. The more you know, the more you _____. The more you _____, the less you know. So why bother to learn?

10. One should love animals. They are so _____.

参考译文

加菲猫

路卡：　你站错地了，肥猫。滚开！

加菲猫：而你呢，路卡，你是投错胎了。

路卡：　够了，那又怎么样?！今天我要让你吃不了兜着走。

加菲猫：我每天都是吃不了兜着走的。不过，路卡，我这回该怎么整你好呢？

路卡：　什么？

加菲猫：要我考考你九九乘法表吗？

路卡：　我知道怎么算。

加菲猫：还是拽着链子带你绕圈圈呢？

路卡：　你是在耍我呀！

加菲猫：我想是的。但是你看上去一点都不好玩。

路卡：　你从来都不知道我的厉害啊！

加菲猫：我想我已经知道了。

路卡：　又是那些鹅卵石。

加菲猫：搞定！我真佩服我自己。

路卡：　要不是这条链子的话，你就死定了。所有的人后退，我不知道这东西会有多大的威力。

加菲猫：我喜欢早上肉桂苹果派的香味。闻起来就像——胜利。

路卡：　噢，我恨死这只肥猫了。

73. Robots

Bigweld:	Welcome. This week I thought you'd like to *take a look around* Bigweld *Industries*. This here is the front gate. Kind of cute, isn't it? ... Good morning, Tim.
Tim the Gate Guard:	Good morning, Mr. Bigweld, sir.
Bigweld:	Tim, who closed the front gate?
Tim the Gate Guard:	Well, I just thought since ...
Bigweld:	We never shut the gate, Tim. Shutting this gate means shutting out fresh ideas. You see, every day, robots come here from here and there ... bringing us new ideas. And I listen to every single one of them. So remember, whether a robot is made of new parts, old parts or *spare* parts, you can shine no matter what you're made of.
Rodney Copperbottom:	He's talking to me, Dad.
Herb Copperbottom:	He sure is, son. He sure is.
Bigweld:	Okay, *folks*, let's get to inventing. You know, I love to *tinker* ... but all the tinkering in the world isn't useful unless it starts with a good idea. So look around for a need and start coming up with ideas to fill that need. One idea will lead to another, and before you know it ... you've done it. See a need, fill a need.
Rodney Copperbottom:	That's it, Dad. I have to look for ... a need.

语言注释

1. take a look around ...　四处看看
2. industry / ˈindəstri / *n*. 工业，产业
3. spare / speə / *a*. 多余的，剩余的，备用的
4. folk / fəʊk / *n*. 人们，人民
5. tinker / ˈtiŋkə / *v*. 笨拙地或不熟练地做或修补

背景介绍

《机器人历险记》是福克斯电影公司继《冰河世纪》(Ice Age)大获好评后，于2005年3月推出的由原班人马创作的动画片。此片是又一动画技术的突破，运用光源应用软件，人物和场景中的金属物品都熠熠闪光，而且不同材质，不同形状的金属放射着独特的光泽，营造出一个梦幻般的机械世界。

逗趣的角色配合高潮起伏的剧情，《机器人历险记》将欢乐带给大人和小孩。故事主要描述乡下机器人罗德尼，自小认为拥有发明家的金头脑，决心前往大城拜见大焊工业总裁大焊先生，闯出人生新天地。主题围绕着冒险和发明，还有二手机器人的友情、机器上班族的生存游戏。虽然是好莱坞一贯的情节与拍摄手法，但有两个细节让我们惊喜，一是档板学金·凯瑞(Jim Carrey)唱"雨中曲"(*Singing in the Rain*)，二是档板在对付邪恶机器人的时候突然学布兰妮·琼·斯皮尔斯(Britney Jean Spears)大跳热舞唱 *Bady One More Time*。

篇目欣赏

这一段是影片开始部分，幼小的罗德尼正在收看大焊先生介绍大焊工业的电视节目。对大焊先生钦佩不已的罗德尼被他那富有激情的讲话激起强烈的发明欲望，开始了自己的发明历程。大焊先生给每个人信心，说道：Remember, whether a robot is made of new parts, old parts or spare parts, you can shine no matter what you're made of.并道出发明的真谛：See a need, fill a need.（需求为创意之母！）父亲的激励之词虽然简单但很肯定（He sure is, son.）。罗德尼的第一项发明尝试就是为父亲发明个洗碗洗碟子的小机器人，把父亲从繁重的工作中解脱出来。随后有着父母的支持，他只身闯荡浮华的大都市，追求自己的发明梦想……

背诵准备

请选择框内的词或词组的恰当形式,填入以下两段话中:

invent	shut	tinker	fill	a new idea
listen to	shine	be made of	lead to	

We never _____ the gate, Tim. _____ this gate means _____ out fresh ideas. You see, every day, robots come here from here and there ... bringing us _____. And I _____ every single one of them. So remember, whether a robot is made of new parts, old parts or spare parts, you can _____ no matter what you _____.

Okay, folks, let's get to _____. You know, I love to _____ ... but all the _____ in the world isn't useful unless it starts with a good idea. So look around for a need and start coming up with ideas to _____ that need. One idea will _____ another, and before you know it ... you've done it. See a need, fill a need.

参考译文

机器人历险记

大焊先生:　　　　　　　大家好! 本周我将为大家介绍大焊工业。这是
　　　　　　　　　　　　公司大门。很 Q 吧? ……早,提姆!

提姆(大焊工业的门卫):早安, 大焊先生!

大焊先生:　　　　　　　提姆,谁把大门关上的?

提姆(大焊工业的门卫):我想……因为……

大焊先生:　　　　　　　大门永远不能关,提姆。关上大门等于拒绝新
　　　　　　　　　　　　观念。你看每天来自各地的机器人将带给我们
　　　　　　　　　　　　新观念。我虚心听取他们每个人的新点子。所
　　　　　　　　　　　　以记住,不管机器人是用新的、旧的、或是备用
　　　　　　　　　　　　零件组装起来的,都能闪耀出众。

罗德尼： 爸爸,他在对我说这番话耶。

赫佰： 是啊,当然是啊,儿子。

大焊先生： 各位! 我们来发明东西吧! 你们知道,我喜欢敲敲打打,但如果没有好点子,怎么敲打也没用。所以要先找出需求,然后想点子满足这个需求。不知不觉中,灵感将接踵而至,源源不绝……成功了! 需求为创意之母!

罗德尼： 没错,爸,我要开始寻找……需求。

74. The Shawshank Redemption

(Red is out of jail and leads a hard life outside. Now he goes all the way to Buxton, he finds the thing Andy buries for him under a special rock there.)

Andy: (A letter from Andy to Red)

Dear Red,

If you're reading this, you've gotten out. And if you've come this far, maybe you'd come a bit further. You remember the name of the town, don't you? I could use a good man to help me *get* my project *on wheels*. I'll *keep an eye out for you*, and the chessboard ready.

Remember, Red, hope is a good thing — maybe the best of things. And no good thing ever dies. I will be hoping that this letter finds you and finds you well.

Your friend,

Andy

Red: (Red recalls what Andy's said in jail.) "Get busy living or get busy dying." That's god damn right.

(Monologue) For the second time in my life, *I'm guilty of committing a crime — parole violation*. Of course I doubt they'll *toss up* any roadblocks for that. Not for an old *crook* like me.

I find I'm so excited I can barely sit still or *hold a thought in my head*. I think it's the excitement only a free man can feel — a free man at the start of a long journey, whose *conclusion* is uncertain.

I hope I can make it across the border. I hope to see my friend and shake his hand. I hope the Pacific is as blue as it has been in my dreams.

I hope ...

语言注释

1. redemption / rɪˈdempʃən/ *n*. 赎罪, 赎救
2. get ... on wheels　开展, 进行

3. keep an eye out for sb.　关注,期待
4. be guilty of　有罪的,犯罪的
5. commit a crime　犯罪
6. parole violation　违反假释条例
7. toss up　投铜板以作决定
8. crook / kruk / *n*. 恶棍,流氓
9. hold a thought in my head　思绪萦绕脑海
10. conclusion / kən'klu:ʒen / *n*. 结束,终结

背景介绍

这篇节选自《肖申克的救赎》———一部"该得奖而没得奖"的影片。1994 年的奥斯卡颁奖典礼上,《阿甘正传》是《肖申克的救赎》最大的竞争对手,如果说《阿甘》是一个梦,那么《救赎》就是一种生活。生活比梦简单,但生活远比梦境残酷。《救赎》获得了包括最佳电影、最佳男演员、最佳编剧、最佳摄影、最佳剪辑、最佳音效、最佳音乐/歌曲七项大奖的提名,却因为遭遇了《阿甘正传》而统统坠马,乘兴而来,空手而归,但是从 IMDB 得分和在影迷心中的地位来看,这部电影绝对是影迷心中的无冕之王。

这部影片改编自史蒂芬·金 (Steven King) 的小说《丽塔·海华丝与肖申克的救赎》,是史蒂芬·金的小说集《春天里的四个故事》中的一个。该片的导演弗兰克·达拉邦特(Frank Dalabont)经过长达五年的时间才获得了这本小说的改编权,并且用八周的时间写完剧本。Get busy living or get busy dying.(要么忙着生存,要么忙着死亡。)《救赎》把生命变成了一种残酷的选择。相信自己,不放弃希望,不放弃努力,耐心地等待生命中属于自己的辉煌。虽然最后找到了通向天堂的那条路,但是这条追寻的过程中却是充满坎坷。最近美国福克斯推出的主打悬疑情节剧《越狱》(Prison Break)有着相似的剧情,不过可看性更强,可以比较观赏。

篇目欣赏

这一篇选自影片的结尾部分。一天夜里,风雨交加,雷声大作,已得到灵魂救赎的银行家安迪越狱成功。原来二十年来,安迪每天都抱有一份希望,忍受着各种煎熬与责难,用那把小鹤嘴锄挖洞,把小鹤嘴锄几乎磨成了圆头。不久,狱中好友瑞德获得假释,狱外生活艰辛,几乎丧失活下去的勇气,但在最后他按约定来到橡树下,找到安迪留给他的东西——一盒钱和一封信。Remember, Red, hope is a good thing — maybe the best of things. And no good thing ever dies. 几句话,又燃起瑞德对生活的希望,对未来的憧憬,他满怀希望,登上去墨西哥的旅程。I hope I can make it across the border. I hope to see my friend and shake his hand. I hope the Pacific is as blue as it has been in my dreams. I hope ...两个老友终于在墨西哥阳光明媚的海滨重逢了。

背诵准备

希望是生命之光,我们一起记住这些激励人心的句子,在遇到困境时,想想它们。请先找出有关 hope 的佳句,并写下你心中的希望。

安迪给予瑞德的希望:

1. Hope is a good thing — maybe the best of things. And no good thing ever dies.

瑞德心中的希望:

1. _____
2. _____
3. _____

我心中的希望:

1. _____
2. _____
3. _____

参考译文

肖申克的救赎

（瑞德获准出狱，狱外生活异常艰难。他一路来到霸士腾小镇，在一块特别的岩石下找到了安迪埋在底下，留给他的东西。）

安迪：　（安迪写给瑞德的一封信）

亲爱的瑞德：

　　若你能看到这封信，那代表你已经出来(狱)了。如果你已跑了这么远，也许可以再前进一点。你还记得那个镇子的名字，是吗？我需要一个人和我一起工作。棋盘已摆好了，我期待你的到来。

　　记住，瑞德，有希望是件好事情，也许是世间最好的事情。美好的事情从不会消逝。我希望你能读到这封信，而且身体健康。

你的朋友
安迪

瑞德：　（瑞德想起安迪在狱中说过的话）"要么忙着生存，要么忙着死亡。"这话一点都没错。

　　（独白）我一生中第二次犯了罪——违反了假释出城条例。当然，我怀疑他们会因此设下路障逮我。像我这样的老家伙可以免了吧。

　　我发现我很激动，几乎坐不住，我的思绪乱飞。这是一个自由人才能感受到的——一个踏上未知旅程的自由人。我希望我能成功越过边界。我希望见到我的老友，跟他握握手。我希望太平洋的海水如我梦中那样的蓝。

　　我希望……

75. The Lion King

(Simba starts walking away. Rafiki follows)

Simba:	*Creepy* little monkey. Will you stop following me? Who are you?
Rafiki:	(In front of Simba, then right in his face.) The question is: whooo ... are you?
Simba:	(*Startled*, then sighing) I thought I knew. Now I'm not so sure.
Rafiki:	Well, I know who you are. Shh, Come here. It's a secret.
Simba:	Enough already. What's that supposed to mean, anyway?
Rafiki:	It means you are a *baboon* — and I'm not. (Laughs)
Simba:	(Moving away) I think ... you are a little *confused*.
Rafiki:	(Magically in front of Simba again) Wrong. I'm not the one who's confused; you don't even know who you are.
Simba:	(Irritated, sarcastic) Oh, and I suppose you know?
Rafiki:	Sure do; you're Mufasa's boy. Bye.
Simba:	Hey, wait ! You knew my father?
Rafiki:	(Monotone) Correction — I know your father.
Simba:	I hate to tell you this, but ... he died. A long time ago.
Rafiki:	Nope. Wrong again! Ha ha hah! He's alive ! And I'll show him to you. You follow old Rafiki, he knows the way. Come on !
Rafiki:	Don't *dawdle*. Hurry up!
Simba:	Hey, whoa, wait, wait.
Rafiki:	Come on, come on.
Simba:	Would you slow down?
Rafiki:	Stop! Shh, look down here.
Simba:	(Disappointed sigh) That's not my father. That's just my *reflection*.
Rafiki:	No. Look harder. You see, he lives in you.
Mufasa's Ghost:	(Quietly at first) Simba ...
Simba:	Father?
Mufasa'S Ghost:	Simba, you have forgotten me.
Simba:	No. How could I?

Mufasa's Ghost：	You have forgotten who you are，and so have forgotten me. Look inside yourself，Simba. You are more than what you have become. You must take your place in the Circle of Life.
Simba：	How can I go back? I'm not who I used to be.
Mufasa's Ghost：	Remember who you are. You are my son，and the one true king. Remember who you are.
Simba：	No. Please ! Don't leave me.
Mufasa's Ghost：	Remember ...
Simba：	Father!

语言注释

1. creepy / ˈkriːpɪ / *adj*.令人毛骨悚然的
2. startled / ˈstɑːtld / *adj*. 吃惊的
3. baboon / bəˈbuːn / *n*.狒狒
4. confused / kənˈfjuːzd / *adj*.糊涂的
5. dawdle / ˈdɔːdl / *v*.行动迟缓，闲荡
6. reflection / rɪˈflekʃn / *n*.倒影

背景介绍

这篇对白节选自《狮子王》。这是一部充满冒险和传奇色彩的动画片。《狮子王》自从 1994 年 6 月 24 日在美国上映以来,以其活泼可爱的卡通形象、震撼人心的壮丽场景、感人至深的优美音乐,以及其所描述的爱情与责任的故事内容,深深地打动了许多人。在欧洲、拉美和非洲等 20 多个国家,该片成为历史上最受欢迎的英语影片,该片的背景取材于莎士比亚的著名作品《哈姆雷特》(王子复仇记),讲述了狮王穆发萨和他的儿子辛巴在森林王国里经历了生、死、爱、责任和生命中的种种考验,从而在周而复始生生不息的自然中体验出生命的真正含义。整个剧情跌宕起伏,富有文学色彩。

篇目欣赏

这 段是辛巴在猴子拉菲吉的帮助下和穆发萨的灵魂的一个精彩对白。这时他已经长大成人了。他由于对父亲的死的内疚逃离了他的王国。而他的内疚和懦弱,使他无力再回去(How can I go back? I'm not I used to be.)。而要认识自己的本能还是让他在拉菲吉的指引下看到了水中的自己,在月色中和父亲进行了心灵上的对话,从而让他意识到他作为一个国王应该承担的责任(Remember who you are.)。这是非常有趣的一个自我实现,自我觉醒。

背诵准备

请选择框内词的适当形式填入下列句中,并背出下列句子。

know	who	die	slow down	more than
used to	inside	follow	confused	take one's place

1. Will you stop _____ me? Who are you?

2. Would you _____? I can't follow you.

3. Look _____ yourself, you are _____ what you have become. Remember you are the king.

4. You are the one true king, you must _____ in the Circle of Life.

5. How can I go back? I'm not who I _____ be.

6. I hate to tell you. My father _____. A long time ago.

7. I am a little _____. I don't even know _____ I am.

8. I thought I _____, now I'm not so sure.

参考译文

狮子王

(辛巴转身走开。拉菲吉跟上。)

辛巴：　　　　　奇怪的瘦猴子。你能不能别跟着我？你是谁？

拉菲吉：　　　　(跳到辛巴身前,接着又凑到了它面前)问题是：你……是谁？

辛巴：　　　　　(起初吃了一惊,接着又叹了一口气)我曾经以为我知道。但现在我不能肯定。

拉菲吉：　　　　嗯,我知道你是谁。嘘,过来。这是个秘密。

辛巴：　　　　　够了。你说的那个秘密究竟是什么意思？

拉菲吉：　　　　它的意思是你是一个狒狒——而我不是。(大笑)

辛巴：　　　　　(转身走开)我想……你有点糊涂了。

拉菲吉：　　　　(又一次神奇地出现在辛巴面前)错。我不是那个犯糊涂的人;你甚至连自己是谁都不知道。

辛巴：　　　　　(恼怒地,讽刺地)哦,难道你知道？

拉菲吉：　　　　当然,你是穆发萨的儿子。再见。

辛巴：　　　　　喂,等一下！你认识我父亲？

拉菲吉：　　　　(拉长声调)对——我认识你父亲。

辛巴：　　　　　尽管我很不情愿告诉你,但是……他死了。很久以前就死了。

拉菲吉：　　　　不。又错了！哈哈哈！他还活着！我这就带你去见他。你跟着老拉菲吉,他认得路。快来！

拉菲吉：　　　　别磨蹭。快点儿！

辛巴：　　　　　喂,哟。等一等,等一等。

拉菲吉：　　　　快来,快来。

辛巴：　　　　　请你慢些好吗？

拉菲吉：　　　　停！嘘！往下看。

辛巴：　　　　　(失望得叹了一口气)那不是我父亲,那只是我的影像。

拉菲吉：　　　　不,仔细看看。你明白了吗,他就活在你的身上。

穆发萨的灵魂：　(一开始很安静)辛巴……

辛巴：　　　　　爸爸？

穆发萨的灵魂：　辛巴,你已经把我忘了。

辛巴：　　　　　不。我怎么能？

穆发萨的灵魂：	你已经忘了自己是谁，因而也就忘记了我。往你的内心深处看看，辛巴。不应该只是你现在这个样子。你必须占据在生命轮回中你应有的位置。
辛巴：	我如何才能回到过去呢？我已不是从前的我了。
穆发萨的灵魂：	记住你是谁。你是我的儿子，而且是唯一合法的国王。记住你是谁。
辛巴：	不！请别离开我！
穆发萨的灵魂：	记住……
辛巴：	爸爸！

76. The Sound of Music

Reverend mother:	You've been unhappy. I'm sorry.
Maria:	Reverend mother.
Reverend mother:	Why did they send you back to us?
Maria:	They didn't send me back, Mother, I left.
Reverend mother:	Sit down, Maria. Tell me what happened.
Maria:	Well, I ... I was frightened.
Reverend mother:	Frightened? Were they unkind to you?
Maria:	Oh, no! No, I was confused. I felt ... I've never felt that way before. I couldn't stay. I knew that here I'd be away from it. I'd be safe.
Reverend mother:	Maria, our *abbey* is not to be used as an *escape*. What is it you can't face?
Maria:	I can't face him again.
Reverend mother:	Him? Captain Von Trapp? Are you in love with him?
Maria:	I don't know. I don't know ... I ... The *baroness* and I ... She said he was in love with me, but I didn't want to believe it. Oh, there were times when we would look at each other ... oh, Mother, I could hardly breathe.
Reverend mother:	Did you let him see how you felt?
Maria:	If I did, I didn't know it. That's what's been *torturing* me; I was there on *God's errand*. To have asked for his love would have been wrong. Oh, I couldn't stay. I just couldn't. I am ready this moment to take my *vows*. Please help me.
Reverend mother:	Maria. The love of the man and the woman is *holy*, too. You have a great *capacity* to love. What you must find out is how God wants you to spend your love.
Maria:	But I *pledged* my life to God, I ... I pledged my life to *His Service*.
Reverend mother:	My daughter, if you love this man, it doesn't mean you love God less. No, you must find out. You must go back.
Maria:	Oh, Mother, you can't ask me to do that! Please let me stay, I beg you.
Reverend mother:	Maria, these walls were not built to shut out problems. You have to face them. You have to live. The life was born to live.

语言注释

1. abbey / ˈæbɪ / *n*. 修道院
2. escape / ɪˈskeɪp / *n*. 逃避，逃脱
3. baroness / ˈbærənɪs / *n*. 男爵夫人
4. torture / ˈtɔːtʃə / *v*. 使受剧烈痛苦；折磨
5. errand / ˈerənd / *n*. 差事
   God's errand   上帝的使命
6. vow / vau / *n*. 誓约，许愿
7. holy / ˈhəulɪ / *adj*. 神圣的
8. capacity / kəˈpæsɪtɪ / *n*. 能力，资格
9. pledge / pledʒ / *v*. 保证，许诺
10. His Service   服务，贡献

背景介绍

《音乐之声》是一部十分适合亲子同乐的影片。这个真实故事发生在1938年的奥地利：见习修女玛丽亚是个性格开朗，热情奔放的姑娘。她爱唱歌跳舞，还十分喜爱大自然的清新宁静。但是修道院院长觉得玛丽亚不适应这种与尘寰隔绝的生活，于是她来到萨尔茨堡当上了前奥地利帝国海军退役军官冯·特拉普家7个孩子的家庭教师。在此期间，玛丽亚关心孩子们在成长过程中的所作所为，很快就成了他们的知心朋友，建立了深厚的感情。她教7个孩子一起练合唱，成立了一支很有素养的家庭合唱队，这激起了上校对生活的热爱，也唤起了他对玛丽亚的爱情，与玛丽亚结成了美满的伴侣。在这部影片中，那有趣的故事、悦耳的歌曲、温馨的人情、天真无邪的笑料，构成了这部曾打破影史上最高卖座纪录的歌舞片，并曾获最佳影片等五项奥斯卡金像奖。同时使它成为一部很受欢迎的家庭电影。

篇目欣赏

本文所选的这一幕是玛丽亚和院长嬷嬷的一段对话。在玛丽亚的一生中,院长嬷嬷是一个非常重要的人物。她信仰信基督教,所以她相信上帝对她和人类的爱。在她的思想中她认为要报答上帝的爱,就要成为上帝让你成为的那个人。她认为上帝赋予了玛丽亚很多能力和智慧和对孩子们的爱心,她应该成为一个有家的人,所以她对玛丽亚说:We ought to be what God wants us to be. 所以玛丽亚必须去完成她的职责:成为一个母亲,成为上校的妻子。因为上校对她的爱情表白,让她很矛盾,她认为她的一生是为上帝服务的。同时,她还相信我们不能逃避自己的问题,我们必须面对它们:These walls were not built to shut out problems. You have to face them. You have to live. The life was born to live. 这些话给了玛丽亚极大的鼓励,也改变了她的一生。

背诵准备

阅读下列问题,并根据内容写上适当的词或词组来完成句子。

1. What is Maria's problem?

   She has been _____, _____, _____. She can't _____ Captain Von Trapp. She thought to have _____ his love would have been _____.

2. How does the Reverend Mother help her out of it ?

   The Reverend Mother first asked what _____ to Maria. Then had a _____ with her. She also encouraged her to _____ the problem and said that the life was _____ to live.

3. What are the most important words Reverend Mother gave to Maria?

   1) Our abbey is not to be used as an _____.

   2) The love of the man and the woman is _____, too.

   3) You have a great _____ to love. What you must _____ is how God wants you to _____ your love.

4) If you love this man, it doesn't mean you love God _____. No, you must find out.

5) These walls were not _____ to _____ problems. You have to face them. You have to live. The life was _____ to live.

参考译文

音乐之声

院长嬷嬷： 你一直不快乐——我很难过。

玛丽亚： 院长嬷嬷。

院长嬷嬷： 他们为什么要把你送回来？

玛丽亚： 院长嬷嬷，不是他们送我回来的，是我自己要离开的。

院长嬷嬷： 玛丽亚，坐下。告诉我发生了什么事？

玛丽亚： 我……我害怕。

院长嬷嬷： 害怕？他们对你不好吗？

玛丽亚： 噢，不，不是。我感到困惑，我觉得……从未有过的感觉。我实在呆不下去，我知道在这儿——院长嬷嬷：远离它，我就会感到安全。

院长嬷嬷： 玛丽亚，修道院不是用来逃避现实的，什么使你无法面对？

玛丽亚： 我不能再面对他了。

院长嬷嬷： 他？冯·特普少校？你爱上他了？

玛丽亚： 我不知道，我不知道。我……男爵夫人和我……她说他爱上我了，但我不愿相信。噢，有几次我们彼此对视时……噢，院长嬷嬷，我几乎喘不过气来。

院长嬷嬷： 你有没有让他看出你的情感？

玛丽亚： 如果有的话，我也不知道，就是这一直折磨着我。我是奉上帝使命去那儿的，要求得到他的爱当然是不对的。我不能待下去了。我真的不能。我已准备好现在就来发誓。请帮帮我。

院长嬷嬷： 玛丽亚，男女之间的爱情同样是神圣的。你有一颗博大的爱心，你要弄明白的是上帝要你怎样去献出你的爱心。

玛丽亚： 但我已向上帝保证奉献一生，我已保证为其服务。

院长嬷嬷： 孩子，如果你爱这个男子，并不意味着你减少了对上帝的爱。不是的，你必须明白，你必须回去。

玛丽亚： 哦，院长嬷嬷，你千万不能让我回去！请让我留下来吧，我求您了。

院长嬷嬷： 玛丽亚，修道院的墙不是用来掩藏问题的，你必须正视它们，你必须热爱你命中注定的生活方式。

77. Forrest Gump

GUMP'S HOUSE — MOM'S BEDROOM

Forrest: What's the matter, Momma?

Mrs. Gump: I'm *dyin'*, Forrest. Come on in, sit down over here.

Forrest: Why are you dyin', Momma?

Mrs. Gump: It's my time. It's just my time. Oh, now, don't you be afraid, sweetheart. Death is just a part of life. It's something we're all *destined* to do. I didn't know it, but I was destined to be your momma. I did the best I could.

Forrest: You did good, Momma.

Mrs. Gump: Well, I *happened to* believe you make your own *destiny*. You have to do the best with what God gave you.

Forrest: What's my destiny, Momma?

Mrs. Gump: You're gonna have to *figure* that out for yourself. Life is a box of chocolates, Forrest. You never know what you're gonna get.

Forrest: (voice-over) Momma always had a way of explaining things so I could understand them.

Mrs. Gump: I will miss you, Forrest.

Forrest: (voice-over) She had got the cancer and died on a Tuesday. I bought her a new hat with little flowers on it.

语言注释

1. dyin' / daɪŋ / *adj*.（dying 的缩写）垂死的
2. destine / ˈdestɪŋ / *v*.命中注定
3. happen to (do) 发生……
4. destiny / ˈdestɪnɪ / *n*.命运
5. figure / ˈfɪɡə / *v*.想象,理解

背景介绍

《阿甘正传》这部影片是通过对一个智商只有 75 的低能儿的生活的描述,反映美国生活的方方面面。它从一个独特的角度对美国几十年来社会政治生活中的重要事件作了展现。它是一部以喜剧形式来表现严肃主题的电影,而且相当成功。它的主题有很多,主要有两个:一,对人生意义的思考,对命运的思索。人的命运是按一定的轨迹运行,还是像羽毛那样飘忽不定呢? 二,它的反主流、反社会、反传统性。影片以一低能儿的视角来观察美国几十年的历史变迁。一个智商为 75 的人,却能看到许多"聪明人"看不到的人生美丽。即使是在危机与彷徨中,他依然有星光、彩云陪伴,让他一步步跑下去,跑出辉煌的人生历程。另外,影片中还穿插着许多小的主题。比如,战友间的友谊;爱情,特别是阿甘对珍妮执著的无邪的爱;对种族主义与对弱智残疾人歧视的责备,不要蔑视任何人,人是生来平等的,只要给他一定发挥空间,人的潜能是无限的;对"阿甘式"乐观精神的向往等等,都是值得我们在欣赏影片的同时去回味、体会的。

篇目欣赏

这段对白是甘太太在临终前和阿甘的一段非常意味深长的对话。阿甘的一生,送走了三位亲人:朋友巴布、妈妈和珍妮。阿甘总是说"如果没有死那该多好"。这句直白的话也是我们的心声。罗素名言,生命是一条江,发源于远处,蜿蜒于大地,上游是青年时代,中游是中年时代,下游是老年时代,上游狭窄而湍急,下游宽阔而平静。什么是死亡,死亡就是江入大海,大海接纳了江河,又结束了江河。人生因为死才有意义,没有结束,过程将会贬值。甘太太临死前,把阿甘叫到身边就是要让他知道人生的过程要自己把握,要做得最好。所以她说:I happened to believe you make your own destiny. You have to do the best with what God gave you. 阿甘的母亲就是这样教育孩子的。因为有死,所以才要不枉此生。也许,人的生命就像夜空中的流星,在一刹那间划过天际,殒身而尽。星光的短暂不能改变,我们唯一能做的,就是使那一瞬间的光辉更美丽。

背诵准备

在这段对白中有一些非常有用的词组,范文中有这些词组的句子,自己也来造个句子吧。同时把例句熟读并背诵。

1. a part of   Death is just a part of life.
   Your sentence：＿＿＿＿＿＿＿＿＿＿＿＿＿＿＿＿＿＿＿＿＿.
2. be destined to (do)   I was destined to be your momma.
   Your sentence：＿＿＿＿＿＿＿＿＿＿＿＿＿＿＿＿＿＿＿＿＿.
3. happened to do   I happened to believe you make your own destiny.
   Your sentence：＿＿＿＿＿＿＿＿＿＿＿＿＿＿＿＿＿＿＿＿＿.
4. figure ... out   You're gonna have to figure that out for yourself.
   Your sentence：＿＿＿＿＿＿＿＿＿＿＿＿＿＿＿＿＿＿＿＿＿.
5. have a way of ...   Momma always had a way of explaining things.
   Your sentence：＿＿＿＿＿＿＿＿＿＿＿＿＿＿＿＿＿＿＿＿＿.

参考译文

阿甘正传

阿甘的家里,妈妈的卧室
阿甘：   你怎么了,妈妈?
甘太太：我要死了,阿甘。过来,坐到这儿来。
阿甘：   你为什么要死呢,妈妈?
甘太太：这是我的时间,我的时间到了。现在,你不要害怕,孩子。死
        亡是人的生命的一部分,是每个人应去的终点,我不知道是怎
        么回事,但我注定是你妈妈,我已尽了全力。
阿甘：   你做得很好,妈妈。
甘太太：而且,我有理由相信你能够把握你自己的命运。你一定要把
        上帝给你的恩赐发挥到极致。
阿甘：   我的命运是什么,妈妈?
甘太太：你会自己弄明白的。生活就像一盒巧克力,阿甘。你永远不
        会知道你将要得到什么(画外音:妈妈总是用一种方法来解释
        事情能让我能明白。)
甘太太：我会想你的,阿甘。
(画外音:她得了癌症,在周二死了。我给她买了一个带花的新帽子。)

78. Shark Tales

Dan Lino:	You see, Sykes. It's a fish-eat-fish world. You either take or you get taken.
Sykes:	Truer words have never been spoken. Is that it? We done?
Dan Lino:	Now, you and me, we work together a long, long, long time.
Sykes:	Please, Dan Lino. It's hardly been like work.
Dan Lino:	You know ...
Sykes:	I love that about you ...
Dan Lino:	Let me finish. That I've lived my life for my sons. Raising them, and protecting them ...
Sykes:	You are the best. (To someone else) He is the best, right? Am I right or am I wrong? Am I right?
Dan Lino:	It's all been to prepare them for the day they run the *reef*. Well, today is that day. Long story short. From now on, you work for Frankie and Lenny.
Sykes:	Lenny? Frankie, I understand. But Lenny? You can't be serious.
Dan Lino:	I'm dead serious. It takes more than *muscles* to run things. Now Lenny, he's got the *brains*. That's something special.
Sykes:	He is special, all right.
Dan Lino:	What does that mean?
Sykes:	Nothing. I'm just saying ...
Dan Lino:	I bring you in here, look you in the eye, tell you what's what, and what?
Sykes:	What?
Dan Lino:	What "what"?
Sykes:	You said "what" first.
Dan Lino:	I didn't say what. I asked you what.

语言注释

1. reef / riːf / *n*. 堡礁
2. muscle / ˈmʌsl / *n*. 肌肉
3. brain / breɪn / *n*. 头脑

背景介绍

《鲨鱼故事》是由梦工厂继《怪物史莱克》后推出的又一部动画片。《鲨鱼故事》展现了一个海底世界。清洗店的小鱼儿职员奥斯卡目睹了黑帮头目鲨鱼丹利诺的儿子弗兰基被渔船抛下的铁锚砸死,于是冒充自己就是打败了庞然大物的"鲨鱼杀手"。他被当成英雄,但这个谎言也导致丹利诺对奥斯卡的一路追杀。《鲨鱼故事》似乎把海底世界拟人化得更彻底,情节亦颇具创意,各种海底族群之间的弱肉强食完全被比拟成人类黑社会帮派斗争的情形。《鲨鱼故事》秉承了梦工厂一贯引以为豪的反传统、反经典的喜剧风格,被认为是动画版的《教父》。

篇目欣赏

这篇节选是丹利诺和塞斯之间的一段有意思的对白。塞斯一直为丹利诺工作。残暴冷酷的丹利诺谋划的净是些巧取豪夺的勾当,不过他对自己的两个宝贝儿子弗兰基和兰尼却是关爱有加,希望把他们培养成为家族合格的接班人。在这段对话里,丹利诺在关照塞斯要开始为弗兰克和兰尼工作。看来丹利诺准备把位置让给两个儿子了。丹利诺在关照塞斯一些生活准则,并希望他能帮助扶持两个儿子。虽然丹利诺非常冷酷,但作为父亲却很尽责。

背诵准备

请选择框内的词的适当形式填入下列句中：

take	bring	true	muscle	be	
raise	run	in	short	dead	

1. You either take or you get _____.

2. _____ words have never been spoken. Is that it?

3. Please, Dan Lino. It's hardly _____ like work.

4. That I've lived my life for my sons. _____ them, and protecting them ...

5. It's all been to prepare them for the day they _____ the reef.

6. Well, today is that day. Long story _____. From now on, you work for Frankie and Lenny.

7. I'm _____ serious. It takes more than _____ to run things.

8. I _____ you in here, look you _____ the eye, tell you what's what, and what?

参考译文

鲨鱼故事

丹利诺：　看,塞斯,这是一个鱼吃鱼的世界。你不吃别人,就会被别人吃。

塞斯：　　没有什么话比这句话更正确了,是不是?

丹利诺：　如今你我已经合作了很久,很久。

塞斯：　　拜托,丹利诺,那几乎不像是工作。

丹利诺：　你知道……

塞斯：　　我喜欢你那样……

丹利诺：　让我说完。这就是我为儿子所做的。抚养他们,保护他们。

塞斯：　　你做得最好。(对其他人说)他是最好的,不是吗? 我是对还是错? 我说得对吗?

丹利诺： 是要让他们准备经营这个礁城，就是今天了。长话短说，现在你就替弗
兰基和列尼工作了。

塞斯： 列尼？弗兰基的话我明白。但列尼，你不是当真吧？

丹利诺： 我是绝对认真的。经营不仅仅靠武力。列尼有头脑，很了不起。

塞斯： 是的，他很特别。

丹利诺： 你什么意思？

塞斯： 没有，我只是说……

丹利诺： 是我带你进来，看着你，告诉你什么是什么，你还要什么？

塞斯： 什么？

丹利诺： 什么"什么"？

塞斯： 是你先说什么的。

丹利诺： 我没有说什么，我是问你什么。

79. Stuart Little — Call of the Wild

Stuart: The Beast took Snowbell.

Reeko: I'm sorry to hear that. Wow, he was a great guy. Let's take a moment of silence. Ok, done. I'm sure we'll all miss him. Take care now.

Stuart: We got to save him.

Reeko: That's *nuts*.

Stuart: Not if we do it together.

Reeko: Yo, now you are really talking *crazy*. I'm staying as far away as I can.

Stuart: But you said you don't sweat the Beast.

Reeko: Yeah, yeah, Stuart. I said that. Listen carefully. I was lying.

Stuart: Lying?

Reeko: Yeah, I do that. I'm just a *skunk*. A *rotten*, unpopular, smelly, *freeloading* skunk. Ask anyone, and they'll tell you I'd never fight the Beast. That was something I just said so. You know ... You'd liked me ...

Stuart: Well, I liked you anyway. Reeko, I'm going with or without you.

Reeko: Then I'd say it's without me. Stuart, wait up, will you? Snowbell's history. Man. There is nothing you can do for him. Stu, why don't you listen to me?

Stuart: Because it's my *fault*. I saw him, but I didn't get to him in time.

Reeko: Dude, you weren't the one who sent him straight into the *paw* of the Beast.

Stuart: Sent him? Wait a minute. What do you mean "sent him"?

Reeko: Listen, Stu ... I can explain.

Stuart: I thought you were my friend. Why would you do that?

Reeko: It's *complicated*. The Beast is a cruel, heartless *monster*. She doesn't care about anybody but herself.

Stuart: Then you two must have a lot in common.

Reeko: Stu, slow down. Slow down and think about what you are doing. It's too *risky*, man.

Stuart: When it comes to friends, sometimes you gotta take a risk.

语言注释

1. nuts / nʌts / *adj*. 发疯的,疯狂的
2. crazy / ˈkreɪzɪ / *adj*. 疯狂的
3. skunk / skʌŋk / *n*. 臭鼬
4. rotten / ˈrɒtn / *adj*. 讨厌的
5. freeloading / friːləʊdɪŋ / *adj*. 靠别人施舍的
6. fault / fɔːlt / *n*. 错,过失
7. paw / pɔː / *n*. 爪子
8. complicated / ˈkɒmplɪkeɪtɪd / *adj*. 复杂的
9. monster / ˈmɒnstə / *n*. 怪物
10. risky / ˈrɪskɪ / *adj*. 冒险的

背景介绍

他是一个聪明、热心的小老鼠,名字叫斯图亚特。斯图亚特一心想寻找自己的家。当他被里特一家收养之后,他开始了一场和各种角色一起的冒险活动。故事讲述斯图亚特和童子军一起到森林冒险后发生的一系列事件。斯图亚特先是认识了臭鼬利科,然后那只猫斯纳贝尔被兽王抓走。斯图亚特想办法把它救出来。最后在斯图亚特的感化下,利科和森林里的动物们帮助斯图亚特一起打败了兽王。

篇目欣赏

节选的这一部分对话是斯图亚特看到斯纳贝尔被兽王抓走后,来找利科帮忙一起去救斯纳贝尔。利科因害怕兽王不肯同去。而斯图亚特说的话令人深思。这段对话揭示了斯图亚特和利科不同的个性和内心世界,也展示了在危难来临时对待朋友的不同态度。

背诵准备

请选择框内的词的适当形式填入下列句中：

silent	crazy	her	if	sweat	smell
nothing	fight	popular	heartless	risky	

1. Wow, he was a great guy. Let's take a moment of _____.

2. Not _____ we do it together.

3. Yo, now you are really talking _____. I'm staying as far away as I can.

4. But you said you don't _____ the Beast.

5. I'm just a skunk. A rotten, _____, _____, freeloading skunk. Ask anyone, they'll tell you I'd never _____ the Beast.

6. Snowbell's history. Man. There is _____ you can do for him.

7. The Beast is a cruel, _____ monster. She doesn't care about anybody but _____.

8. When it comes to friends, sometimes you gotta take a _____.

参考译文

精灵鼠小弟——野外求生记

斯图亚特：　兽王抓走了斯纳贝尔。

利科：　　　真为他难过。他是好人。让我们为他默哀。好了。我们会想念他的。再见。

斯图亚特：　我们得救他。

利科：　　　那是不可能的。

斯图亚特：　如果我们齐心协力就行。

利科：　　　你真是在说疯话，我向来对他敬而远之。

斯图亚特：　但是你说过你不怕她的。

利科：　　　是，我是说了。听着，我是骗人的。

斯图亚特： 骗人的？

利科： 是的，我只是一只臭鼬。一只令人讨厌的，不受欢迎的，有臭味的，靠别人施舍而活的臭鼬。不管问谁，他们都会说我不会和兽王对着干。我这么说，你也不会喜欢我了。

斯图亚特： 不管怎么样，我都喜欢你。不管你帮不帮我，我都要走。

利科： 那我还是帮不了你。等等，斯图亚特，斯纳贝尔死定了。你现在不能为他做什么。你为什么就不听我的呢？

斯图亚特： 因为那是我的错。我看见他，却没能及时帮助他。

利科： 小家伙，又不是你送他到兽王手里的。

斯图亚特： 送他？等等。你说"送入"是什么意思？

利科： 听着，我来解释。

斯图亚特： 我还认为你是我的朋友呢。你为什么那样做？

利科： 原因很复杂。兽王是一个残忍无情的怪物。她不在乎任何人，只在乎她自己。

斯图亚特： 那你们两个有很多共同之处。

利科： 慢着，斯图亚特。想想你在干什么，天那，这太冒险了。

斯图亚特： 为朋友；有时我们得冒险。

80. Free Willy 3

Max:	I have a question.
Father:	Hey, Max. Take this.
Max:	Why is it wrong if you hurt other people?
Father:	That's a rule, Max. Just is.
Max:	But don't you want to do what you want no matter who hurts?
Father:	Maybe, but I just don't do it.
Max:	Why?
Father:	Why what?
Max:	Why don't you do it?
Father:	People have rights.
Max:	Even people you hate?
Father:	Yup.
Max:	I didn't know I had rights.
Father:	You do.
Max:	Dad?
Father:	Yes. Max?
Max:	What if whales are like people?
Father:	They aren't.
Max:	What if they are?
Father:	Max. Whales are animals that were put here by God for us to hunt. You don't get *upset* when you eat a *cheeseburger*, do you?
Max:	Why not?
Father:	Whales don't feel. They aren't people. They are just fish.
Max:	You are wrong.
Father:	You know better than me? You're ten years old.
Max:	But you are wrong.
Father:	And I've been wrong all my life. My dad was wrong and his dad too. We are all wrong and you are right.
Max:	You are hurting people.
Father:	Who am I hurting? I'm not hurting anyone.

... (Max's father was saved by the whale Willy after falling down into the water.)

Max:	Cheeseburger saved your life.

Father：　You were right.

Max：　　Hey，you made a mistake.

Father：　What am I supposed to do now?

...（Max's father tried to kill Willy, but Willy saved him when his life was in danger in the water.）

Woman：　It's not what I would have done.

Man：　　What do you mean?

Woman：　I mean some guy tried to kill me. I wouldn't have saved his life. I would have *bitten* his *butt*.

Rodolph：Maybe he's smarter than we are.

Man：　　Or more human.

语言注释

1. upset / ʌpˈset / *adj*. 难过
2. cheeseburger / ˈtʃiːzbɜːgə / *n*. 乳酪肉饼汉堡包
3. bite / baɪt / *v*. 咬
4. butt / bʌt / *n*. 屁股

背景介绍

《人鱼的童话3》讲述鲸鱼威利和它的小伙伴们重新回到了久别的海域。此时，从前的杰西已经长大，并成为海岸科考队的成员。十岁的男孩麦克斯住在海域附近，他父亲是一个非法捕鲸手。麦克斯第一次跟父亲出海捕鱼，遇到了威利和它的鲸群。危难时刻，杰西出现，拯救了鲸群。但这一次并没有打消麦克斯父亲非法捕鲸的念头。庆幸的是，经过杰西的启发，麦克斯懂得了鲸鱼对人类的重要性。一次捕鲸时，麦克斯的父亲不幸落入水中，生死关头，威利却将麦克斯的父亲救起。此时此刻，麦克斯的父亲恍然大悟，并与威利成了好朋友。从此，海域又恢复了它的宁静与和谐。本片揭示了人与自然，人与动物的关系，表明保护动物就是保护自己。

篇目欣赏

> 麦克斯在杰西启发下,一起和鲸鱼在海里玩耍并意识到鲸鱼也通人性。节选部分是在这之后他与父亲的一段对话。他告诉父亲不该再猎杀鲸鱼。事实表明,鲸鱼在他父亲落入海中的时候没有以牙还牙,而是以德报怨。证明鲸鱼是一种非常有人情味的动物,我们应该爱护它们而不是猎杀它们。

背诵准备

请选择框内的词的适当形式填入下列句中:

smart	save	rights	all	upset
bite	do	who	too	have

1. But don't you want to do what you want no matter _____ hurts?
2. People have _____.
3. You don't get _____ when you eat a cheeseburger, _____ you?
4. And I've been wrong _____ my life. My dad was wrong and his dad _____. We are all wrong and you are right.
5. Cheeseburger _____ your life.
6. I mean some guy tried to kill me. I wouldn't _____ saved his life. I would have _____ his butt.
7. Maybe he's _____ than we're.

参考译文

人鱼的童话 3

麦克斯: 我有一个问题。

父亲: 嘿,麦克斯,拿着这个。

麦克斯： 为什么伤害别人不对？

父亲： 因为这是个规矩，麦克斯。就是这样。

麦克斯： 但你能随心所欲做你想做的事，不管伤害到谁吗？

父亲： 可能，但我不会做。

麦克斯： 为什么？

父亲： 你指什么？

麦克斯： 你为什么不做？

父亲： 每个人都有权利。

麦克斯： 甚至你恨的人？

父亲： 是的。

麦克斯： 我不知道我有权利。

父亲： 你当然有。

麦克斯： 爸爸？

父亲： 什么事？

麦克斯： 鲸鱼会不会也和人一样？

父亲： 它们不一样。

麦克斯： 如果是一样的呢？

父亲： 麦克斯，鲸鱼是动物，是上帝赐给我们的猎物。你吃汉堡时不会难过，
是吗？

麦克斯： 为什么不？

父亲： 鲸鱼没有感情。他们不是人，只是鱼。

麦克斯： 你错了。

父亲： 你比我懂得多？你才十岁。

麦克斯： 但你错了。

父亲： 难道我错了一辈子，我爸爸，我爷爷都错了，只有你对？

麦克斯： 你在伤害别人。

父亲： 伤害谁？我谁也没有伤害。

（麦克斯的爸爸掉入海中，生死关头是鲸鱼威利救起了他。）

麦克斯： 汉堡救了你的命。

父亲： 你是对的。

麦克斯： 嘿，你错了。

父亲： 我现在该怎么办？

（麦克斯的父亲想杀威利，但当他掉入水中，生死关头威利却救了他。）

女人： 如果是我，我就不会做。

男人： 你什么意思？

女人： 我的意思是有人想杀我，我就不会救他的命。我会咬他屁股。

鲁道夫： 或许他比我们更聪明。

男人： 或许更有人情味。

81. Confidence

from The Sound of Music

I have *confidence* in sunshine. I have confidence in rain. I have confidence that spring will come again. *Besides* which you see, I have confidence in me. *Strength* doesn't lie in numbers. Strength doesn't lie in *wealth*. Strength lies in nights of *peaceful slumbers*. When you wake up, it's healthy. All I trust I give my heart to. All I *trust* becomes my own. I have confidence in confidence alone. Besides which you see, I have confidence in me.

语言注释

1. confidence / ˈkɒnfɪdəns / *n*. 信心
2. besides / bɪˈsaɪdz / *prep*. 除……之外
3. strength / streŋθ / *n*. 力量
4. wealth / welθ / *n*. 财富
5. peaceful / ˈpiːsfʊl / *adj*. 宁静的
6. slumber / ˈslʌmbə / *n*. 睡眠
7. trust / trʌst / *v*. 信任

背景介绍

《音乐之声》取材于 1938 年发生在奥地利的一个真实故事:见习修女玛丽亚是个性格开朗,热情奔放的姑娘。她爱唱歌、爱跳舞,还十分喜爱大自然的清新、宁静和美丽。只要修道院的门开着,她就常在苍翠的群山间像云雀一样歌唱,在洁净的小溪边与潺潺的流水合唱。修道院院长觉得玛丽亚不应该过这种与尘寰隔绝的生活,该放她到外面看看。就这样,她来到萨尔茨堡当上了前奥地利帝国海军退役军官冯·特拉普家 7 个孩子的家庭教师。冯·特拉普是个心地善良的爱国者,他在服役期间功勋卓著。几年前,心爱的妻子不幸去世,现在心灰意冷。家里没有歌声,没有笑声,也不许人家提到他的妻子。他爱自己的孩子,但是并不了解他们,老是像指挥水兵一样管理着他们。这首歌是玛丽亚在去萨尔茨堡路上为了消除焦虑,提高自信而唱的。

篇目欣赏

成 功源于自信。玛丽亚是一个很自信的人。只有相信自己,才能使别人相信你。一个没有自信的人如何能取得别人的信任呢? 居里夫人曾说:"我们应有恒心,更要有自信心。"自信心是所有伟人发明创造的巨大动力,有了自信,才会勇敢、坚强、敢于创新,没有自信,就没有独创,就难以成功。你有信心学好英语吗? 请别迟疑,回答"Yes"!

背诵准备

这段文字句式统一,请用文章中的词语填空,帮助记忆。

I have confidence in _____. I have confidence in _____. I have confidence that _____ _____ _____ _____. Besides which you see, I have confidence in _____. Strength doesn't lie in _____. Strength doesn't lie in _____. Strength lies in _____ _____ _____ _____. When you wake up, it's _____. All I trust _____ _____ _____ _____ _____. All I trust _____ _____ _____. I have confidence in _____ alone. Besides which you see, I have confidence in _____.

参考译文

信 心

选自《音乐之声》

我相信阳光。我相信雨露。我相信春天终会再次来到。除了你看得到的,我还相信我自己。力量不存在于数字中。力量不存在于财富里。平静的夜里安然入睡,力量在此积蓄,让你健康地醒来。我把我的心交给我所信任的,我所信任的变成了我的一部分。我相信信心本身。除了你看得到的,我还相信我自己。

82. The Little Prince (excerpt)

By Antoine de Saint-Exupery

I showed my *masterpiece* to the grown-ups, and asked them whether the drawing frightened them.

But they answered, "Frighten? Why should anyone be frightened by a hat?"

My drawing was not a picture of a hat. It was a picture of a *boa constrictor digesting* an elephant. But since the grown-ups were not able to understand it, I made another drawing: I drew the inside of the boa constrictor, so that the grown-ups could see it clearly. They always need to have things explained.

The grown-ups' *response*, this time, was to advise me to lay aside my drawings of boa constrictors, whether from the inside or the outside, and devote myself instead to geography, history, arithmetic and grammar. That is why, at the age of six, I gave up what might have been a magnificent career as a painter. I had been *disheartened* by the failure of my Drawing Number One and my Drawing Number Two. Grown-ups never understand anything by themselves, and it is *tiresome* for children to be always and forever explaining things to them.

语言注释

1. masterpiece / ˈmɑːstəpiːs / *n*. 杰作
2. boa constrictor　蟒蛇
3. digest / daɪˈdʒest / *v*. 消化
4. response / rɪsˈpɒns / *n*. 回答,响应,反应
5. dishearten / dɪsˈhɑːt(ə)n / *v*.
使……气馁,使……沮丧
6. tiresome / ˈtaɪəsəm / *adj*. 无聊的,烦人的

背景介绍

圣·德克旭贝里(Antoine de Saint-Exupery),1900 年出生于法国里昂,1921—1923 年在法国空军中服役,曾是后备飞行员,后来又成为民用航空驾驶员,参加了开辟法国——非洲——南美国际航线的工作。在这期间,他还从事文学写作,作品有《南线班机》(1930),《夜航》(1931)等等。

1939 年德国法西斯入侵法国。经他坚决要求,圣·德克旭贝里参加了抗德战争。1940 年法国在战争中溃败。随后,他只身流亡美国。在美国期间,他继续从事写作,1940 年发表了《战斗飞行员》,1943 年发表了《给一个人质的信》以及《小王子》。

篇目欣赏

本文节选自圣·德克旭贝里的童话《小王子》。它被誉为一则关于生命和生活的寓言。

"这就像花一样。如果你爱上了一朵生长

在一颗星星上的花,那么夜间,

你看着天空就感到甜蜜愉快,

所有的星星上

都好像开着花。"

它所讲述的是一个美丽的伤感故事:

飞行员因为飞机出了故障,被迫降落在远离人烟的撒哈拉沙漠上,这时一位迷人而神秘的小男孩出现了,执拗地请飞行员给他画一只绵羊。他就是小王子,纯洁、忧郁,来自太阳系中某个不为人知的小行星,爱提问题,对别人的问题却从不作答。在攀谈中小王子的秘密逐渐被揭开了,他是因为与他的美丽、骄傲的玫瑰发生了感情纠葛才负气出走的。他在各星球中漫游,分别造访了国王、自负的人、酒鬼、商人、掌灯人和地理学家的星球,最后降临到地球上,试图找到疏解孤独和痛苦的良方,小王子结识了狐狸,同狐狸建立了友谊,也从狐狸那里学到了人生的真谛。他决定回到他的玫瑰那里去,但是他的躯壳是难以带走的,于是他决定求助于那条 30 秒钟内就能置人于死地的毒蛇。

就是这样一个平实无华的童话,既没有离奇的情节,也没有惊天动地的壮举,故事在平淡的铺叙中展开。然而自1943年问世以来,被译成42种文字,多次再版,经久不衰,被选入许多教科书。无论在西方或东方,阅读《小王子》长久以来被视为一种必修的文化学分,从九岁到九十九岁,每个人都可以以自己的方式来体会书中深远的柔情和哲理。

背诵准备

下面这两幅图,哪一幅是 Drawing Number One? 哪一幅又是 Drawing Number Two?

根据上面的两幅图,你能完成以下的填空吗?

I showed my masterpiece to the _____, and asked them whether the drawing frightened them.

But they answered, "Frighten? Why should anyone be frightened by a _____?"

My drawing was not a picture of a _____. It was a picture of a boa constrictor _____ an elephant. But since the grown-ups were not able to understand it, I made another drawing: I drew the _____ of the boa constrictor, so that the grown-ups could see it clearly. They always need to have things explained.

参考译文

小王子(节选)

圣·德克旭贝里

我把我的这幅杰作拿给大人看,我问他们我的画是不是让他们害怕。

但他们回答说:"害怕?一顶帽子有什么可怕的?"

我画的不是帽子,是一条巨蟒在消化着一头大象。既然大人们无法理解,我就又画了一幅画。我把巨蟒肚子里的情况画了出来,以便让大人们能够看懂。这些大人总是需要解释。

这次,大人们劝我把这些画着开着肚皮的,或闭上肚皮的蟒蛇的图画放在一边,把兴趣放在地理、历史、算术和语法上。就这样,在6岁那年,我就放弃了当画家这一美好的职业。我的第一号、第二号作品的不成功,使我泄了气。这些大人们自己什么也弄不懂,还得不断地给他们作解释。这真叫孩子们厌烦。

83. Beautiful Smile and Love

By Mother Teresa

The poor are very wonderful people. One evening we went out and we picked up four people from the street. And one of them was in a most terrible condition, and I told the Sisters: You take care of the other three. I take care of this one who looked worse. So I did for her all that my love can do. I put her in bed, and there was such a beautiful smile on her face. She took hold of my hand as she said just the words "thank you" and she died. I could not help but examine my *conscience* before her and I asked what would I say if I was in her place. And my answer was very simple. I would have tried to draw a little attention to myself. I would have said I am hungry, that I am dying, I am cold, I am in pain, or something, but she gave me much more — she gave me her *grateful* love. And she died with a smile on her face. As did that man whom we picked up from the *drain*, half eaten with worms, and we brought him to the home. "I have lived like an animal in the street, but I am going to die like an *angel*, loved and cared for." And it was so wonderful to see the greatness of that man who could speak like that, who could die like that without *blaming* anybody, without *cursing* anybody, without comparing anything. Like an angel — this is the greatness of our people. And that is why we believe what Jesus had said: I was hungry, I was naked, I was homeless, I was unwanted, unloved, uncared for, and you did it to me.

语言注释

1. conscience / ˈkɒnʃəns / *n*. 良知
2. grateful / ˈgreɪtful / *adj*. 感谢(激)的
3. drain / dreɪn / *n*. 下水道,排(废)水管
4. angel / ˈeɪndʒəl / *n*. 天使
5. blame / bleɪm / *v*. 责怪,把……归究于
   blame sb. / sth. for ... 因……而责怪某人
6. curse / kɜːs / *v*. 诅咒

背景介绍

特 蕾莎修女(Mother Teresa, 1910－1997)，原名艾格妮丝·巩霞·博杰舒，是印度著名的慈善家，印度天主教仁爱传教会创始人，1979 年被授予诺贝尔和平奖。艾格妮丝诞生在马其顿斯科普里的一个富裕的阿尔巴尼亚家庭，在浓郁的天主教生活氛围中长大。37 岁正式成为修女，1948 年远赴印度加尔各答，并于两年后正式成立仁爱传教修女会，竭力为贫困中的最穷苦者服务。她创建的修女会有 7000 多名正式会员，还有数不清的追随者和义务工作者分布在世界 100 多个国家。她认识众多的总统、国王、传媒巨头和企业巨子，并受到他们的仰慕和爱戴。可是，她住的地方，唯一的电器是一部电话；她一共只有 3 套衣服，而且自己洗换；她只穿凉鞋没有袜子……她的一生，用她自己的话来说就是："怀大爱心，做小事情。"

篇目欣赏

本 文是她在领取诺贝尔和平奖时的演讲词节选，语言简洁质朴而感人至深。诺贝尔领奖台上响起的声音往往都是文采飞扬、热烈而激昂的，而特雷莎修女的演说朴实无华，其所举事例听来似平凡之至，然而其中所蕴含的伟大而神圣的爱感人至深。The poor are very wonderful people. 总起整段，之后，她用平实的语言讲述了发生在身边的两个平凡小故事——一位生命岌岌可危的小女孩临终前仍不忘面带微笑对特蕾莎修女表达感激之情；在排水道几乎全身都快被虫子吃掉了的一位男子在临终前宽慰地说道："I have lived like an animal in the street, but I am going to die like an angel, loved and cared for." 平凡中孕育着伟大，真情才能动人。Like an angel — this is the greatness of our people. 特雷莎修女最后以《圣经》中 Jesus 的话作总结。

背诵准备

一篇优秀的演讲稿就像一件杰出的艺术品,无论从哪一个角度去欣赏,它都会给人留下品位不尽的美感。排比的句式往往使文章增添韵律美,加快节奏感,增强气势和说服力。你不妨试着从排比句开始着手记忆本篇美文。

I would have tried to _____ _____ _____ _____ _____ _____. I would have said _____ _____ _____, that _____ _____ _____, _____ _____ _____, _____ _____ _____, or something, but she gave me _____ _____ — she gave me _____ _____ _____.

It was so wonderful to see the greatness of that man who could _____ _____ _____, who could _____ _____ _____ without _____ _____, without _____ _____, without _____.

Like an angel — this is the greatness of our people. And that is why we believe what Jesus had said: I was _____, I was _____, I was _____, I was _____, _____, _____, and you did it to me.

参考译文

美丽的微笑与爱心

特蕾莎修女

穷人是非常了不起的。一天晚上,我们外出,从街上带回了四个人,其中一个生命岌岌可危。于是我跟修女们说:"你们照料其他三个,这个濒危的人就由我来照顾了。"就这样,我为她做了我的爱所能做的一切。我将她放在床上,看到她的脸上绽露出如此美丽的微笑。她握着我的手,只说了句"谢谢您"就去世了。我情不自禁地在她面前审视起自己的良知来。我问自己,如果我是她的话,会说些什么呢?答案很简单,我会尽量引起旁人对我的关注,我会说我饥饿难忍,奄奄一息,冷得发抖,痛苦不堪,诸如此类的话。但是她给我的却更多更多——她给了我她的感激之情。她死时脸上却带着微笑。我们从排水道带回的那个男子也是如此。当时,他几乎全身都快被虫子吃掉了,我们把他带回了家。"在街上,我一直像个动物一样地活着,但我将像个天使一样地死去,有人爱,有人关心。"真是太好了,我看到了他的伟大之处,他竟能说出那样的话。他那样地死去,不责怪任何人,不诅咒任何人,无欲无求。像天使一样——这便是我们人的伟大之所在。因此我们相信耶稣所说的话——我饥肠辘辘——我衣不蔽体——我无家可归——我不为人所要,不为人所爱,也不为人所关心——然而,你却为我做了这一切。

84. Of Beauty

By Sir Francis Bacon

In beauty, that of favor, is more than that of color; and that of decent and gracious motion, more than that of favor. That is the best part of beauty, which a picture cannot express; no, nor the first sight of the life. There is no excellent beauty, that hath (old use of *has*) not some strangeness *in the proportion*. A man cannot tell whether *Apelles*, or *Albert Durer*, were the more *trifler*; whereof (old use of *which*) the one, would make a *personage* by *geometrical* proportions; the other, by taking the best parts out of *divers* faces, to make one excellent. Such personages, I think, would please nobody, but the painter that made them. Not but I think a painter may make a better face than ever was; but he must do it by a kind of *felicity* as a musician that maketh (old use of *makes*) an excellent air in music, and not by rule. A man shall see faces, that if you examine them part by part, you shall find never a good; and yet altogether do well. If it be true that the principal part of beauty is in decent motion, certainly it is no *marvel*, though persons in years seem many times more *amiable*; pulchrorum autumnus pulcher; for no youth can be *comely* but by pardon, and considering the youth, as to make up the comeliness.

Beauty is as summer fruits, which are easy to *corrupt*, and cannot last; and for the most part it makes a *dissolute* youth, and an age a little out of *countenance*; but yet certainly again, if it light well, it maketh virtue shine, and *vices* blush.

语言注释

1. in the proportion   成比例;相称
2. Apelles   阿佩利斯(公元 4 世纪希腊画家)
3. Albert Durer   艾伯特·杜勒(德国大画家)
4. trifler / ˈtraɪflə / *n*. 不务正业的人;吊儿郎当的人
5. personage / ˈpɜːsənɪdʒ / *n*. 人物
6. geometrical / dʒɪəˈmetrɪkəl / *adj*. 几何的,几何学的
7. divers / ˈdaɪvəz / *adj*. 各种各样的

8. felicity / fɪˈlɪsɪtɪ / *n.* 恰当;巧妙

9. marvel / ˈmɑːvəl / *n.* 令人惊奇的事

10. amiable / ˈeɪmjəbl / *adj.* 和蔼可亲的,友好的,亲切的

11. comely / ˈkʌmlɪ / *adj.* (女性)标致的,秀丽的

12. corrupt / kəˈrʌpt / *v.* 使堕落,变坏;腐蚀

13. dissolute / ˈdɪsəljuːt / *adj.* 放纵的

14. countenance / ˈkaʊntɪnəns / *n.* 面容;面部表情

15. vice / vaɪs / *n.* (涉及性或毒品的)罪恶,邪恶行径

背景介绍

弗兰西斯·培根(Francis Bacon,1561－1626)是 17 世纪英国著名思想家、政治家和经验主义哲学家,同时又是实验科学的前驱者。新贵族出身,毕业于剑桥。此后从政,1621 年被指控犯有受贿罪而下台。

在培根有生的 65 年中,他始终矢志于推进人类知识与文明的发展。其一生著述颇丰,且涉及的领域广泛,包括政治、经济、哲学、历史、法律、宗教、艺术、教育、科学、婚姻与道德、社交与休闲、民风与习俗等。1597 年,培根发表了他的处女作《论说随笔文集》。他在书中将自己对社会的思考,以及对人生的理解,浓缩成许多富有哲理的名言警句。

篇目欣赏

《论美》一篇深刻地表达了培根对美的精深理解。文章是在论美,语言本身也很美,最后一段用比喻的修辞手法:"Beauty is as summer fruits, which are easy to corrupt, and cannot last." 形象地唤起了我们的想象。文中提到了很多的美,有颜色美、状貌美,有优雅的动作之美,以及那种图画所不能表现、初睹所不能见及的德行美。在对这些"美"的论述中,最看重的是德行美。容貌美、状貌美、优雅动作之美都属于外形美,德行美却是属于一种内在的美。最理想的美是"内外兼美乃至上之美",这是培根在这篇文章中所阐述的主要观点。

背诵准备

请尝试说说以下的关键句讲到的是哪种"美"及所传达出作者怎样的美学观点？不妨也在心中记下这些佳句吧！

1. In beauty, that of favor, is more than that of color; and that of decent and gracious motion, more than that of favor. That is the best part of beauty, which a picture cannot express; no, nor the first sight of the life.
2. A man shall see faces, that if you examine them part by part, you shall find never a good; and yet altogether do well.
3. pulchrorum autumnus pulcher
4. Beauty is as summer fruits, which are easy to corrupt, and cannot last; and for the most part it makes a dissolute youth, and an age a little out of countenance; but yet certainly again, if it light well, it maketh virtue shine, and vices blush.

参考译文

论 美

弗兰西斯·培根

美不在颜色艳丽而在面目端庄，又不尽在面目端庄而在举止文雅合度。美之极致，非图画所能表，乍见所能识。举凡最美之人，其部位比例，必有异于常人之处。阿贝尔与杜勒皆画家也，其画人像也，一则按照几何学之比例，一则集众脸形之长于一身，二者谁更不智，实难断言。窃以为此等画像除画家本人外，恐无人喜爱也。余不否认画像之美可以超绝尘寰，但此美必为神笔，而非可依规矩得之者，乐师之谱成名曲亦莫不皆然。人面如逐部细察，往往一无是处，观其整体则光彩夺目。美之要素既在于举止，则年长美过年少亦无足怪。古人云："美者秋日亦美。"年少而著美名，率由宽假，盖鉴其年事之少，而补其形体之不足也。

美者犹如夏日蔬果，易腐难存；要之，年少而美者常无行，年长而美者不免面有惭色。虽然但须托体得人，则德行因美而益彰，恶行见美而愈愧。

85. On the Weather

By Jerome . K . Jerome

In her own home, the country, Nature is sweet in all her moods. What can be more beautiful than the snow, falling big with mystery in silent softness, *decking* the fields and trees *with* white as if for a fairy wedding! And how delightful is a walk when the frozen ground rings beneath our swinging tread — when our blood *tingles* in the rare keen air, and the sheep-dogs' distant bark and children's laughter peals faintly clear like Alpine bells across the open hills! And then skating! *Scudding* with wings of steel across the *swaying* ice, making whirring music as we fly. And oh, how *dainty* is spring — Nature at sweet eighteen!

When the little hopeful leaves *peep* out so fresh and green, so pure and bright, like young lives pushing shyly out into the *bustling* world; when the fruit-tree blossoms, pink and white, like village maidens in their Sunday *frocks*, hide each white-washed cottage in a cloud of *fragile* splendor; and the cuckoo's note upon the breeze is *wafted* through the woods! And summer, with its deep dark green and drowsy hum — when the rain-drops whisper solemn secrets to the listening leaves and the *twilight lingers* in the lanes! And autumn! Ah, how sadly fair, with its golden glow and the dying *grandeur* of its *tinted* woods — its blood-red sunsets and its ghostly evening mists, with its busy murmur of reapers, and its *laden* orchards, and the calling of the gleaners, and the festivals of praise!

语言注释

1. deck ... with ...   用……装饰
2. tingle / ˈtɪŋgl / v. (尤指皮肤)感到刺痛
3. scud / skʌd / v. (文)云飘过,掠过
4. sway / sweɪ / v. (使)摇摆,(使)摇晃
5. dainty / ˈdeɪntɪ / adj. 小巧的,精致的
6. peep / piːp / v. 隐约出现
7. bustling / ˈbʌslɪŋ / adj. 繁忙的,热闹的

8. frock / frɒk / *n*. (过时)长服,整身长裙

9. fragile / ˈfrædʒaɪl / *adj*. 脆弱的,易碎的,易损坏的

10. waft / wɒft / *v*. (在空气中缓缓地)飘落

11. twilight / ˈtwaɪlaɪt / *n*. 暮色,黄昏的天色

12. linger / ˈlɪŋə / *v*. 逗留,徘徊

13. grandeur / ˈgrændʒə / *n*. 壮丽,雄伟

14. tint / tɪnt / *v*. 稍微改变

15. laden / ˈleɪdn / *adj*. 装满的,满载的

背景介绍

罗姆·凯·杰罗姆(Jerome K. Jerome,1859 – 1927)是英国著名的现代幽默大师、小说家、散文家和戏剧家。出生在英国斯坦福特郡,他小时候经历了家境由盛到衰的种种变故。他的第一份工作是铁路职员,后来又跟着一个巡回团周游英伦诸岛,再往后又做过记者、佣金代理、律师事务所助理等工作。变幻不定的角色给了他丰富的社会阅历,为以后写作预备了充足的素材。

杰罗姆在艺术上是个多面手,也是个多产作家。幽默杰作《三人同舟》(*Three Men in a Boat*)和《懒人懒思录》(*Idle Thoughts of an Idle Fellow*)奠定了作者在世界文坛的独特地位。

篇目欣赏

罗姆是英国的幽默大师。《事关天气》节选的前两段,他写道:The weather is like the government — always in the wrong. 天气就像政府,总是在做错误的事情。紧随幽默而来的是一种积极生活的态度。他从不掩饰自己对于世界的热爱。在这段关于乡村四季的描写中,他写下自己最真切的感受:In her own home, the country, Nature is sweet in all her moods. 随后,他的思绪在空中放飞驰骋,一个个灵动的词汇跃然纸上,让我们也醉心于乡村四季,有立刻拥抱大自然的冲动。

背诵准备

在杰罗姆的笔下,乡村四季充满生机与活力、想象与魅力。其中,动词的适当运用是关键。请你再细细品味,朗读一篇原文后将那些富有灵气的动词填入文中划线处。有兴趣试试背诵这一段。

What can be more beautiful than the snow, _____ big with mystery in silent softness, _____ the fields and trees with white as if for a fairy wedding! And how delightful is a walk when the frozen ground _____ beneath our swinging tread — when our blood _____ in the rare keen air, and the sheep-dogs' distant bark and children's laughter _____ faintly clear like Alpine bells across the open hills! And then skating! ... And oh, how dainty is spring — Nature at sweet eighteen! When the little hopeful leaves _____ out so fresh and green, so pure and bright, like young lives _____ shyly out into the bustling world; when the fruit-tree _____, pink and white, like village maidens in their Sunday frocks, _____ each whitewashed cottage in a cloud of fragile splendor; and the cuckoo's note upon the breeze is _____ through the woods! And summer, with its deep dark green and drowsy hum — when the rain-drops _____ solemn secrets to the listening leaves and the twilight _____ in the lanes! And autumn!

参考译文

事关天气

杰罗姆·凯·杰罗姆

大自然在她自己的家园——乡村里时,她的一切情态都是美妙的。冬天雪花纷飞,充满静谧柔和的神秘情调。皑皑白雪,装点着田野和森林,宛若童话中的婚礼场面,还有什么比这更美! 我们散步时步履蹒跚,冻土在脚下叮咚作响,空气凛冽稀薄,使我们的血管感到刺痛。远处牧羊犬的叫声和孩子们的笑声清晰可闻,光秃秃的小山上空传来教堂的钟声。此时在野外散步是何等惬意啊! 滑冰! 冰刀的钢翼在飞奔,掠过倾斜的冰面,我们飞驰着,耳畔响起回旋的音乐。啊! 春天是多么秀丽——

那是 18 岁的大自然啊!

初度绽露的嫩叶充满生机,那么新鲜葱翠,那么纯净明亮,如同年轻的生命怯生生地赶到这喧嚣的世界上。果树上开满粉色和白色的花,宛若乡村少女的节日盛装。座座农舍刷得雪白,掩蔽在果林绚丽娇嫩的花园后面。微风吹过果林,送来杜鹃的啼啭。夏天,蓊郁的暗绿,令人昏昏欲睡的蜂音虫鸣。点点雨滴,向谛听的叶片低语着庄严的秘密,浓阴在小巷里流连。还有秋天!啊,多么哀婉而晴朗的秋日!瑰丽的金光渐渐褪去,树林的秋色渐渐变浓——血红的夕照,缥缈的暮霭,收割者忙碌的低语,硕果累累的果园,还有拾穗人的呼唤,以及赞美上苍的丰收庆典!

86. God's Jobs

By Dan Sutton, Christ Church

Danny Sutton, eight years old, wrote this for his third-grade Sunday school teacher, who asked her students to explain God.

One of God's main jobs is making people. He makes these to put in the place of the ones who die so there will be enough people to take care of the things here on earth. He doesn't make grownups, he just makes babies. I think because they are smaller and easier to make. That way he doesn't have to take up his *valuable* time teaching them to walk and talk. He can just leave that up to the mothers and fathers. I think it works out pretty good.

God's second most important job is listening to *prayers*. An *awful* lot of this goes on, *'cause* some people, like *preachers* and things, pray other times besides bedtimes, and Grandpa and Grandma pray every time they eat, except for *snacks*. God doesn't have time to listen to the radio or watch TV *on account of* this. 'Cause God hears everything, there must be a terrible lot of noise in his ears unless he has thought of a way to turn it down.

God sees and hears everything and is everywhere, which keeps him pretty busy. So you shouldn't go wasting his time asking for things that aren't important, or go over parents' heads and ask for something they said you couldn't have. It doesn't work anyway.

语言注释

1. valuable / ˈvæljʊəbl / *adj*. 珍贵的,宝贵的
2. prayer / preɪə / *n*. 祷告
3. awful / ˈɔːfʊl / *adj*. 可怕的
4. 'cause = because
5. preacher / priːtʃə / *n*. 布道者
6. snack / snæk / *n*. 点心
7. on account of 由于

背景介绍

作 者是美国马里兰州一个教堂里的工作人员。所以对教堂里发生的一切非常熟悉。而且能以特别的角度看待这些问题。

篇目欣赏

本 文选自《心灵鸡汤》。文章构思新颖。从一个小孩的眼中描述上帝的工作，非常有意思。文章语言浅显易懂，但语言地道，读后会让人有会心的微笑。

背诵准备

本文结构清晰，语言明快。像 One of God's main jobs is making people. 只要记住一些基本结构和要点词汇，一定会很快背出这篇短文。

One of God's main jobs is _____ people. He make these to put in the _____ of the ones who die so there will be enough people to take care of the things here on earth. He doesn't make _____, he just makes babies. I think because they are smaller and _____ to make. That way he doesn't have to take up his valuable time _____ them to walk and talk. He can just leave that up to the mothers and fathers. I think it _____ out pretty good.

God's _____ most important job is listening to prayers. An _____ lot of this goes on, 'cause some people, like preachers and things, pray other times _____ bedtimes, and Grandpa and Grandma pray every time they eat, except for _____. God doesn't have time to listen to the radio or watch TV _____ account of this. 'Cause God hears everything, there must be a terrible lot of noise in his ears _____ he has thought of a way to turn it down.

God sees and hears everything and is everywhere, which keeps him _____ busy. So you shouldn't go _____ his time asking for things that aren't important, or go over parents' heads and ask for something they said you couldn't have. It doesn't work _____.

参考译文

上帝的工作

丹尼·桑顿

丹尼·桑顿,八岁,写了这篇文章作为作业,交给星期天学校的老师。老师叫他们解释上帝。

上帝主要的工作之一是造人。他制造这些人去填补那些死去的人的位置,使得有足够的人照料地球。他不制造成人,只制造婴儿。我想主要是因为婴儿小一点,容易制造。那样的话,他不需要花宝贵的时间去教他们走路和说话。他把那个工作留给他们的爸爸和妈妈。我认为那样也不错。

上帝的第二项工作是倾听祈祷。这种事很多。因为有些人,像布道者,除了睡前,其他时候也祈祷,爷爷和奶奶每次吃饭前,除了吃点心之前,都祈祷。上帝为此没有时间听收音机或看电视。因为上帝听见了每一件事,他耳朵里肯定有很多噪音,除非他可以想出办法把声音关小一点。

上帝看见和听见了每一件事,而且无所不在,使得他非常忙碌。所以你不要为一些无关紧要的事去浪费他的时间,或者猜测父母的心思去要求父母说过不能要的东西。无论如何都不行的。

87. The Sounding of the Call

By Jack London

To Buck it was boundless delight, this hunting, fishing, and *indefinite* wandering through strange places. For weeks at a time they would hold on *steadily*, day after day; and for weeks upon end they would camp, here and there, the dogs *loafing* and the men burning holes through frozen *muck* and *gravel* and washing countless pans of dirt by the heat of fire. Sometimes they went hungry, sometimes they feasted *riotously*, all according to the *abundance* of game and the fortune of hunting. Summer arrived, and dogs and men, packed on their backs, rafted across blue mountain lakes, and *descended* or *ascended* unknown rivers in slender boats whipsawed from the standing forest.

Two months came and went, and back and forth they twisted through the uncharted vastness, where no men were and yet where men had been if the Lost Cabin were true. They went across *divides* in summer *blizzards*, *shivered* under the midnight sun on naked mountains between the timer line and the *eternal* snows, dropped into summer valleys amid swarming *gnats* and flies, and in the shadows of *glaciers* picked strawberries and flowers as ripe and fair as any the Southland could boast. In the fall of the year they *penetrated* a weird lake country, sad and silent, where wild-fowl had been, but where then there was no life nor sign of life — only the blowing of chill winds, the forming of ice in sheltered places, and the *melancholy* rippling of waves on lonely beaches.

语言注释

1. indefinite / ɪnˈdefənɪt / *adj*. 不确定的,不明确的
2. steadily / ˈstedɪlɪ / *adv*. 均匀规律地,稳定地
3. loaf / ləʊf / *v*. 虚度光阴
4. muck / mʌk / *n*. 污秽,脏物
5. gravel / ˈɡrævl / *n*. 砾石
6. riotously / ˈraɪtəslɪ / *adv*. 极端地

7. abundance / ə'bʌndəns / *n.* 丰富,充裕

8. descend / dɪ'send / *v.* 下来,下去,下降

9. ascend / ə'send / *v.* 上升,升高

10. divide / dɪ'vaɪd / *n.* 分水岭,分水线

11. blizzard / 'blɪzəd / *n.* 暴风雪

12. shiver / 'ʃɪvə / *v.* 颤抖(尤指因寒冷或恐惧)

13. eternal / ɪ'tɜːnəl / *adj.* 永久的,永恒的

14. gnat / næt / *n.* 蚋,蠓,蚊

15. glacier / 'gleɪʃɪə / *n.* 冰川,冰河

16. penetrate / 'penətreɪt / *v.* 进入或穿过某物

17. melancholy / 'melənkəlɪ / *adj.* 悲哀的,沮丧的

背景介绍

杰克·伦敦(Jack London)于 1876 年出生于旧金山。由于家庭生活艰难,他十岁时就上街卖报,先后在罐头厂、麻纺厂、发电厂做工。1896年,在克朗代克发现了金矿,他加入了淘金的队伍。从此,杰克·伦敦开始了创作生涯。杰克·伦敦是 19、20 世纪之交美国最富有批判精神的现实主义作家。在文学史上素有"美国高尔基"之称。

篇目欣赏

《野性的呼唤》是杰克·伦敦最为出名的动物小说之一。作品的主题是描写了大狗巴克与群狗的斗争,他野性未驯,在狼群的呼唤下切断了和人类的联系,逃入了原始森林,变成了狼。作品以犬作为故事的主角,从狗的角度来描写观察人类社会的诸种表现,目的在于通过动物世界中"人性"的沦丧和野性的复发以及他们之间的勾心斗角和残酷争夺来揭示当时美国社会的现实本质。本文节选的是小说的最后一章中的两段。文中对巴克当时生存状态的描写非常到位,而文字也如散文般非常优美。

背诵准备

这节选的两段描写文字中有一些平行结构的运用使文章工整优美。例如：day after day，here and there。如果能记住这些结构，一定能够很快背诵这一段。(试背第二段)

Two months _____ and _____, and _____ and _____ they twisted _____ the uncharted vastness, where no men _____ and yet where men _____ if the Lost Cabin were true. They went _____ divides in summer blizzards, _____ under the midnight sun on naked mountains _____ the timer line and the eternal snows, _____ into summer valleys amid swarming gnats and _____, and in the shadows of glaciers _____ strawberries and flowers as ripe and fair as any the Southland could _____. In the fall of the year they _____ a weird lake country, sad and _____, where wild-fowl had been, but where then there was no life _____ sign of life — only the _____ of chill winds, the _____ of ice in sheltered places, and the melancholy _____ of waves on lonely beaches.

参考译文

呼唤的声音

杰克·伦敦

对于巴克而言，这样打猎，捕鱼，在奇境异乡无拘无束地游荡真是其乐无穷。有时一连几周，他们会一天接着一天地走下去；有时随处宿营，逗留好几个星期。这时，那群狗闲荡着，而人们就用火烤化冰冻的腐殖层和沙砾，然后淘洗数不清的一盘盘泥沙。他们有时忍饥挨饿，有时则尽情吃喝，一切都取决于打猎的运气好环和野味的多寡。夏天来了，狗和人都把行李驮在背上，乘着木筏渡过群山间一片片蓝色的湖泊，乘着用森林里锯下的大木头做成的小船，在不知名的河流里逆流而上或顺流而下。

两个月过去了，他们在地图上都不曾标示的无名荒山野岭间迂回曲折地来回往返，那里渺无人烟。如果传说中地点不明的金矿确有其事的话,就曾经有人早已到过。他们冒着夏天的暴风雪翻过了一座座分水岭;在森林和终年积雪分界的地区,在午夜的阳光照射下瑟瑟发抖;也曾不小心跌入蚊蝇成群的山谷;在冰河的隐藏处摘采丝毫也不逊于南国成熟的草莓和美丽的花朵。那年秋天,他们进入了一片神秘怪异而令人毛骨悚然的湖沼地带。这里静谧而悲凉,曾是野兽栖息的场所,可眼下没有一丁点生命或生命的迹象,有的只是寒风呼啸,隐蔽处冻结的冰雪,寂寥的河岸上凄凉的波涛声。

88. Smell of Time

By Ray Bradbury

It was a long road going into darkness and hills and he held to the wheel, now and again reaching into his lunch *bucket* and taking out a piece of candy. He had been driving steadily for an hour, with no other car on the road, no light, just the road going under, the *hum*, the roar, and Mars out there, so quiet. Mars was always quiet, but quieter tonight than any other. The deserts and empty seas swung by him, and the mountains against the stars.

There was a smell of time in the air tonight. He smiled and turned the *fancy* in his mind. There was a thought. What did time smell like? Like dust and clocks and people. And if you wondered what Time sounded like? It sounded like water running in a dark cave and voices crying and dirt dropping down upon hollow box lids, and rain. And going further, what did Time look like? Time looked like snow dropping silently into a black room or it looked like a silent film in an ancient theater, one hundred billion faces falling like those New Year balloons down and down into nothing. That was how Time smelled and looked and sounded. And tonight — Tomas shoved a hand into the wind outside the truck — tonight you could almost touch the time.

He drove the truck between hills of Time. His neck *prickled* and he sat up, watching ahead.

语言注释

1. bucket / ˈbʌkɪt / *n*. 小桶
2. hum / hʌm / *n*. 嗡嗡声
3. fancy / ˈfænsɪ / *n*. 遐想
4. prickle / ˈprɪkl / *v*. 刺痛

背景介绍

美国作家雷·布拉德伯里(Ray Bradbury)于 1920 年 8 月 22 日出生于伊利诺伊州。小时一直生活在大家庭中,为他以后的创作提供了一定的素材。他在 1931 年开始写作,1934 年全家搬到洛杉矶。布拉德伯里在洛杉矶读高中的时候,参加了戏剧俱乐部,期望成为一名演员。然而他的两个老师发现了他的天才,鼓励他成为一名作家。后来他慢慢向这方面发展。他的第一篇短篇故事在 1938 年发表在《想象》杂志上。在 1950 年写了科幻小说《火星人》获得成功。1953 年发表了最著名的作品《华氏 451》。他的很多作品被收入《美国最佳短篇故事选》,也曾获得很多奖项。他的一些作品曾被改编成电视剧和广播剧。他还为很多组织做顾问及写稿。2002 年 4 月 1 日,在"一本书,一个城市"的读书活动中,他在世界著名的好莱坞星光大道上作为第 2193 颗星永载史册。

篇目欣赏

本篇节选自美国作家雷·布拉德伯里(Ray Bradbury)的《二零零二年八月:邂逅》(August 2002: Night Meeting)。故事从一个老人和一个年轻的旅行者——汤姆斯·戈麦兹的对话开始。老人说他喜欢来火星是因为他喜欢新奇的东西,每天生活中的小事都使他兴奋不已,他就像回到了童年。后来汤姆斯·戈麦兹碰到了火星人。每个人所看到的是不同的东西。汤姆斯·戈麦兹所看到的是城市的废墟,而火星人看到的是欣欣向荣的城市。他们都不知道自己能否在时光隧道中再遇到对方。雷·布拉德伯里想暗示的是所有的文明都是短暂的。本文阐述了一种对未知的想象。文章空灵、奇异,给我们一种异样的感觉。

背诵准备

这篇《二零零二年八月:邂逅》中运用了很多不同动词-ing 形式,使得文章能描绘一种动作在时间中的延续。如果能记住不同的动词,一定能够很快背诵这篇文章。

There was a smell of time in the air tonight. He smiled and turned the _____ in his mind. There was a thought. What did time _____ like? Like dust and clocks and people. And if you wondered what Time _____ like? It sounded like water _____ in a dark cave and voices _____ and dirt _____ down upon hollow box lids, and rain. And going further, what did Time _____ like? Time looked like snow _____ silently into a black room or it looked like a silent film in an ancient theater, one hundred billion faces _____ like those New Year balloons down and down into nothing. That was how Time smelled and looked and sounded. And tonight — Tomas _____ a hand into the wind outside the truck — tonight you could almost _____ the time.

He drove the truck between hills of Time. His neck prickled and he sat up, _____ ahead.

参考译文

<h1 style="text-align:center">时间的味道</h1>

雷·布拉德伯里

此去路漫漫,伸向黑暗,深入群山。他掌握着方向盘,不时伸手从小提桶里拿糖果吃。沉着向前,开了一小时,不见别的车辆,不见灯光,只见古道从车下滑过。发动机如吟如啸。汽车外,火星一片静寂。火星一直这么安静,不过今夜比往常更静。荒漠沧海,沧海荒漠,悠悠然飘过他身旁。还有那衬着星空的群山。

今夜仿佛闻到时间的气味。他微微一笑,顿生遐想。有意思。时间是什么气味?如尘埃如时钟,如众人。时间的声音呢?如黑洞流泉,如百姓呼号,如尘去洒在空箱上,如降雨。再有时间的形象呢?如雪片悄悄掉进暗室;如古老的电影院中无声影片上亿万人的面孔像新年的气球纷纷坠落,落呀,落呀,落入虚无。这就是时间的气味、声音和形象。而今夜——汤姆斯伸手探探车外的风——今夜似乎摸得着时间。

他驾车穿过时间的万重山岭。忽然脖子感到刺痛,他警觉起来,注视前方。

89. On Pleasure

By Epicurus

Since pleasure is the first good and natural to us, for this very reason we do not choose every pleasure, but sometimes we pass over many pleasures, when greater discomfort *accrues* to us as the result of them: and similarly we think many pains better than pleasures, since a greater pleasure comes to us when we have *endured* pains for a long time. Every pleasure then because of its natural *kinship* to us is good, yet not every pleasure is to be chosen; even as every pain also is an evil, yet not all are always of a nature to be avoided. Yet by a scale of comparison and by the consideration of advantages and disadvantages we must form our judgment on all these matters. For the good on certain occasions we treat as bad, and *conversely* the bad as good.

We must consider that of desires some are natural, others vain, and of the natural some are necessary and others merely natural; and of the necessary some are necessary for happiness, others for the repose of the body, and others for very life ...

Insofar as you are in difficulties, it is because you forget nature; for you create for yourself unlimited fears and desires. It is better for you to be free of fear lying upon a *pallet*, than to have a golden couch and a rich table and be full of trouble.

语言注释

1. accrue / əˈkruː / v. 自然增加,产生
2. endure / ɪnˈdjʊə / v. 忍耐
3. kinship / ˈkɪnʃɪp / n. 血族关系
4. conversely / kənˈvɜːslɪ / adv. 相反地
5. insofar / ɪnsəʊˈfɑː / adv. 在⋯⋯的范围
6. pallet / ˈpælɪt / n. 草床,小床

背景介绍

伊壁鸠鲁(Epicurus,BC 342 – BC 270)是古希腊著名哲学家,创立了伊壁鸠鲁学派。伊壁鸠鲁生于萨摩斯,早年学习柏拉图和德谟克利特学说。18 岁时来到雅典服兵役,之后在外地学习和教学。伊壁鸠鲁著述传说有三百余卷,但只有部分残篇流传下来。伊壁鸠鲁认为,最大的善来自快乐,没有快乐,就不可能有善。快乐包括肉体上的快乐,也包括精神上的快乐。他的哲学最显著的与众不同之处就是强调感官的快乐:"快乐是幸福生活的起点和目标"。

篇目欣赏

本文节选自伊壁鸠鲁的《论快乐》。伊壁鸠鲁主张人生的目的是避免痛苦,寻求快乐或幸福。快乐论更是提出快乐成为人生的最高幸福,追求快乐是人生的目的与道德的标准。他认为,快乐乃至高的善,趋乐避苦是人的本性,但重要的是快乐的持久度而不是强度,是心灵无忧虑,身体无痛苦,而不是感官的不断刺激。快乐的生活人人可以享受,为此人们必须清除不必要的欲望,以达到一种理想中的快乐。伊氏主要著作有《论自然》、《准则学》、《论目的》等,本文选自他的书信集。

背诵准备

这篇《论快乐》中运用一些对等的结构,如果能记住这些不同的结构,一定能够很快背诵这篇文章。

Since pleasure is the first good and _____ to us, for this very reason we do _____ choose every pleasure, _____ sometimes we pass over many pleasures, when greater discomfort _____ to us as the result of them: and _____ we think many pains better than pleasures, since a greater _____ comes to us when we have endured _____ for a long time. Every pleasure then because of its natural _____ to us is good, yet not every pleasure is to be chosen; even as every pain also is an _____, yet not all are always of a nature to be avoided. Yet by a scale of _____ and by the consideration of _____ and _____ we must form our judgment on all these _____. For the good on certain occasions we treat as bad, and _____ the bad as good.

参考译文

论快乐

伊壁鸠鲁

快乐于我们乃至善且自然之追求,正因为此,我们并不选择每一种快乐,而是偶尔放弃多种快乐,因为这些快乐会带来更大的不安;同样,我们认为许多痛苦优于快乐,因为当我们长期忍受痛苦之后,更大的快乐便随之而来。就其与我们之自然联系而言,每一种快乐都是善的,然而并非每一种快乐都是可取的;同理,虽然每一种痛苦都是恶的,但并非每一种痛苦从本质上都应当加以躲避。不过,我们必须依据某种鉴别的尺度,通过权衡利弊来形成对一切事物的判断。因此我们有时将好事视为坏事,反之则将坏事视为好事。

必须看到,有些欲望是自然的,而另一些欲望则是无益的;在自然的欲望之中,有些是必需的,而另一些纯属自然而已;在必需的欲望之中,有些是幸福之所需,有些是身体安康之所需,而另一些则旨在维持生计……

你之所以困难重重,乃因为忘却天性;是你为自己设置了无穷的恐惧与欲望。与其锦衣玉食却忧心忡忡,不如粗茶淡饭却无忧无虑。

90. January Wind

By Hal Borland

The January wind has a hundred voices. It can scream, it can bellow, it can whisper, and it can sing a *lullaby*. It can roar through the leafless oaks and shout down the hillside, and it can murmur in the white pines rooted among the granite *ledges* where *lichen* makes strange *hieroglyphics*. It can whistle down a chimney and set the *hearth*-flames to dancing. On a sunny day it can pause in a sheltered spot and breathe a promise of spring and violets. In the cold of a lonely night it can rattle the *sash* and stay there muttering of ice and snow banks and deep-frozen pond.

Sometimes the January wind seems to come from the farthest star in the outer darkness, so remote and so impersonal is its voice. That is the wind of a January dawn, in the half-light that trembles between day and night. It is a wind that merely quivers the trees, its force sensed but not seen, a force that might almost hold back the day if it were so directed. Then the east brightens, and the wind relaxes — the stars, its source, grown dim.

And sometimes the January wind is so intimate that you know it came only from the next hill, a little wind that plays with leaves and *puffs* at chimney smoke and whistles like a little boy with *puckered* lips. It makes the little cedar trees quiver, as with delight. It shadow-boxes with the weather-*vane*. It *tweaks* an ear, and whispers laughing words about *crocuses* and daffodils, and nips the nose and dances off.

But you never know, until you hear its voice, which wind is here today. Or, more important, which will be here tomorrow.

语言注释

1. lullaby / ˈlʌləbaɪ / *n.* 催眠曲,摇篮曲
2. ledge / ledʒ / *n.* 暗礁,矿层
3. lichen / ˈlaɪkɪŋ / *n.* (植)青苔,地衣
4. hieroglyphic / ˌhaɪərəˈglɪfɪks / *n.* 象形文字

5. hearth / hɑ:θ / *n*. 炉边,炭盘

6. sash / sæʃ / *n*. 窗框

7. puff / pʌf / *v*. 喷出,向……吹气

8. pucker / ˈpʌkə / *v*. 折叠

9. vane / veɪn / *n*. 风向标,风信旗

10. tweak / twi:k / *v*. 拧

11. crocus / ˈkrəʊkəs / *n*. 番红花

背景介绍

汉尔·波兰(Hal Borland)于 1900 年 5 月 14 日出生在内布拉斯加的大草原上。汉尔·波兰曾先后在科罗拉多大学和哥伦比亚大学学习,然后成了一名记者,曾担任《纽约时报》周末版户外专栏作家。他在写作中渗透着个人在自然中的体验以及美国农村的生活方式。他的 *High , Wide and Lonesome* 在 1957 年被授予最佳散文奖;他的 *When the Legends Die* 在 1972 年被译成九国文字;他的 *An American Year* 在 1968 年曾因对自然出色描写而获奖章。

篇目欣赏

这篇《一月的风》文字优美,描写精到。让我们似乎感到一月的风在我们窗外呼啸。作者运用了比喻,拟人等多种手法,用想象的描绘性语言来描写一月的风。作者在文中用了各种各样的动词从不同角度来描写风的情状,令人叫绝。

背诵准备

这篇《一月的风》中运用了很多不同的动词,使得文章灵动精致。如果能记住不同的

动词,一定能够很快背诵这篇文章。

The January wind has a hundred _____. It can scream, it can _____, it can _____, and it can _____ a lullaby. It can _____ through the leafless oaks and _____ down the hillside, and it can _____ in the white pines rooted among the granite ledges where lichen makes strange hieroglyphics. It can _____ down a chimney and _____ the hearth-flames to dancing. On a sunny day it can _____ in a sheltered spot and _____ a promise of spring and violets. In the cold of a lonely night it can _____ the sash and stay there muttering of ice and snow banks and deep-frozen pond.

Sometimes the January wind _____ to come from the farthest star in the outer darkness, so _____ and so impersonal is its voice. That is the wind of a January dawn, in the half-light that _____ between day and night. It is a wind that merely _____ the trees, its force sensed but not seen, a force that might almost _____ back the day if it were so directed. Then the east _____, and the wind relaxes — the stars, its source, grown dim.

参考译文

一月的风

汉尔·波兰

　　一月的风有百种声音。它时而尖声呼叫,时而大声咆哮,时而柔声细语,时而哼起轻轻的摇篮曲;它时而怒吼着冲过光秃的橡树,呐喊着冲下山谷,时而登上爬满苔藓的悬崖峭壁,在松林间喃喃自语;它时而吹着口哨沿烟囱而下,让炉膛的火苗欢蹦乱跳。在阳光明媚的日子,它会在屋檐下驻足,喃喃低语:春天的脚步近了,紫罗兰就要盛开了;在寂寞的寒夜,它会来到窗沿,敲开窗户,轻声提醒人们:明天会有冰冻,道旁会有雪堆,池塘会冻结。

　　有时,一月的风似乎源自星际间最遥远的星球,其声音是如此缥缈、淡漠! 那是一月灰暗的黎明时的风,在昼夜交替中颤抖。树上的枝丫只是微微颤动,其风势只可感知却无法察觉。若是得到命令,它或许会把白天阻截回去。这时,东方泛白,风声渐歇,星星——风的源头——开始变得暗淡了。

有时,一月的风又是如此亲密,你知道它就从附近那座山过来。它像一个嘟起双唇的淘气的小男孩,时而与树叶嬉戏,时而吹动烟囱喷出的缕缕轻烟,时而吹起阵阵口哨。它时而让小雪松欢快地抖动,时而与风向标踢几脚拳。它时而拧拧你的耳朵,轻轻告诉你有关番红花、水仙花的事,然后捏捏你的鼻子,蹦蹦跳跳走开了。

然而,如果没有听到风的声音,你绝不知道这里今天吹的是什么风,或者,尤其重要的是,明天吹的又是什么风。

$91.$ On Doors

By C. D. Morley

The opening and closing of doors are the most significant actions of man's life. What a mystery lies in doors!

No man knows what awaits him when he opens a door. Even the most familiar room, where the clock ticks and the hearth glows red at dusk, may harbor surprise. The *plumber* may actually have called (while you were out) and fixed that leaking *faucet*. The cook may have had a *fit* of the *vapors* and demanded her passports. The wise man opens his front door with humility and a spirit of acceptance.

There are many kinds of doors. Revolving doors for hotels, shops, and public buildings that are typical of the brisk, *bustling* ways of modern life. Can you imagine John Milton or William Penn skipping through a revolving door? Then there are the curious little slanted doors that still swing outside *denatured* bar-rooms and extend only from shoulder to knee. There are trap doors, sliding doors, double doors, stage doors, prison doors, glass doors. But the symbol and mystery of a door resides in its quality of concealment. A glass door is not a door at all, but a window. The meaning of a door is to hide what lies inside; to keep the heart in suspense.

Also, there are many ways of opening doors. There is a cheery push of an elbow with which the waiter shoves open the kitchen door when he bears in your tray of supper. There is the suspicious and *tentative* withdrawal of a door before the unhappy book agent or peddler. There is the genteel and carefully modulated recession with which footmen swing wide the oaken barriers of the great. There is the sympathetic and awful silence of the dentist's maid who opens the door into the operating room, and, without speaking, implies that the doctor is ready for you. There is the brisk *cataclysmic* opening of a door when the nurses come in, very early in the morning — "It's a boy!"

语言注释

1. plumber / ˈplʌmə / n. 水管工
2. faucet / ˈfɔːsɪt / n. 水龙头
3. fit / fɪt / n. (感情等的)突发
4. vapors / ˈveɪpəz / n. (古)郁气,忧郁病
5. bustling / ˈbʌslɪŋ / adj. 繁忙的
6. denature / ˈdɪneɪtʃə / v. 使失去自然属性
7. tentative / ˈtentətɪv / adj. 试探的
8. cataclysmic / ˌkætəˈklɪzmɪk / adj. 剧变的,剧烈的

背景介绍

C. D. 莫利(Christopher Darlington Morley)是美国作家和编辑。于1890 年生于宾夕法尼亚州的哈佛。他是《星期六文学评论》的创始人和编辑。他的小说《基迪·福伊尔》(1939)是一本畅销书,是一本关于描写一个爱尔兰美国女孩的现实主义小说。根据小说拍成的电影还获得奥斯卡奖。C. D. 莫利是一个多产的小说家、散文家和诗人。

篇目欣赏

本文节选自 C. D. 莫利的散文《论门》。他的这篇散文描写细腻,文笔流畅,文字高雅。以非常独特的角度阐述了他对门的思索。《论门》从门上洞察人生百态,并借此揭示人生哲理。

背诵准备

这篇《论门》中运用了一些排比结构,使得文章绘态淋漓尽致。如果能记住这些结构,一定能够很快背诵这篇文章。

The _____ and _____ of doors are the most significant actions of man's life. What a mystery lies in doors!

No man knows what _____ him when he opens a door. Even the most _____ room, where the clock ticks and the hearth glows red at dusk, may _____ _____. The plumber may actually have called (while you were out) and fixed that leaking _____. The cook may have had a fit of the vapors and demanded her passports. The wise man opens his front door with _____ and a spirit of acceptance.

There are many kinds of doors. _____ doors for hotels, shops, and public buildings that are typical of the brisk, bustling ways of modern life. Can you imagine John Milton or William Penn skipping through a revolving door? Then there are the curious little _____ doors that still swing outside denatured bar-rooms and extend only from shoulder to knee. There are _____ doors, sliding doors, _____ doors, stage doors, _____ doors, glass doors. But the symbol and mystery of a door resides in its quality of concealment. A glass door is not a door at all, but a window. The meaning of a door is to _____ what lies inside; to keep the heart in suspense.

参考译文

论　门

C.D. 莫利

开门和关门是人生中最有意思的行动,门内是怎样的神秘莫测啊!

没有人知道打开门后,等待他的是什么。即使是最熟悉的房间,那里钟在滴答作响,壁炉在暮色里闪着红光,也可能会藏着叫人吃惊的事情。水管工可能真的来过(在你出门的时候),修好了滴水的水龙头。厨师可能忧郁症发作,要求同意她离开。聪明的人总是带着谦恭和接受的态度打开前门。

门有许多种类。旅馆,商店和公共大楼的旋转门。这些门代表着典型的活泼而忙碌的现代生活方式。你能想象约翰·弥尔顿或威廉·佩恩匆匆忙忙地走过一扇旋转门吗?还有那开起来乒乓响的古怪的小门,这种门只有从膝盖到肩那么高,仍在老旧的酒吧外面摆动。还有活板门,拉门,双折门,舞台门,监狱门,玻璃门等。不过一扇门的标志和神秘在于它的隐秘性。玻璃门根本算不上门,仅是一扇窗户而已。门的意义就在于把里面的东西隐藏起来,使你的心悬虑不安。

同样,开门也有许多种方式:有一种是用胳膊肘轻快地一推,侍者端着你的晚餐盘,打开厨房门的时候总这样。有在愁苦的书籍代理商或小贩面前总是颇有戒心地和犹犹豫豫地一点点地拉开后退的门。有随着有礼貌又小心的逐渐退出的男仆而敞开的大人物的栎木门。还有牙医女助手富于同情而悄然无声地打开的手术室的门,她一声不吭,暗示医生已经在等你了。另有一种,在清晨很早的时候,护士欢快而突然地打开门进来,嘴里喊着:"是个男孩!"

92. Flowery Tuscany (excerpt)

By D. H. Lawrence

In the morning, the sun shines strong on the horizontal green cloud-puffs of the pines, the sky is clear and full of life, the water runs hastily, still browned by the last juice of crushed olives. And there the earth's bowl of crocuses is amazing. You cannot believe that the flowers are really still. They are open with such delight, and their pistilthrust is so red-orange, and they are so many, all reaching out wide and marvelous, that it suggests a perfect ecstasy of *radiant*, thronging movement, lit-up violet and orange, and surging in some invisible rhythm of concerted, delightful movement. You cannot believe they do not move, and make some sort of *crystalline* sound of delight. If you sit still and watch, you begin to move with them. Like moving with the stars, and you feel the sound of their radiance. All the little cells of the flowers must be leaping with flowery life and *utterance*.

And now that it is March, there is a rush of flowers. Down by the other stream, which runs sideways to the sun, and tangles the *brier* and *bramble*, down where the *hellebore* has stood so wan and dignified all winter, there are now white tufts of *primroses*, suddenly come. Among the tangle and near the water-lip, tufts and bunches of primroses, in abundance. Yet they look more wan, more *pallid*, more flimsy than English primroses. They lack some of the full wonder of the northern flowers. One tends to overlook them, to turn to the great, solemn-faced purple violets that rear up from the bank, and above all, to the wonderful little towers of the grape-*hyacinth*.

This is the time, in March, when the sloe is white and misty in the hedge-tangle by the stream, and on the slope of the land the peach tree stands pink and alone. The almond blossom, silvery pink, is passing, but the peach, deep-toned, bluey, not at all *ethereal*, this reveals itself like flesh, and the trees are like isolated individuals, the peach and the apricot.

It is so conspicuous and so individual, that pink among the coming green of spring, because the first flowers that emerge from winter seem always white or yellow or purple. Now the celandines are out, and along the edges of the pond, the big, sturdy, black-purple anemones, with black hearts.

语言注释

1. radiant / ˈreɪdɪənt / *adj*. 光彩的
2. crystalline / ˈkrɪstəlaɪn / *adj*. 水晶般的，清晰透明的
3. utterance / ˈʌtərəns / *n*. 表达
4. brier / ˈbraɪə / *n*. 多刺的木质茎植物
5. bramble / ˈbræmbl / *n*. 荆棘
6. hellebore / ˈheləbɔː / *n*. 藜芦，菟葵
7. primrose / ˈprɪmrəuz / *n*. 樱草花
8. pallid / ˈpælɪd / *adj*. 苍白的
9. hyacinth / ˈhaɪəsɪns / *n*. 风信子
10. ethereal / iːˈθɪərɪəl / *adj*. 轻柔的

背景介绍

D. H. 劳伦斯（David Herbert Lawrence）是英国小说家、诗人和散文家，英国本世纪最重要也是最具有争议的小说家之一。于 1885 年生于诺丁汉郡的伊斯特伍德村。父亲是煤矿工人，母亲当过小学教师。劳伦斯少年时代在诺丁汉矿区上学，后到诺丁汉大学学院学过植物学和法律。他的主要作品有《白孔雀》、《儿子与情人》、《虹》和《查泰莱夫人的情人》等。他敢于打破传统方式，以其独特的风格揭示人性中的本能力量。劳伦斯文笔生动，充满诗意，描写细腻、优美。

篇目欣赏

本文描绘了阿尔卑斯山南麓在春末三月时的风光。劳伦斯描写了各种花在太阳光下绽开的盛景。它们的千姿百态和瑰丽的色彩使劳伦斯觉得它们在动,在发出声音。劳伦斯细腻优美的描写让我们觉得大自然是如此的美丽。寒暑易节,花开花落,自然界的变化是永恒的,又是如此妙不可言。劳伦斯以景寓情,表达了他对生活的乐观态度。

背诵准备

劳伦斯是个非常善于描写的作家。在不同的地方,他用了不同的描写手法。有描写太阳、天空、水的,有描写花的情状的,有描写花的各种颜色的。有各种动词和介词的穿插使用,有排比的运用。只要找到规律,一定能够很快背诵这篇文章的。

In the morning, the _____ shines strong on the horizontal green cloud-puffs of the pines, the _____ is clear and full of life, the _____ runs hastily, still browned by the last juice of crushed olives. And there the earth's bowl of crocuses is amazing. You cannot believe that the flowers are really still. They are open with such _____, and their pistilthrust is so _____, and they are so _____, all reaching out wide and marvelous, that it suggests a perfect ecstasy of radiant, thronging _____, lit-up violet and orange, and surging in some invisible rhythm of concerted, delightful movement. You cannot believe they do not move, and make some sort of crystalline sound of delight. If you _____ still and _____, you begin to move with them. Like moving with the stars, and you feel the sound of their radiance. All the little cells of the flowers must be leaping with flowery life and utterance.

And now that it is March, there is a rush of flowers. Down _____ the other stream, which runs sideways to the sun, and tangles the brier and bramble, down _____ the hellebore has stood so wan and dignified all winter, there are now white tufts of primroses, suddenly come. _____ the tangle and _____ the water-lip, tufts and bunches of primroses, in abundance. Yet they look more

_____ , more _____ , more _____ than English primroses. They lack some of the full wonder of the northern flowers. One tends to overlook them, to turn to the great, solemn-faced purple violets that rear up from the bank, and above all, to the wonderful little towers of the grape-hyacinth.

参考译文

如花的托斯卡纳(节选)

D. H. 劳伦斯

　　清晨,强烈的阳光照射在地平线上松树喷出的团团绿雾上,晴朗的天空充满了生命的气息,最后压榨出的橄榄汁把匆匆的流水变成了棕色。满地的番红花让人感到惊奇,你简直不能相信这些花是立在原地静止的,它们愉快地绽放,花蕊是橙红色的,花儿是这样异乎寻常的多,到处都是,团团锦簇,让人心醉神迷:花儿一齐在舞动,那明亮起来的紫和橙的色调,随着看不见的和谐节奏在快乐地摇动。你一定会觉得它们在动,而且发出了一些愉快的,透明般的声音。如果你坐着不动,看着看着,你就会开始随着它们摆动,它们就像星星一样,你会感受到它们那明快而响亮的声音。花的每一个细胞都在带着花一样的生命和它们的思想在跳跃。

　　已经是三月了,这是一个花儿竞相开放的时节。在其他一些朝太阳方向奔跑的溪流边,荆棘灌木缠在一起,在冬日里菟葵曾无力但却高傲伫立的地方,突然出现了一丛丛白色的樱草花。在这些纠缠中和溪水拐弯处,丛丛束束的樱草花满目都是。不过,它们是那样的苍白无力,比英格兰樱草花还单薄,不像北面的花儿那样充满神奇色彩。人们常常会忽视它,而将目光转向那长在河岸边庄重的美丽紫罗兰,更会去看那些深紫色的风信子小花格。

　　三月正是时候,溪边灌木乱丛中白色的野李花朦朦胧胧的,健壮的桃树独自站立在山坡,开着粉红色的花。银粉色的杏花已渐渐离去,桃树披着深色调的蓝色,一点也不轻柔,却是有血有肉的,而桃树与杏树看起来就像是孤立的。

　　粉色在春天萌发的绿色中,很显眼,独特,因为第一批从冬天冒出来的花总是白色的或黄色的或紫色的。白屈菜也长起来了:在池塘边上,有高大强壮,深紫色,黑色花蕊的银莲花。

93. A Pair of Socks

By William Lyon Phelps

One fine afternoon, I was walking along Fifth Avenue, when I remembered that it was necessary to buy a pair of socks. Why I wished to buy only one pair is unimportant. I turned into the first sock shop that caught my eye, and a boy clerk who could not have been more than seventeen years old came forward. "What can I do for you, sir?" "I wish to buy a pair of socks." His eyes *glowed*. There was a note of *passion* in him voice. "Did you know that you had come into the finest place in the world to buy socks?" I had not been aware of that, as my entrance had been *accidental*. "Come with me," said the boy, *ecstatically*. I followed him to the *rear* of the shop, and he began to *haul* down from the shelves box after box, displaying their contents for my *delectation*.

"Hold on, lad, I am going to buy only one pair!" " I know that," said he, "but I want you to see how marvelously beautiful these are. Aren't they wonderful!" There was on his face an expression of *solemn and holy rapture*, as if he were *revealing* to me the mysteries of his religion. I became far more interested in him than in the socks. I looked at him in amazement. "My friend," said I, "if you can keep this up, this is not merely the *enthusiasm* that comes from *novelty*, from having a new job, if you can keep up this *zeal* and excitement day after day, in ten years you will own every sock in the United Sates."

语言注释

1. glow / ɡləʊ / *v*. 发光
2. passion / ˈpæʃən / *n*. 激情，热情
3. accidental / ˌæksɪˈdentl / *adj*. 偶然的
4. ecstatically / ɪkˈstætɪklɪ / *adv*. 欣喜若狂地
5. rear / rɪə / *n*. 后部,背面
6. haul / hɒːl / *v*. 用力拖拉

7. delectation / ˌdɪlekˈteɪʃn / n. (文学用语)
愉快, 款待

8. solemn and holy rapture 庄严和神圣的狂喜

9. reveal / rɪˈviːl / v. 展现, 显示

10. enthusiasm / ɪnˈθjuːzɪæzəm / n. 热心, 热情

11. novelty / ˈnɒvltɪ / n. 新鲜, 新奇的事物

12. zeal / ziːl / n. 热心, 热情, 热诚

背景介绍

威廉·莱昂·费尔普斯(William Lyon Phelps, 1865 - 1943)是耶鲁大学四十年来最著名的一位英国文学教授和演说家。费尔普斯因其普及古典文学知识的若干讲座而闻名。他也是一个出色的作家。其最早的学术著作有《早期英国浪漫主义文学运动》(1893)、《如何理解布朗宁》(1915)。他著有二十余册文学论著。

篇目欣赏

这是费尔普斯教授生活中经历的一件小事,但那个年轻的小店员却给他留下了深刻的印象。他的描述很简洁,但确细腻而生动。这个少年做买卖的自豪感(Did you know that you had come into the finest place in the world to buy socks?)和喜悦的心情(His eyes glowed. There was a note of passion in his voice.)就好像他正向我解释他所信仰的玄妙宗教。这些都给作者带来了惊喜。在各行各业中都有许许多多的人在生活的道路上走下坡路,意气消沉。机械的干活必然导致失败。所以,让我们向这个小伙子学习,怀着希望和热情工作,学习。

背诵准备

　　这篇短文是一个节选,中间出现了一段作者和小伙子的对白。围绕着这个对白,作者进行了一些细致的描述。请阅读以下句子,排出对白的正确顺序,然后和同学一起背诵并表演这个小对话。

1. I wish to buy a pair of socks.
2. I know that, but I want you to see how marvelously beautiful these are.
3. Come with me .
4. My friend, if you can keep this up, this is not merely the enthusiasm that comes from novelty, from having a new job, if you can keep up this zeal and excitement day after day, in ten years you will own every sock in the United Sates.
5. Did you know that you had come into the finest place in the world to buy socks?
6. Aren't they wonderful!
7. What can I do for you, sir?
8. Hold on, lad, I am going to buy only one pair!

_____ _____ _____ _____ _____

参考译文

一双袜子

威廉·莱昂·费尔普斯

　　一个晴朗的下午,我沿第五大街而行,忽然想起需要买双袜子。为何我只想买一双并不重要。我拐进看到的第一家袜店,一个不到17岁的少年售货员迎上来:"先生,我能为您效劳吗?""我想买双短袜。"他双眸满是热情,声音饱含激情:"您知道您来到了世界上最好的袜店吗?"我倒并未意识到这点,我不过是随便进来的。"随我来,"男孩欣喜若狂地说。我跟着他往里走。他开始从货架上拽下一个又一个盒子,向我展示里面的袜子,让我欣赏。

　　"停一停,孩子,我只买一双!""我知道,"他说,"但我想让您瞧瞧这些袜子是多么漂亮、难道它们不棒吗！"他的脸色庄严而虔诚，就像是在向我透露他的信仰中的奥秘似的。我对他的兴趣远远超过了对袜子的兴趣。我吃惊地打量着他。"我的朋友，"我说，"如果你能这样保持下去，如果这热情并不仅仅缘于新奇，缘于找到份新工作，如果你能日复一日地保持这种热心和激情，不出十年，全美的每一双袜子都将是从你手中卖出去的。"

94. Attitude

By Charles Swindoll

"The longer I live, the more I realize the *impact* of attitude on life. Attitude, to me, is more important than facts. It is more important than the past, the education, the money, than *circumstances*, than failure, than successes, than what other people think or say or do. It is more important than appearance, *giftedness* or skill. It will make or break a company ... a church ... a home. The remarkable thing is we have a choice everyday regarding the attitude we will *embrace* for that day. We cannot change our past ... we cannot change the fact that people will act in a certain way. We cannot change the *inevitable*. The only thing we can do is play on the one string we have, and that is our attitude. I am *convinced* that life is 10% what happens to me and 90% of how I *react* to it. And so it is with you ... we are *in charge of* our Attitudes."

语言注释

1. impact / ˈɪmpækt / *n*. 强烈印象或影响
2. circumstances / ˈsɜːkəmstəns / *n*. 环境
3. giftedness / ˈɡɪftɪdnɪs / *n*. 天赋
4. embrace / ɪmˈbreɪs / *v*. 拥抱
5. inevitable / ɪnˈevɪtəbl / *adj*. 不可避免的
6. convince / kənˈvɪns / *v*. 使人信服,相信
7. react / rɪˈækt / *v*. 反应,起作用
8. in charge of (使)负责管理

背景介绍

查 尔斯·斯威道尔(Charles Swindoll)出生于 1943 年,毕业于美国达拉斯神学院。他是达拉斯地区的 Stonebriar 社区的主任牧师。51 岁时,他成了这个学院的第四任院长。同时他也是国际联合电台节目"生活透视"的主持人。他著有三十多本畅销书,如《伟大生命系列》,《再笑一次》等。

篇目欣赏

查 尔斯·斯威道尔对生活有他独特的看法,他认为:"The longer I live, the more I realize the impact of attitude on life."他还认为自己的态度最重要。它是人生的催化剂,选择不同的人生态度,对人生有不同的重大影响。在人生的航程上,高举积极达观的旗帜,是正确的人生态度。拥有积极达观的人生态度,便拥有绚丽多彩的人生!

背诵准备

本文是作者对态度的一个看法,在句式上他用了很多比较句。下面就给出的两个名词进行一下比较吧。

例如:attitude & facts (important)

Attitude is more important than facts.

Attitude is not as important as facts.

1. his Chinese handwriting & his English handwriting (beautiful)

   _____.

2. travel by night & travel by day (good)

   _____.

3. I can walk & a younger man can walk (far)

   _____.

4. he plays basketball & his brother plays basketball (well)

5. the Summer Palace & Beihai Park (many people)

参考译文

态　度

查尔斯·斯威道尔

　　随着年龄增长阅历增加,我越来越认识到态度对生活的影响。态度对我而言是比事实还重要,比过去、教育、金钱、境遇、成败还重要,也比别人说什么、怎么想和怎么做还重要。态度比相貌、天赋或技能还重要。态度能建立也能打垮一个公司、一个教会和一个家庭。我们每一天面临一个选择,选择那天所持的态度是一个非凡的事情。我们不能改变过去。我们不能改变别人将必定怎么做的事实。我们不能改变无法避免的事情。只有一个我们能改变的,就是我们的态度,态度也是我们继续拥有的。我深信,生命力的10%取决于发生在我周围的人和事,而90%取决于我对这些人和事的反应。生命力掌握在你手里。我们对我们的态度负全责。

95. Hints to Those That Would Be Rich

By Benjamin Franklin

The use of Money is all the *advantage* there is in having money. For £6 a Year you may have the Use of £100 if you are a man of known *prudence* and honesty.

He that spends a *groat* a day *idly*, spends idly above £6 a year, which is the price of using £100.

He that wastes idly a groat's worth of his time per day, one day with another, wastes the *privilege* of using £100 each day.

He that idly loses 5 s. worth of time, loses 5 s. and *might as prudently* throw 5 *s.* in the river.

He that loses 5 s. not only loses that *sum*, but all the advantage that might be made by turning it in *dealing*, which, by the time that a young man becomes old, *amounts to* a comfortable bag of money.

...

A penny sav'd is two pence clear.

A pin a day is a groat a year.

语言注释

1. advantage / əd'vɑːntɪdʒ / *n*. 办法，益处
2. prudence / 'pruːdəns / *n*. 精打细算，谨慎从事
3. groat / grəut / *n*. 古时英国四便士的银币。
4. idly / 'aɪdlɪ / *adv*. 闲散地,懒惰地
5. privilege / 'prɪvɪlɪdʒ / *n*. 利益,好处
6. might as prudently   反正一样,倒不如
7. s. (shilling 的缩略形式)先令
8. sum / sʌm / *n*. 金额,款项
9. deal / diːl / *v*. 经营
10. amount to   等于或相当于

背景介绍

杰明·富兰克林(Benjamin Franklin, 1760－1790)美国政治家和科学家。他没有受过多少正规教育,但博览群书,后来被授予三所英国大学的学位。他对各种自然现象极感兴趣,做过许多科学实验。他曾参与起草美国"独立宣言",美国独立后他被派往巴黎拟定和约。他的最后一次政治活动是签署一份提交国会的关于废除奴隶制的备忘录。

篇目欣赏

杰明·富兰克林由于家里贫穷,只上过两年学,但他的学习从未间断过,他从伙食费中省下钱来买书。同时,利用工作之便,他结识了几家书店的学徒,将书店的书在晚间偷偷地借来,通宵达旦地阅读,第二天清晨便归还。这篇短文是选自富兰克林给贫穷的理查德的一封信。它不仅告诉了他一个致富之道,同时也告诉大家,时间更是最大的财富。只有节约时间,才能得到财富。

背诵准备

这篇短文出现了很多的名词所有格。把他们整理出来加以单独背诵可以帮助你理解句式,易于背诵。

1. 有钱的好处 _____

2. 节俭而诚实的人 _____

3. 一百英镑的使用价值 _____

4. 每天值四便士的时间 _____

5. 每天使用一百英镑的权利 _____

6. 损失了价值五先令时间的人 _____

参考译文

致富之道

本杰明·富兰克林

有钱的唯一好处就在于用钱。如果你是一个节俭而诚实的人，一年六英镑就可以当一百英镑的钱使用。

一天消费四便士的人，一年就消费六个多英镑，而六英镑相当于一百英镑的使用价值。

每天虚度值一便士的时间的人，日复一日，等于消费了每天使用一百英镑的权利。

一个游手好闲而损失了价值五先令时间的人，就是失去了五个先令，他还不如把五先令扔进河里的好。

一个失去五先令的人，不仅失去了那笔钱，还失去了把钱用于经商可能带来的好处，而一个年轻人到年老的时候这笔钱就会等于一笔可观的财产。

……

省下的一便士是不折不扣的两便士，

每天节约一丁点儿一年就是一大笔。

96. Night

By Nathanial Hawthorne

Night has fallen over the country. Through the trees rises the red moon, and the stars are scarcely seen. In the vast shadow of night the coolness and the dews *descend*. I sit at the open window to enjoy them; and hear only the voice of the summer wind. Like black *hulks*, the shadows of the great trees ride at *anchor* on the *billowy* sea of grass. I cannot see the red and blue flowers, but I know that they are there. Far away in the meadow gleams *the silver Charles*. *The tramp of horses' hoofs* sounds from the wooden bridge. Then all is still save the continuous wind of the summer night. Sometimes I know not if it be the wind or the sound of the neighboring sea. The village clock strikes; and I feel that I am not alone.

How different it is in the city! It is late, and the crowd is gone. You step out upon the balcony, and lie in the very bosom of the cool, *dewy night* as if you folded her garments about you. Beneath lies the public walk with trees, like a fathomless, black gulf, into whose silent darkness the spirit plunges, and floats away with some beloved spirit clasped in its embrace. The lamps are still burning up and down the long street. People go by with *grotesque* shadows, now foreshortened, and now lengthening away into the darkness and vanishing, while a new one springs up behind the walker, and seems to pass him revolving like the sail of a windmill. The iron gates of the park shut with *a jangling clang*. There are footsteps and loud voices; — a *tumult*; —a *drunken brawl*; — an alarm of fire; — then silence again. And now at length the city is asleep, and we can see the night. The belated moon looks over the roofs, and finds no one to welcome her. The moonlight is broken. It lies here and there in the squares, and the opening of the streets — *angular* like blocks of white marble.

语言注释

1. descend / dɪ'send / *v*. 下来,下降
2. hulk / hʌlk / *n*. (旧船的)船体
3. anchor / 'æŋkə / *n*. 锚

4. billowy /ˈbɪləʊɪ/ *adj*. 如波浪起伏的
5. the silver Charles　银色的查尔斯河(美国马萨诸塞州的一条河流)
6. the tramp of horses' hoofs　踢嗒踢嗒的马蹄声
   dewy /ˈdjuːɪ/ *adj*. 带露水的
7. dewy night　露水弥漫的夜幕中
8. grotesque /grəʊˈtesk/ *adj*. 奇形怪状的
9. a jangling clang　哨啷一声
10. tumult /ˈtjuːmʌlt/ *n*. (尤指一大群人的)骚乱
11. a drunken brawl　酒醉后的吵架声
12. angular /ˈæŋgjʊlə/ *adj*. 有棱角的

背景介绍

纳撒尼尔·霍桑是美国十九世纪最杰出的浪漫主义小说家。1828年,他以自己的大学时代为题材,写出了小说《范·肖》,自己出资匿名出版。第一部成功的小说《红字》(*The Scarlet Letter*)于1850年出版。霍桑的短篇小说细致深刻,风格独特,不少作品立意新颖,取材得当,富于诗意。内容与形式的和谐统一产生了完美强烈的艺术效果,对美国短篇小说这一突出文学类型的发展具有积极深远的影响。

篇目欣赏

这篇短文是对夜晚的景色的描述。霍桑通过对夜色在乡村和城市的不同景色的对比,表达了他对乡村自然景色的热爱,甚至是夜晚也不例外。夜晚的乡村是朦胧的、美丽的、安静的。安静得能听到风声(hear only the voice of the summer wind. 耳边只听到那夏天的风声)。红月(the red moon),树林(the shadows of the great trees),踢嗒踢嗒的马蹄声(the tramp of horses' hoofs),邻近的海涛声(the sound of the neighboring sea),时钟(the village clock)都让作者感到一种安逸和满足。

背诵准备

在这篇对夜的描写的短文中,作者分别对乡村的夜景和城市的夜景进行对比。请你说说作者分别提到了哪些城市或乡村的事物。

1. trees	2. flowers
3. grass	4. the Charles
5. wooden bridge	6. horse
7. village clock	8. balcony
9. the public walk with trees	10. The iron gates of the park
11. The lamps	12. -an alarm of fire
13. a drunken brawl	14. the squares
15. the opening of the streets	

A. night in the country

a. _____ b. _____ c. _____ d. _____ e. _____

f. _____ g. _____

B. night in the city

a. _____ b. _____ c. _____ d. _____ e. _____

f. _____ g. _____ h. _____

参考译文

夜

纳撒尼尔·霍桑

夜幕也笼罩乡间。一轮红月正从树林后面冉冉升起,天上几乎看不到星星。在这苍茫的夜色中,寒气与露水降下来了。我坐在敞开的窗前欣赏着这夜色,耳边只听到夏天的风声。大树的阴影像黑色的大船停泊在波浪起伏的茫茫草海上。虽然我见不到红色和蓝色的花朵,但我知道他们在那儿。在远处的草地上,银色的查尔斯河闪闪发光。木桥那边传来了踢嗒踢嗒的马蹄声。接着,一片寂静,留下的只是夏夜不断的风声。有时,我根本辨别不出它究竟是风声,还是邻近的海涛声。村子里的时钟敲起来了,于是我觉得并不孤独。

　　城市的夜晚可是多么不同呀!夜深了,人群已经散去。你走到阳台上,躺在凉快和露水弥漫的夜幕中,仿佛你用它作为外衣裹住了你的身子。阳台下面是栽着树木的人行道,像一条深不可测的黑色海湾,飘忽的精灵就投入了漆黑沉静的海湾,拥抱着某个所爱的精灵随波荡漾而去。漫长的大街上,街灯依然到处亮着。人们灯下走过,拖着各种各样奇形怪状的影子时而缩短,时而伸长最后消失在黑暗中;同时,一个新的影子又突然出现那个行路人的身后,这影子似乎像风车上翼板一样,转到他身体的前方去了。公园的铁门当啷一声关上了。耳边可以听见脚步声和响亮的说话声;——一阵喧闹;——一阵酒醉后的吵架声;——一阵火灾的报警声;——接着,又是一片寂静。于是,城市终于沉睡,我们终于能看到夜的景色。姗姗来迟的月亮从屋顶后面探出脸来,发觉没有人在欢迎她。破碎的月光东一块,西一块地散落在各个广场上和各条大街的开阔处——像一块块白色的大理石一样棱角分明。

97. Life Is What We Make It

By Orison Swett Marden

Are you dissatisfied with today's success? It is the harvest from yesterday's sowing. Do you dream of a golden *morrow*? You will *reap* what you are sowing today. We get out of life just what we put into it.

Nature takes on our moods: she laughs with those who laugh and weeps with those who weep. If we *rejoice* and are glad the very birds sing more sweetly, the woods and streams murmur our song. But if we are sad and *sorrowful* a sudden *gloom* falls upon Nature's face; the sun shines, but not in our hearts; the birds sing, but not to us.

The future will be just what we make it. Our purpose will give it its *character*. One's *resolution* is one's *prophecy*. Leave all your discouraging *pessimism* behind. Do not prophesy evil, but good. Men of hope come to the front.

语言注释

1. morrow / ˈmɒːrəʊ / *n*. （文学古语）次日

2. reap / riːp / *v*. 收割庄稼(尤指谷物);收获

3. rejoice / rɪˈdʒɔɪs / *v*. 为胜利而欢欣

4. sorrowful / ˈsɒrəʊfʊl / *adj*. 悲伤的,伤心的

5. gloom / gluːm / *n*. 忧郁的心情;沮丧的气氛

6. character / ˈkærɪktə / *n*. 性质;特色

7. resolution / ˌrezəˈluːʃən / *n*. 决心;决定

8. prophecy / ˈprɒpɪsɪ / *n*. 预言

9. pessimism / ˈpesɪmɪzəm / *n*. 悲观;悲观情绪

背景介绍

奥 里森·S·马登(Orison Swett Marden, 1850－1924),出生于新英格兰的一个贫穷的农场家庭。7 岁时,他成了孤儿,于是他只能独自寻找住宿和食物。年少的时候,他读了苏格兰作家斯玛而斯的《自己拯救自己》一书。这本书的思想种子在马登的心中形成了强烈的愿望,从而发展成了崇高的信念,使他的世界成了一个值得生活得更美好的世界。后来他成功创办了杂志《成功》,被奉为美国成功学运动的先驱,著有《成功学原理》等。马登相信人的品质是取得成功和保持成果的基石。他认为达到了真正完美无缺的品质本身就是成功。

篇目欣赏

从 题目(*Life Is What We Make It*)所示,我们知道这篇短文强调的是个人的意志力能决定个人的前途。作者在第一段连续使用两个修辞问句,自问自答,用发自内心的感情来拉近和你的距离。文中第二段提到,"大自然反映我们的心情"。随着人们的悲喜,大自然有着相应的变化。但其实这只是表面的。其实这是个人情绪,心境的"感受"而已。主宰的权利还是在个人手上。何不保持愉快的心情,共享大自然的美好而开创自己的前途呢? 未来靠我们去创造。

背诵准备

在这篇短文中出现了很多活用的单词和词组,掌握好这些词组的用法能有效地帮助你体会这篇励志短文。请选择框内的词的适当形式填入下列句中。

take on	dream of	put into	laugh with
come to	weep with	fall upon	get out of
leave ... behind	be satisfied with		

1. _____ you _____ today's success? It is the harvest from yesterday's sowing.

2. _____ you _____ a golden morrow ?

3. We _____ life just what we _____ it.

4. Nature _____ our moods.

5. Nature _____ those who laugh and _____ those who weep.

6. If we are sad and sorrowful a sudden gloom _____ Nature's face.

7. The future will be just what we make it. _____ all the discouraging pessimism _____ .

8. If we always prophesy good, men of hope _____ the front.

参考译文

生活全靠我们自己创造

奥里森·S·马登

你是否对今日的成功不甚满意? 它是昨日播下的种子结成的果实。你是否梦想能拥有金色的明天? 今日的播种,便是你明日的收获。我们付之于生活,亦取之于生活。

自然传达着我们的心情:她与欢笑者同欢,与哭泣者同泣。假若我们欢欣愉悦,鸟儿的歌声就会更甜美,树叶沙沙,溪流潺潺,吟唱着我们的歌。倘若我们悲伤哀愁,忧郁就会瞬间罩在她的脸庞;阳光依旧灿烂,却照不进我们的心房;鸟儿依旧欢唱,但拨不动我们的心弦。

未来是我们创造的。我们的旨意赋予其秉性。决心预示着将来的成败。将一切令你气馁的悲观情绪都抛诸脑后。莫要预言挫折,多思益处。满怀希望的人才能勇往直前。

98. I Have a Dream (excerpt)

By Martin Luther King, Jr.

This is our hope, and this is the faith that I go back to the South with. With this faith, we will be able to *hew* out of the mountain of despair a stone of hope. With this faith, we will be able to transform the *jangling discords* of our nation into a beautiful symphony of brotherhood. With this faith, we will be able to work together, to pray together, to *struggle* together, to go to jail together, to stand up for freedom together, knowing that we will be free one day.

语言注释

1. hew / hjuː / *v.* 砍倒;劈开
2. jangle / ˈdʒæŋg(ə)l / *v.* 发出噪音
3. discord / ˈdɪskɔːd / *n.* 噪音,刺耳的声音
4. struggle / ˈstrʌg(ə)l / *v.* 努力,斗争

背景介绍

马丁·路德·金(Martin Luther King. Jr., 1929－1968)是美国黑人运动的著名领袖。他生于佐治亚州一个牧师家庭,受过高等教育,获神学博士学位。1955 年他参加领导了蒙哥马利市黑人拒乘公共汽车运动,并发起组织了"南方基督教领袖会议"。1963 年又组织了伯明翰黑人争取自由平等权利的大游行,把黑人运动由南方推向北方。1964 年获诺贝尔和平奖,被誉为"为世界有色人民树立了一个榜样"。1968 年 4 月 4 日在田纳西州孟菲斯城遇刺身亡。

篇目欣赏

> 这 篇演说是 1963 年 8 月 28 日 10 个黑人组织在华盛顿举行 25 万人参加的"自由进军"时,在林肯纪念堂发表的,被人称为"黑人之音"。这篇演说感情激昂,比喻精辟,语言犀利,行文流利,气势非凡。

背诵准备

整段文字用了工整的排比句,共四句话。记住结构和内容就可以轻松背诵此段。下面来试试吧:

This is our hope, and this is the faith that I go back to the South with. With this faith, we will be able to _____

_____. With this faith, we will be able to

_____.

With this faith, we will be able to _____

_____, knowing that we will be free one day.

参考译文

我有一个梦想(节选)

马丁·路德·金

　　这是我们的希望。这是我将带回南方去的信念。有了这个信念,我们就能从绝望之山开采出希望之石。有了这个信念,我们就能把这个国家的嘈杂刺耳的争吵声,变为充满手足之情的悦耳交响曲。有了这个信念,我们就能一同工作,一同祈祷,一同斗争,一同入狱,一同维护自由,因为我们知道,我们终有一天会获得自由。

99. Our Family Creed (excerpt)

By John D. Rockefeller, Jr.

I believe in the *dignity* of labor, whether with head or hand; that the world owes no man a living but that it owes every man an *opportunity* to make a living.

I believe that *thrift* is essential to well — ordered living and that economy is a *prime requisite* of a sound financial *structure*, whether in government, business or personal affairs.

I believe that truth and justice are *fundamental* to an *enduring* social order.

I believe in the *sacredness* of a promise, that a man's word should be as good as his bond, that character — not wealth or power or position — is of supreme worth.

I believe that the *rendering* of useful service is the common duty of mankind and that only in the *purifying* fire of *sacrifice* is the *dross* of selfishness *consumed* and the greatness of the human soul set free.

语言注释

1. dignity / ˈdɪgnɪtɪ / *n*. 尊贵,高尚
2. opportunity / ɒpəˈtjuːnɪtɪ / *n*. 机会
3. thrift / θrɪft / *n*. 节俭,节省
4. prime / praɪm / *adj*. 主要的
5. requisite / ˈrekwɪzɪt / *n*. 必需品,必要条件
6. structure / ˈstrʌktʃə / *n*. 体系,结构
7. fundamental / fʌndəˈment(ə)l / *adj*. 基础的;根本的
8. enduring / ɪnˈdjʊərɪŋ / *adj*. 持久的
9. sacredness / ˈseɪkrɪdnɪs / *n*. 神圣,庄严
10. render / ˈrendə(r) / *v*. 给予;提供
11. purify / ˈpjʊərɪfaɪ / *v*. 净化,变干净
12. sacrifice / ˈsækrɪfaɪs / *n*. 牺牲

13. dross / drɒs / *n*. 废物；杂质

14. consume / kən'sju:m / *v*. 被毁灭，耗尽

背景介绍

约翰·戴维森·洛克菲勒(John Davison Rockefeller Jr., 1874 - 1960)是美国慈善家,生于俄亥俄克利夫兰,美国石油大王老洛克菲勒的唯一儿子。就读于布朗大学,后进入父亲的企业工作。1910 年起致力于发展慈善事业。曾领导洛克菲勒医学院研究所,建成纽约市洛克菲勒中心(1939)。他最为主要的事迹包括出资重建了英国殖民时期在北美建立的威廉斯堡古城(Colonial Williamsburg)以及向联合国捐赠了位于纽约的 18 英亩土地作为联合国总部的永久地址。

篇目欣赏

这是一篇很特别的演说——在文字上具有格言警语风格,而在内容上则属励志性的演说。当时电台进行一项由"联合服务组织"所主持的系列节目,主题是"使日子最值得活下去的事物"。这个主题对身处战争情境的广大电台听众而言具有特殊的意义。在此背景下,小洛克菲勒家族的信条也就很自然地格外引起广泛的注意。在战火纷飞和法西斯势力猖獗肆虐时产生过积极影响。

背诵准备

洛氏家训向世人宣示几个极为珍贵的信念,这里包括以下五点:劳动的尊严;节俭的重要性;真理正义对社会秩序的重大贡献;诺言的神圣;良好品格之崇高价值;服务人群之美德。如果能分条记住,则能帮助背诵全文。下面就来试着记住它们:

I believe in the dignity of labor, _____; that the
world owes no man a living but that _____.

I believe that _____ is essential to well — ordered living and
that _____ is a prime requisite of a sound financial structure, whether in government, business or personal affairs.

I believe that truth and justice are _____.

I believe in the sacredness of a promise, _____,
that character — not wealth or power or position — is of supreme worth.

I believe that _____ and that only in the purifying
fire of sacrifice is the dross of selfishness consumed and the greatness of the human
soul set free.

参考译文

我们的家庭信条(节选)

小约翰·戴维森·洛克菲勒

我相信劳动的尊严,不论是脑力或体力的劳动;世界不欠任何人生计,但它欠每人一个谋生的机会。

我相信俭朴是井然有序的生活所必需;节约是健全的财务结构之主要条件,不论是政府、企业或个人之事务皆是如此。

我相信真理与正义是社会秩序长久维系的基础。

我相信诺言的神圣,一句承诺应该如同契约一般有效;品格——而非财富或权势或地位——具有至为崇高的价值。

我相信提供有用的服务是人类共同的责任,唯有在牺牲奉献的炼火中,自私自利的渣滓始能烧毁,而人类灵魂的伟大也才能发挥出来。

100. The Gettysburg Address (excerpt)

By Abraham Lincoln

It is rather for us to be here *dedicated* to the great task remaining before us: that from these honored dead we take *increased devotion* to that cause for which they here gave the last full measure of devotion; that we here highly *resolve* that these dead shall not have died *in vain*; that the nation, under God, shall have a new birth of freedom, and that government of the people, by the people, for the people, shall not *perish* from the earth.

语言注释

1. dedicate / ˈdedɪkeɪt / v. 献身，致力
2. increase / ˈɪnkriːs / v. 增加，增大
3. devotion / dɪˈvəʊʃ(ə)n / n. 献身，贡献
4. resolve / rɪˈzɒlv / v. 做决定
5. in vain　徒劳毫无收益的；未成功
6. perish / ˈperɪʃ / v. 消亡

背景介绍

伯拉罕·林肯（Abraham Lincoln，1809－1865）是美国伟大的民主主义政治家，共和党人，美国第 16 任总统。他出生于社会底层，具有勤劳、俭朴、谦虚和诚恳的品格。他进白宫后，在奴隶制等问题上，政界发生倾轧，国家出现分裂，遇到了很多困难。在日常工作中他不顾个人安全，每天挤出大量时间接见群众，听取申诉，尽力解决他们的问题。在他任职期间，由于各种反动势力的影响，政策上有过踌躇和动摇，但在人民群众的支持和推动下，能够顺应历史潮流，最终签署了著名的《解放宣言》，解决了当时美国社会经济政治生活中存在的主要矛盾。在四年国内战争中，他亲自指挥作战。领导联邦政府同南部农场奴隶主进行了坚决斗争，维护了国家的统一，有力地推动了美国社会的发展。林肯于 1865 年 4 月 14 日遇刺身亡。由于林肯在美国历史上所起的进步作用，人们称赞他为"新时代国家统治者的楷模"。

篇目欣赏

林肯不仅是位杰出的政治家,还是美国历史上不可多得的演说家。他的演说素以朴实无华、情感真挚、逻辑严密、思想深邃著称。此篇演讲短小精悍,言简意赅,抚今追昔,旨在凭吊牺牲的英烈,激励人们为争取自由和统一而不懈奋斗,具有极强的感染力和鼓舞力。

背诵准备

这段文字运用了对比、排比等手法,句式精练,值得仔细研究。

It is rather for us to be here _____ to the great task remaining before us: that from these _____ dead we take _____ _____ devotion to that cause for which they here gave the last full measure of devotion; that we here highly resolve that these dead shall not have died in vain; that the nation, under God, shall have a new birth of freedom, and _____ _____, shall not perish from the earth.

参考译文

葛底斯堡演说(节选)

亚伯拉罕·林肯

　　我们倒是应该在这里献身于留在我们面前的伟大任务:那就是继承这些光荣的先烈,对他们在这里作出最后全部贡献的事业,作出我们进一步的贡献;那就是我们在这里狠下决心,决不让这些先烈的死成为白白的牺牲;那就是我们的国家一定要在上帝底下获得新的自由;那就是让这个民有、民治、民享的政府永世长存。

1. Crawled up, Down came, washed, out, Out came, dried up, Crawled up

2. howl, cry

3. / aʊt /, stout, spout, shout, out

4. 1. The more; the fewer 2. The less, the healthier 3. The faster, the more 4. The more, the greener 5. The richer, the more

5. Puffer Bellies; engine driver; handle; Chug, chug, toot, toot

6. Small, white, Clean, bright, happy

7. traveler

8. Alabama, Louisiana, The weather it was dry, The sun so hot I froze to death

9. Far, Tea, Sew, Me, Doe, La, Ray

10. won't sing, turns brass, gets broke, won't pull, turn over, won't bark, fall down

11. white as snow, sure to go, followed, made, lingered near, waited patiently

12. wood and clay, wood and clay, will not stay, iron and steel, iron and steel, will be stolen away

13. Witches, broomsticks, jack-o'-lanterns, painted, bobbing, gypsies

14. drumming, piping, lords, dancing, milking, swans, laying

15. 1. Just as he was about to fly off, he made a buzzing noise and asked the bull if he would like him to go.

    2. The bull replied to the mosquito, "I do not know you have come, and I shall not miss you when you go away."

16. 1. The fox was strolling through an orchard when he saw a bunch of ripe grapes.

    2. Drawing back a few steps, the fox took a run and a jump, but just missed the bunch.

    3. The fox tried again and again, but still failed to reach the bunch.

    4. The fox walked away with his nose in the air, saying, "I am sure they are sour."

17. sitting, was telling, ran, told, had broken, was stealing, hastened, saw, running, foretell, foresee

18. 1. Suddenly he noticed a face glaring down on him.

    2. Looking more closely he found it was only a Mask like the ones actors use to put over their faces.

    3. You look very fine, but it is a pity that you haven't got any brains.

19. 1. While he was wandering through the suburbs looking up to observe the stars, he fell into a deep ditch accidentally.

2. When he got out of the ditch, he found he got black and blue all over the body.

3. After his neighbor learned the whole story, he said, "..."

20. pitcher, happily, water, discovered, beak, everything, efforts, pebbles, dropped, rose

21. 1. He put his hands into a pitcher which was full of hazelnuts.

   2. He was prevented by the neck of the pitcher.

   3. He burst into tears and cried for help.

   4. His mother said, "You can take out your hand if you give up half of that."

22. lived, dried, left, look, live, like, came, looked, said, looks, jump, settle, replied, get

23. 1. A hunter, not very brave, was searching for the tracks of a lion.

   2. He asked a man felling oaks in the forest if he had seen any tracks of the lion or knew where the lion was.

   3. The hunter, turning very pale and chattering with his teeth from fear, replied

24. 1. The one who has the most handsome children will be able to get the award.

   2. A monkey presented, with a mother's tenderness, a flat-nose, hairless, ugly, young monkey.

   3. She seriously said, "I don't know if Jupiter will give the award to me, but I DO know that in my eyes, my son is the dearest, and the most handsome of all."

25. 1. A war was about to break out between the Birds and the Beasts.

   2. When the two armies were collected together, the Bat hesitated which to join.

   3. He said he was a beast when the Birds invited him and he said he was a bird when the Beasts invited him.

   4. Peace was made between the Beasts and the Birds at the last moment.

   5. Both the Bird and the Beast turned against him.

26. 1. The scorpion and the frog met on the bank of a stream.

   2. The scorpion asked the frog to carry him across on its back.

   3. The frog worried, "How do I know you won't sting me?"

   4. When they were in the middle of the stream, the scorpion stung the frog.

   5. The frog felt the onset of paralysis.

27. was driving, sank, frightened, stood, did not know, cried, asked, appeared, addressed, Put, Whip, pray, tried, thanked, helped

28. out, in, across, down, at, in, up, at, away, into, away

29. How are you? How are things with you?

Everything is fine, but I have only one wish, that there may be a heavy rain, so that the plants may be well watered.

I want nothing but only one wish. I hope the dry weather may continue, and the sun shines hot and bright, so that the bricks might be dried.

Which side shall I take?

30. went, was carried, drowned, was noticed, was sitting, plucked, let, fall, climbed, floated, came, stood, laid, was, sitting, stung, was, threw, made, coming, deserves

31. 1. He found a yellow and glittering egg in his goose's nest.

2. He thought it was a trick played on him, so he was about to throw the egg away.

3. He soon found it was an egg of pure gold.

4. He became rich by selling these gold eggs.

5. He wanted to get all the gold eggs, but killed it only to find nothing.

32. they were doing all the work but the Belly was having all the food; refused to take the food; refused to receive it; had no work to do; could hardly move; was dry; were unable to support the Body; was still doing necessary work for the Body quietly; will go to pieces

33. were traveling, met, climbed, hid, found, be attacked, fell, came, touched, smelt, held, pretended, be, left, is said, will, touch, was, gone, climbed, joked, had whispered, gave, replied, travel, deserts, comes, tests

34. 1. I'll buy some hens from Farmer Brown.

2. I will sell these eggs to the priest's wife.

3. I'll buy a new dress and a new hat.

4. I will go to the market.

5. I will just look at her and toss my head like this.

35.

Season	Ants	Grasshopper
Summer	The ants are busy collecting grain.	The grasshopper is having fun.
Winter	The ants have plenty of grain collected in summer.	The starving grasshopper passes by and earnestly begs for a little food.

36. 1. It was just a ruse to make the other animals come pay their respects.

    2. The lion jumped at them and ate them up, one by one.

    3. She greeted him from outside the cave.

    4. Because she saw the tracks of those going in, but none coming out.

    5. He is wise who is warned by the misfortunes of others.

37. 2, 1, 4, 6, 3, 5

38. stork, wolf, arrived, house, bowls, quickly, asked, soup, angry, beak, hungry, laughed, idea, wolf, pitchers, eating, if, mouth, so, that, hungry, stork

39. 1. They were frightened of the cat.

    2. They decided to hold a meeting and talk over the problem.

    3. That cat was always sneaking up and surprising him.

    4. He said they had to run for their lives every day.

    5. He said, "Let's tie a bell around the cat's neck. Then we can hear him coming, and have plenty of time to run and hide."

    6. They got a bell and a piece of ribbon.

    7. None of them was brave enough to bell the cat.

40. 1. The partridge was strutting along, looking very beautiful.

    2. She wished she could walk as beautifully as the partridge

    3. The crow tried to copy the partridge's wonderful strut.

    4. "What do you think you're doing?"

    5. "Walk like a crow!"

    6. The crow never did learn how to strut. And finally she forgot how to walk like a crow!

41. was sleeping, ran, woke, grabbed, opened, begged, laughed, let, go, heard, roaring, ran, see, was caught, said, worry, get, began, nibbled, nibbled, squeezed

42. "Help, help!";

"Wolf! Wolf! The wolves are attacking my sheep."

"There are no wolves. I was just fooling."

"Wolf! Wolf!"

"Wolf! Wolf!"

"Help! The wolves are attacking my sheep!"

"You won't fool us again."

43. 1. The hare laughed at the tortoise, and was far ahead at the beginning, so he

stopped to talk with some friends.

2. He was so busy talking that he didn't see the tortoise run past him.

3. He thought that he had a lot of time, so he stopped to eat a big lunch.

4. He was too full to run fast after the lunch, so he stopped to rest.

5. While he was sleeping, the tortoise passed him again.

44. "Well, Mr. Wolf, I know that I shall be your prey, but before I die, could you just do me a favor?"

"What do you want?"

"I really like dancing. Could you play me a piece of music, so I can dance with the music?"

"I am a butcher, but not a piper. I deserve it."

45. Hold fast, die, broken-winged, Hold fast, go, barren, Frozen

46. 1. About living and dying

I think the difference lies

Between tears and crying.

2. About here and there —

I think the distance

Is nowhere.

47. depends, upon, red, glazed, white

48. nobody, nobody, banish, somebody, frog, bog

49. prairie, clover, bee, revery, Revery, bees

50. （略）

51. Only a house warm as bonfire, a space for myself to admire, flowery as in May that everyone may desire.

52. two; have; pulled; many; foot.

53. （略）

54. diverged, traveler, undergrowth

55. vales, hills, daffodils, lake, trees, breeze

56. immortal, fearful, dread, dread

57. roving, loving, loving, roving

58. Work, work, work, Seam, gusset, band, Band, gusset, seam

59. （略）

60. （略）

61. 1. the grass beyond the door,

    The sweet keen smell,

   2. Your neck turned so,

    Some veil did fall,

   3. But when or how

    the grass beyond the door,

   4. You have been mine before,

    How long ago

62. entered, ascended, grown, grow, Tree, Moss, violets, child

63. （略）

64. （略）

65. （略）

66. year, day, Morning, hillside, lark, snail, God, world

67. （略）

68. （略）

69. breeding, mixing, stirring, covering, feeding

70. （略）

71. Raindrops on roses; warm woolen mittens; Brown paper package tied up with strings; Cream colored ponies; Door bells and sleigh bells; Wild geese that fly with the moon on their wings; in white dresses with blue satin sashes; stay on my nose and eyelashes; Silver white winters; bites; stings; am feeling sad; sad

72. 1. I hate Mondays. 我恨星期一。

   2. Money is not everything. There's Mastercard & Visa. 钞票不是万能的，有时还需要信用卡。

   3. Never put off the work till tomorrow what you can put off today.
不要把工作拖到明天才做，今天就可以拖着不做。

   4. "Your future depends on your dreams." So go to sleep.
"你的梦想决定着你的将来"，所以睡一会吧。

   5. There should be a better way to start a day than waking up every morning.
应该有更好的方式开始新的一天，而不该是千篇一律的由醒来开始。

   6. Success is a relative term. It brings so many relatives.
成功是一个相关名词，它会给你带来很多不相关的亲戚(联系)。

   7. "Hard work never killed anybody." But why take the risk?

"努力工作不会导致死亡!"但为何拿自己去冒险呢?

8. "<u>Work</u> fascinates me." I can look at it for hours!

"工作好有意思耶!"我可观察其好几小时了。

9. The more you learn, the more you know. The more you know, the more you <u>forget</u>. The more you <u>forget</u>, the less you know. So why bother to learn?

学得越多,知道得越多;知道得越多,忘记得越多;忘记得越多,知道得越少。那为什么学来着呢?

10. One should love animals. They are so <u>tasty</u>. 每个人都应该热爱动物,因为它们太美味了。

73. shut, Shutting, shutting, new ideas, listen to, shine, are made of, inventing, tinker, tinkering, fill, lead to

74. 瑞德心中的希望:

1. I hope I can make it across the border.

2. I hope to see my friend and shake his hand.

3. I hope the Pacific is as blue as it has been in my dreams.

75. 1. following 2. slow down 3. inside, more than 4. take your place 5. used to

6: died 7. confused, who 8. knew

76. 1. unhappy, frightened, confused, face, asked, wrong

2. happened, talk, face, born

3. 1) escape 2) holy 3) capacity, find out, spend 4) less 5) built, shut out, born

77. (略)

78. 1. taken 2. Truer 3. been 4. Raising 5. run 6. short 7. dead, muscles

8. bring, in

79. 1. silence 2. if 3. crazy 4. sweat 5. unpopular, smelly, fight 6. nothing

7. heartless, herself 8. risk

80. 1. who 2. rights 3. upset, do 4. all, too 5. saved 6. have, bitten 7. smarter

81. sunshine, rain, spring, will, come, again, me, numbers, wealth, nights, of, peaceful, slumbers, healthy, I, give, my, heart, to, becomes, my, own, confidence, me

82. Drawing Number One   Drawing Number Two

grown-ups, hat, hat, digesting, inside

83. draw a little attention to myself; I am hungry; I am dying; I am cold; I am in pain; much more; her grateful love; speak like that; die like that; blaming anybody; cur-

sing anybody; comparing anything; hungry; naked; homeless; unwanted; unloved; uncared for

84. 1. 颜色美、状貌美、优雅的动作之美、德行美

    2. 和谐之美

    3. 内外兼美乃至上之美

    4. 内外兼美乃至上之美

85. falling, decking, rings, tingles, peals, peep, pushing, blossoms, hide, wafted, whisper, lingers

86. making, place, grownups, easier, teaching, works, second, awful, besides, snacks, on, unless, pretty, wasting, anyway

87. came, went, back, forth, through, were, had been, across, shivered, between, dropped, flies, picked, boast, penetrated, silent, nor, blowing, forming, rippling

88. fancy, smell, sounded, running, crying, dropping, look, dropping, falling, shoved, touch, watching

89. natural, not, but, accrues, similarly, pleasure, pains, kinship, evil, comparison, advantages, disadvantages, matters, conversely

90. voices, bellow, whisper, sing, roar, shout, murmur, whistle, set, pause, breathe, rattle, seems, remote, trembles, quivers , hold, brightens

91. opening, closing, awaits, familiar, harbor surprise, faucet, humility, Revolving, slanted, trap, double, prison, hide

92. sun, sky, water, delight, red-orange, many, movement, sit, watch, by, where, Among, near, wan, pallid, flimsy

93. 7, 1, 5, 3, 8, 2, 6, 4

94. 1. His Chinese handwriting is more beautiful than his English handwriting.

    His English handwriting is not as beautiful as his Chinese handwriting.

    2. Travel by night is better than travel by day.

    Travel by day is not as good as travel by night.

    3. I can walk farther than a younger man.

    A younger man cannot walk as far as I.

    4. He plays basketball better than his brother.

    His brother doesn't play basketball as well as he.

    5. There are more people in the Summer Palace than in Beihai Park.

    There aren't as many people in Beihai Park as in the Summer Palace.

95. 1. the advantage in having money

2. a man of prudence and honesty

3. the price of using £ 100

4. a groat's worth of his time per day

5. the privilege of using £ 100 each day

6. he that loses 5 s. worth of time

96. A.

a. trees b. flowers c. grass d. the Charles e. wooden bridge f. horse

g. village clock

B.

a. balcony b. the public walk with trees c. the iron gates of the park d. the lamps e. an alarm of fire f. a drunken brawl g. the squares h. the opening of the streets

97. 1. Are, satisfied with 2. Do, dream of 3. get out of, put into 4. takes on

5. laughs with, weeps with 6. falls upon 7. Leave, behind 8. come to

98. hew out of the mountain of despair a stone of hope; transform the jangling discords of our nation into a beautiful symphony of brotherhood; work together, to pray together, to struggle together, to go to jail together, to stand up for freedom together

99. whether with head or hand, it owes every man an opportunity to make a living, thrift, economy, fundamental to an enduring social order, that a man's word should be as good as his bond, the rendering of useful service is the common duty of mankind

100. dedicated; honored; increased; that government of the people, by the people, for the people